Renny
A Henchmen MC Novel
--

Jessica Gadziala

RENNY

Cover image credit: Shutterstock.com/ Olena Yakochuk

DEDICATION:

This one goes out to you gals who have trusted me enough to know I would show you the method to my madness. I don't even know most of you, but I know that, for that, you're the bees knees.

RENNY

-

ONE

Mina

"It's not the Grassis."

Really, what were they even thinking in suspecting them? I mean, it was easy to jump to conclusions when you had an eye-witness who made a positive ID. You know, especially when you are a bunch of headstrong, testosterone-filled bikers running on fumes after a devastating blow to their organization and the rage of not being able to pin it on anyone.

But that, in my humble opinion, was no excuse for going balls to the wall on a completely crazy, asinine theory.

That, however, did not stop the men from ranting and raving and making plans on taking out what I knew to be a mostly-unthreatening mob family that they had had a peace with since well before Reign even came into power.

I was leaning back against the wall, arms crossed over my chest, letting myself be ignored. I was pretty sure no one had even heard me about it not being the Grassis. But they were on a tear and I was an outsider, so they weren't going to listen to me until they calmed down anyway.

I wasn't sure what Lo was thinking when she pulled me away from another job I was on, a job I was doing really well at, and brought me back to Navesink Bank to oversee the damn improvements of The Henchmen compound and see what I could do about helping them create a profile for the people that were after them.

Really, she knew better.

It wasn't that I wasn't good at my job; I was. There weren't many profilers, working outside of law enforcement, who were better than me. But that being said, she knew I had preferences. She knew I liked to work from a distance. I liked to watch over the situation and get a bird's eye view of the whole thing. It helped me to stay objective. It kept me from being fed the bullshit lies most people would feed me one way or another. And, in the end, it saved me a lot of frustration.

But there I was amid the chaos in the common room of their compound, all of it recently redone because, well, everything had been covered in blood. I hadn't seen that part myself seeing as the guys had cleaned it up, but I could only imagine it was a complete and utter bloodbath given how many men they had lost the night of the ambush.

It wasn't that I shied away from blood. To be perfectly honest, the stuff I had seen in pictures of brutal rapes, tortures, and murders, yeah, it was enough to turn anyone half-crazy. But, it was always in that sterile form- I always saw it in pictures.

Again, giving me my distance.

I liked my life, as much as possible, to be clean and compartmentalized.

It was something, in the past, Lo had always accepted and accommodated. While the rest of the team were heavy into dark stuff a lot of the time, I got to watch from a distance.

How I preferred it.

It wasn't because I didn't play well with others; I just focused better on work when I didn't have a bunch of strong personalities breathing down my neck or questioning my every theory.

"It's not the Grassis, huh?" a voice asked beside me, bringing with it the faintest hint of smoke and the perfect amount of cologne.

Of course *he* would be the only one of them to have heard me, to be listening to me. Then again, he was always listening to me.

It should have been flattering. Really, were it anyone else, it probably would have been. But Renny was not someone I wanted listening to me all the time. Because Renny, like me, never just listened to the words. Renny picked up the inflection, theorized on the motives behind the words, picked pieces of your soul out of the things that came out of your mouth.

Renny profiled.

And just like doctors make bad patients, profilers make bad profiling subjects.

I didn't like that he could read more into what I said than what I meant to put out there. Which was hypocritical of me, I know, being in the field I was, but it was how it was.

So Renny's borderline obsessive flirting with me for the past few weeks, while charming, sweet, and at times, very tempting, was going to get him nowhere.

Because, come on let's face it, it was hard enough for someone who profiled people to be in a relationship with just an average person. Two profilers getting hot and sweaty or getting serious? Yeah, no.

It would be explosive in both good and bad ways.

But mostly bad.

If I wanted to see shit blow up, I would let Lo ship me overseas again.

Besides, like my professional life, I liked my personal life clean and compartmentalized as well.

So Renny was not going to be a part of my life.

Case closed.

"It's not the Grassis," I repeated, nodding, looking away from Duke and Penny, finding myself a bit too invested in their little love story. You know, from a professional standpoint. Or, at least, I was telling myself that lie.

"What makes you say that?" he pressed, making me have to turn and look at him, finding him much closer than I expected, his shoulder almost brushing mine.

Alright, so, I had never actually been into redheads before. Yes, that was a bit prejudiced of me, but what can I say, politically correct to admit it or not, it had just never been my thing. I liked darker features- dark hair, dark eyes, tanned skin. That was just my personal preference.

That being said, Renny was entirely too good looking for his, or any woman within twenty feet of him, good.

He was tall and a lithe kind of strong. You might even say skinny as a descriptor if you hadn't seen him shirtless. I had. On multiple occasions. And, well, sometimes a lean strong was just as hot as a thick strong. Because he had an eight-pack. Yes, eight. And he had the deepest Adonis belt I had ever seen in my life. Given that I lived half my life at Hailstorm around a ton of fit and often shirtless men, that was saying something. He was also covered in tattoos. They were across his chest, his back, his arms, his hands.

Then of course, there was the money maker.

He had a fantastic face. I was a sucker for some good bone structure and he had it in spades. He had a somewhat thin, but strong face with proportionate features, high and strong cheekbones, inviting lips, and striking light blue eyes.

He was whatever the male equivalent of gorgeous was.

So, despite it being my first time being into his particular brand of copper hotness, I *was* into it.

As such, I tried to keep as much distance as possible between us at all times. It was no easy task given how he was dead set on getting in my pants. So whenever possible, he scooted in beside me, he found reasons to be alone with me, he casually touched me.

Just like he was doing right then, scooting in close when there was no reason to be almost touching me.

"Because it doesn't fit. If they would stop ranting and raving for five seconds and *think* about it, they would come to the same conclusions. The Grassis are into some dark stuff, but they don't beat up women. They don't wage war on other organizations around here. For all intents and purposes, they are a peaceful little criminal enterprise. The only people they put their hands on are people who screw them over or threaten *them.* They do imports. You guys are no threat to them. Hell, they even import the freaking guns for you at times. Why would they step to you now? Why

8

would they break a three-generation pattern of not
involving families, of not hurting women, now?"

"They wouldn't," he said with a shrug. "But there's no
talking to the rest of them until they burn through this. We
lost a lot of fucking men; they're angry and they've been
sitting on their hands. They need to burn through this for a
few before you try to reason with them."

"You're sure it was the Grassis you all saw?" I pressed,
it finally being the chance to get a calm, rational response
out of someone.

"Oh, it was the fucking Grassis, alright. Luca and
Antony. Matteo wasn't there. Thing is, when Penny told the
story, she didn't say shit about any of them being older,
graying like Antony. Luca could maybe fit the description.
But aside from knowing they just aren't the type to beat
women for no fucking reason or even if they had a reason,
her eyewitness account from the attack was off because she
was either too traumatized or wasn't seeing right, or her ID
today was just off. We were in a moving car. She couldn't
have gotten a great look."

"Why didn't you..."

"We did," he cut me off.

"But by the time you circled back," I started.

"They were already gone."

The finishing each other's sentences thing was only cute
in movies and TV. In real life, it was annoying. Just in case
you were wondering about that. Annoying.

I exhaled a breath and looked back toward the group-
what was left of The Henchmen- Reign, Cash, Repo, Duke,
and Renny beside me. And Wolf in the hospital.

I couldn't imagine having your numbers decimated like
that.

RENNY

Hailstorm was a massive operation. But when we lost someone, there was a noticeable shift in energy for a good couple of weeks. There was a solemnness to the walls. Everyone was more on-edge. I think only twice had we ever lost more than one person at a time.

Losing over a dozen, I couldn't imagine what they were all going through.

They all coped in their own ways. Reign, most noticeably, took the only action he could given the situation. He secured the compound. He made it impenetrable so he could protect what was left of his men and their families.

Cash lost a little of his easy, carefree, flirtatious charm and clung a little tighter to Lo, was a bit more over-protective than ever before.

Repo was a mostly silent ticking time bomb. His life was the club. True, he had Maze and his son and the baby on the way now and that had given him something outside of his brotherhood to cling to, but that didn't change the fact that for many, many years, all he had was brotherhood and loyalty. He dedicated everything to the club. He was weighted and he was ready to shed blood.

Duke was Duke. He was silent and in-control. But he was fuming too. He was ready to take action, to even the score. Especially because his woman was the recipient of a nasty beating then disposed of like garbage.

Renny was, well, that depended.

See, the thing with Renny was, you could tell there were scars there. Not the physical kind, though he did have those and I found them oddly sexy, but he had emotional ones. The ones from childhood. The kind that never really healed. The thing was, I didn't know what they were.

10

Because while I had files on every single other member of The Henchmen MC, I didn't have one for Renny.

Whether Lo had one at all was beyond my pay grade.

All I knew was- I didn't have one for him.

So I had no idea what those scars were, but judging from what I had seen over the past few weeks, they were deep.

Because Renny could be a completely different person at the drop of a dime.

It wasn't that he was schizophrenic or anything like that.

But if I had to put my money on anything, I'd say there was some definite borderline personality issues going on there.

He was too up and down, too hot and cold, too severe in his swings to just say he was a moody guy.

Because, as a whole, he was light, upbeat, funny, charming, and rational. But when he hit a low, he was low. He was dark. He was obsessive and cold and even occasionally, cruel. He didn't think clearly. He reacted on impulse and he did things that he knew were not normal.

The vast majority of the time, he was his light self. He joked around, tried to keep the spirits up around the compound after all the darkness. He played ball with the boys and he let the girls do his hair or even, once when Ferryn was particularly insistent, his makeup. He seemed to be handling things well.

But there were times when he and Duke went at it or he and Repo had words that almost went to blows, there were even a few times when he and Cash got into it and Cash was almost impossible to rile, but those times were when you could see that he was still coping. Fact of the matter was, he was the one to charge into the clubhouse and find the men dead and dying. And he was the one to make Duke get Penny out of there and safe while he stayed behind, surrounded by death, sitting next to a man he loved as a brother as he took his last breath.

Then when the bodies were removed, he had been there with the bucket and the bleach, cleaning up the blood of his fallen brothers.

True, they were one-percenters and were perhaps a bit more used to blood and death than the average citizen, but he was still human. He still had to have been dealing with the aftermath of that experience.

And the fact that he was spending most of his time trying to keep everyone else from falling apart tended to point to the fact that he himself was going to blow apart one day.

I didn't want to imagine the wreckage from that.

I reached for my phone as the argument slowly started to fizzle out, as Reign got control and demanded the others do as well so they could talk about it rationally.

I went through my files and brought up two pictures, moving away from Renny without saying anything, but I could feel his eyes on me the whole way across the room where I sat down next to Penny and put my phone in her hands.

"Who are they?" she asked, looking up at me, brows drawn together.

That had Duke's attention, stopping mid-sentence, making everyone else look toward us as well.

"Baby, those are the Grassis," he told her, his voice guarded. "That was who was on the street today."

"Ah, no," she said, shaking her head. She glanced back down at my phone then handed it back to me. "I mean, maybe they were there too, but this isn't who I was talking about."

For reasons I didn't want to analyze, my head lifted and my gaze found Renny's across the room. He watched me for a second before a slow smile lifted one side of his lips. And if I wasn't entirely mistaken, which what were the chances of that, he almost seemed... proud.

But that was ridiculous.

"Who the fuck else were the Grassis with then?" Reign demanded, looking between Duke and Renny.

Renny held up his hands, "All I saw was Luca and Anthony and the backs of other men. I thought they were just standing there too. Didn't realize they were with the Grassis."

"So back to fucking square one?" Repo growled.

"Not exactly," I reasoned. "If one or two of you can calm down a bit and maybe pay the Grassi family a visit and *ask* who they were with this afternoon that Penny fingered as her attackers, you can get an answer. They're decent men. They will want to help."

"Well," Cash said, smile toying at his lips that I didn't trust, "that kind of sounded like you just volunteered for the task. Didn't it sound like that, Reign?" he asked as Reign's mouth spread into a nearly identical little smile.

"Did sort of sound that way to me," he agreed.

I huffed out my breath, shaking my head. "I'm not a Henchmen, guys. I can't show up there and say I am speaking for you. They won't have any respect for that."

"Which is why Renny should tag along," Cash added, looking downright giddy at the idea.

"You can't..." I started.

"Sounds like a plan," Reign cut me off. "Famiglia should be opening in a couple of hours so Antony and Luca at least should already be around. You guys can head out now and we can finally get some answers."

RENNY

"Really, I think this would be better coming from you, Reign," I insisted. "No offense to Renny, but he's not the president or vice, or even road captain. Why would they want to talk to him instead of you?"

"Because they're smart men and when shit goes down in their own business, they get themselves safe. That's what leaders do. They can't do shit for their people if they're dead. They will understand why I need to stay here. And Cash too for that matter and since Wolf is clinging to life in a fucking hospital bed, they will have to accept that Renny is who is showing up."

"Fine then," I sighed, understanding that logic. "But why am I being ordered to go?"

I didn't work for them in the traditional sense.

I worked for Lo. I worked for Hailstorm.

But so long as my assignment from my higher-ups had me at The Henchmen compound, Reign was, in a way, in charge of me.

"Honestly, babe," Reign said, lips twitching, "just for fucking fun."

The bastard.

TWO

Renny

I was wearing her down.

Alright, that was bullshit.

But it was a nice thought to entertain.

I didn't buy into a lot of the romantic bullshit. I watched men, much better men than me, slowly fall for women over the past several years. All the while I'd sit there believing the shit was just a trick of the brain, a heady concoction of sex hormones and oxytocin bound to burn out eventually.

Then that fucking woman walked into the back door of the compound and interrupted a fight between me and Duke- sexy as fuck voice telling us she thought are

15

scrapping was "interesting," and I turned and saw her, and fuck if I wasn't half goddamn in love with her right then.

Only half, mind you.

And most of that love was my dick doing the thinking.

I wasn't a fucking sap.

She was possibly the most gorgeous woman I had ever seen though. She was tall and leggy, with definite but understated curves to her hips, breasts, and ass. But it was the face, man, that was what brought a man to his knees.

I had always been a sucker for exotic, especially the kind that hinted at a mixed ancestry that was hard to put your finger on. And Mina's round face and hazel eyes and long shiny brown hair hinted as something European and something Asian.

Dutch and Japanese as it turned out.

Then of course there was the fact that she was in Hailstorm garb- utility pants in a khaki color and a white tank that in no way hid how fucking perfectly formed she was.

See, in the past, I thought I liked soft. I'd had a lot of hard and cold in my life, when I aged up and started chasing skirts, I wanted sweet, I wanted gentle. For the most part, that was what I had too.

I had a lot of respect for hardass women like Lo, Janie, and Maze. I knew what it took for a man in the world to get respect and I knew that, for women, it was about three times as hard and the job was never-ending. You never had to stop fighting for it.

But while I loved and respected them as colleagues and the old ladies of my brothers, they just weren't what I wanted. I liked cups of tea. They were shots of whiskey.

Then there was Mina.

And Mina worked at Hailstorm.

16

And Mina was hard.

You didn't notice it at first. It was a sneaky kind of hard. She wasn't in your face aggressive and her niche skills weren't of the bomb-making or ass-kicking variety. She wasn't physically hard. She was emotionally hard.

Maybe that was what made the difference for me. See, when people had guards, when they obsessively kept their life in order, when they made actual effort to come off cool and detached, it usually went to follow that all of that was a mask. Underneath, there was chaos, not order. Underneath, they were warm and cared too much, not cold and withholding.

It could have been as simple as me being obsessive, being a bit too into seeing how the goddamn clock ticked, so I liked pulling it apart and seeing the insides. I could have just been interested in seeing her warm and gushy, in seeing why she was so afraid to let that show.

But there was a part of me, as the weeks passed, that thought maybe it was a bit more than that.

I was also impressed by her insane amount of self-discipline. See, I wasn't overly cocky, but I knew I was goddamn charming when I wanted to be. And I pulled my A-game on her. Constantly. And she kept shooting it down. I wasn't exactly a glutton for punishment, but I couldn't help it with her. I wasn't willing to give up.

It was something the guys found hilarious when they weren't stressing out about threats.

So that was why I was pushing off the wall and snatching the keys out of the air as Reign tossed them to me.

"I'm driving," Mina said, walking toward me, tucking her phone into one of the bulky leg pockets of her sage-colored utility pants. They shouldn't have been sexy. They

17

were meant for practicality, not sexuality. But regardless of the designer's intentions, they looked hot as shit on her shapely, long legs. The black wifebeater she had on wasn't exactly hiding her somewhat small, but perfect tits either.

"Angel face, whatever blows up your skirt," I said, jiggling the keyring on my finger. Her eyes flashed, knowing I was fucking with her because I knew she knew that I knew she didn't like being touched. Or, maybe more accurately, she didn't like me touching her. And no matter how carefully she pulled that keyring off, she would have to touch me a little.

"Don't call me angel face," she said, her tone empty, as it always was when she told someone not to call her an endearment. It was knee-jerk. She told men not to do it all the time. Why, I wasn't sure. But it was just one of the many things I wanted to figure out about her.

She surprised me by reaching out, ripping the keyring off, and turning away. It happened so fast that I barely felt her touching me. Apparently she was a 'rip the bandaid off' kind of woman.

I liked that.

"Are you coming?" she asked, not looking over at me as she rounded toward the door to the new garage where we kept the bullet-resistant SUV parked, so we wouldn't have to walk out into the open and risk getting shot before we got inside the safe car.

"Sweets, I would follow you into an apiary slathered in honey," I agreed, falling into step behind her. "I know, I know," I said when she was silent as she walked toward the driver's side, "you're struck silent by the mental image of me shirtless and covered in sweet, sticky..."

"Renny," she cut me off, turning to face me in the passenger seat.

"Yeah?" I asked when she didn't say anything.

She paused for a second like she'd lost her train of thought. And I knew she either must have or didn't want to admit whatever she was thinking because she clumsily tripped out, "Don't call me sweets," before clicking her buckle, turning over the car, and hitting the button for the garage door.

"I can do that," I admitted. I was running out of names for her. Every time she shot one down, I agreed to not call her it. And I didn't again. She liked her boundaries. And if I was going to get to know her in a more carnal way, I had to respect them. Even if my end game was to finally get to know her well enough to rip out the boundary markers and throw them away. "So," I said as we drove through town in complete and utter silence, "what kind of music do you like?"

"Just give up, Renny," she said, tone almost a little sad.

"If you were looking for some lily-livered beta, Mina, coming into an MC compound was likely not your smartest move."

"I wasn't *looking* for any kind of man," she said, slanting those fucking hypnotic hazel eyes at me for the barest of seconds. "I was doing a job. I *am trying* to do a job. You are just trying to..."

"Get you hot and sweaty and naked underneath me?"

She actually snorted a bit at that, likely not expecting it, and I got to see her rare smile light up her profile. "I was going to say mix business and pleasure."

"That's what I said too. But with a better visual," I said, smiling too as we pulled down the path toward the marina where Famiglia was situated- a dark blue building sitting on stilts out of the water with a giant deck I had yet to sit

19

on and have a meal or a drink. Lived in the town for years and still barely saw the sights.

Out of all of the guys at the compound, I probably knew the Grassi family the least. I knew of them. I knew how their business operated. But I had maybe only exchanged a handful of words with them over the many years I had been around. We just didn't brush elbows much.

There was a hierarchy of criminals just like any type of society. Drug dealers, gangs, pimps, all that shit was at the very bottom. Then, somewhere around the middle, you had your arms dealers and cartels and the underground gambling and whatnot. Higher up, you had your established syndicates: the mob in all its varieties- Italian, Russian, Irish, etc.

So the Grassi family with their docks and their old school Italian mob values, were a couple rungs above us arms-dealing bikers. They dressed, acted, and socialized as such. You didn't exactly run across Luca or Matteo at Chaz's on a Friday night.

Hell, as we climbed out of the car and I looked around, I actually felt no small ping of discomfort going into Famiglia in my jeans, boots, white tee, and leather cut. Mina, fucking knockout she was, looked similarly uncomfortable as we walked toward the doors. It was the kind of place you wore a suit or at least dress shirt or a little black dress.

But we weren't dining. And the restaurant wasn't even open yet.

"Henchmen?" the doorman asked, brows drawing together.

"Renny," I nodded. "And this is Mina, from Hailstorm. We need to talk to Antony and Luca."

"You know," Mina said when he nodded and moved inside to find his bosses, "I think that guy used to be a big shot in Notre Dame."

"Big college football fan?" I asked, surprised.

"Do I *look* like a big college football fan?" she shot back with a smirk. "No. I'm not much for sports, but I live in a place full of men. I can't go anywhere without overhearing some kind of sport conversation. But I'm telling you, that guy was a Fighting Irish."

"Go on in," the door guy said as he moved back outside to his post.

I reached for the door and held it open for her. She moved to step inside then stopped and turned to the guy. "Did you blow out your knee or were you kicked for performance drugs?"

The guy's brow rose slowly, a smile pulling at his lips. "Knee. Ruined my chances at pro. Woulda went all the way too."

Mina looked at me, brow lifted in a very 'told you so' way before she went inside.

"Thanks a lot, man," I said, chuckling. "Like she needed a bigger ego than she's already got."

"Nah, she's a marshmallow inside," he surprised me by saying. "Get past the tough outer layer and it's all sickening sweet. Antony doesn't like being kept waiting, man," he reminded me and I nodded and moved inside.

"Renny!" Antony called as I walked up to where Mina was already standing with the two men. Antony, either thanks to owning a restaurant and therefore needing to be hospitality friendly or because he was just like that naturally, greeted most people like they were old friends. Apparently that included me. "How is everyone holding up?" he asked, eyes grave, understanding a loss as big as ours.

"We're ready for it to stop," I said and he nodded. "Luca," I greeted, inclining my chin to him.

It didn't exactly escape me that Mina's eyes lingered on him for a long minute either. If she had a type, and most people did, apparently Luca with his tall, dark, and handsome was hers.

"So what brings you here today?" Antony went on, gesturing toward the table we were all standing near and pulling out a chair for Mina himself. If there was one thing the Grassi family had, aside from shittons of money, a great reputation in the community despite their illegal endeavors, and good looks, it was impeccable manners.

"You heard about Penny, the girl who got beat up and dropped at our compound. What started this all..."

"Yes," Luca said, wincing a little.

"Well, she got a good look at her attackers before she was knocked out. And this morning we were taking her out and she saw them. Freaked the fuck out." I paused, looking between them for any reaction. Seeing none, I went on. "At first, we thought it was you."

"Us?" Antony scoffed, mouth agape, clearly offended.

"You can't be serious, Renny," Luca added, shaking his head. "When have we ever had a reputation for hurting innocents?"

"Never," Mina piped in. "Which is why we are here. When I showed her your pictures, she said it wasn't you guys who she saw. So, we figure it was whoever you were having brunch with today. And we're going to need those names," she added as the two shared a long, hard look.

"We're not trying to step on anyone's toes here," I added. "But those fuckers beat up an innocent woman, nearly killed our road captain, and decimated the rest of our numbers. I don't care who the fuck you are in bed with, even you guys know they need to pay for that."

Luca nodded to his father and Antony sighed. "We were trying to make peace with them. They've been a thorn in our side for years now, trying to move in. I guess they realized they couldn't get the docks after all and set their sights on you. Maybe they thought they could take over the arms trade in the area and that our families would need to get along since we import..."

"Families?" Mina cut in at the exact same moment I was going to ask the same question.

"As in... *family*?" I put in for good measure.

We didn't fuck with the mob. We had scuffled with a bunch of the smaller organizations over the years, but we never had to deal with the truly organized side of organized crime.

Luca nodded. "They have slowly been trying to get off the Island and moving this way. The Abruzzo family."

Mina's entire body stiffened at that name, her eyes going active for a long second before she stood suddenly, the chair scratching hard against the floor.

"We have to go," she said, looking down at me, tone serious. Then she turned and walked away.

I stood up more slowly, unsure what the fuck just happened, but figuring the Abruzzos must be bad news to make her react that strongly. "I guess that's my cue, guys," I said, shrugging. "Thank you for the name. I think."

"If there's any more information you need," Antony said, waving a hand and I was impressed with how carefully he worded that. Not- *if there's anything you need*, but *if there's any more information you need*. Smart on his

23

part to not pick sides when a war was waging, knowing he would benefit from either side's win.

"We appreciate it. Reign will be in touch," I added as I turned away and walked toward the door.

Mina was already gone, situated in the running car.

"Something got her spooked. She ran out here yelling into her phone. Saying they needed to warn the Mallicks."

"The Mallicks?" I asked, brows drawing together, knowing I was missing a big part of the picture and not liking that one bit. "Sucks about the knee man, but the Grassis will take care of you," I said, clamping a hand on his shoulder before moving toward the stairs.

"You'll wear her down," he called to me as I made my way toward the car, seeing Mina talking rapidly on her cell.

Even freaked, she was goddamn perfect.

I was going to wear her down alright.

But not before I figured out who the fuck the Abruzzo family was, what the fuck they wanted from us, and what the fuck that had to do with the fucking Mallick family.

Priorities, in this case, meant to make sure *my* ass was still breathing long enough to get *her* pretty ass in my bed.

THREE

Mina

The Abruzzos?

In what freaking universe was that who was stepping to The Henchmen?

"I'm putting a call into Charlie Mallick now," Lo said, sounding calm though I know she was likely as freaked as I was. "He needs to warn Eli."

"Isn't Eli still..."

"Not as of this morning," she cut me off. "Are you heading back now?"

"Yeah, Renny just got in the car. We will be there in five."

"I'll be there in twenty. Janie is at the hospital, but I don't want to involve her in this. I'll call Alex instead. We need all hands on deck if we are going to figure out how the fuck some nobodies from Long freaking Island are taking down one of the longest-standing organizations in Navesink Bank."

She ended the call and I tossed my phone toward Renny as I threw the car into reverse and peeled out of the marina. "So are you going to let me..."

"I only want to tell it once and it's a short drive. You'll just have to wait."

I knew he wanted to say something to that; I could feel the air in the car getting thicker, more oppressive and I knew that fun-loving Renny was taking a short vacation and dark Renny was making an appearance. But, really, there was no time to coddle him.

We pulled into the garage and flew out of the car in unison, both getting to the door at the same time, but Renny held it open for me despite his mood.

Everyone was in the common room, kids included.

Reign's head jerked up when the door closed. He looked at me for a long minute before turning to Summer and giving her a look that managed to communicate that the kids needed to disappear.

"Come on guys, let's go see the glass room!" Summer declared cheerfully, but I could hear the tension there. She was stressing out. And given that she was pregnant, things needed to calm down so she and Maze, who was also expecting, could finish out their pregnancies with as little stress and worry as possible.

The kids jumped up, excited, knowing they weren't usually allowed to go up there and it was novel to be able to. Even though Ferryn was old enough to give everyone a look that suggested she knew she was being shooed away so the adults could talk and that she didn't care for that one bit.

She was going to be a handful when she was a teenager. I hoped Reign and Summer were aware of that.

"Alright," Reign said when it was just the men left, Penny going with the women and kids because she was the only one who could climb the ladder with them. "What'd they say?"

I swallowed a little hard, not particularly liking being the one bringing the information to them. Again, it was messy. I never had to be the one to deal with the outrage and the questioning and everything like that. I was hoping Lo was hauling ass so I only had to deal with it for a few minutes.

"The Abruzzo family."

"You've got to be *fucking* kidding me," Reign seethed, standing suddenly to pace a few feet, raking a hand through his hair.

"Who the fuck is the Abruzzo family?" Duke asked, looking at his brothers.

"Remember that time Wolf got locked up?" Reign asked the group at large.

"Which time?" Duke snorted. Wolf's uncontrollable temper was not exactly a secret to anyone.

"The time he ripped mother fucking Lex Keith to shreds," Reign said, stopping pacing suddenly and standing almost freakishly still.

"Know Lex Keith was a rapist scumbag..." Duke offered, shaking his head.

"Yeah, he was. And once upon a time a long fucking time ago, he got ahold of Janie. Way before Wolf and she shacked up, but when she told him, he flipped his shit and got locked up for it. But, along the way, Janie kind of lost her shit around here..."

"Janie loses her shit all the time," Renny said, smiling affectionately.

"Yeah, no. She snapped. Was ordering us around and shit. It was nuts. And the cop on the case, Marco, would not be bribed. He was a fucking hardhead. Was in no one's pockets. Janie enlisted Eli and had his ass kicked, found out something was off with him, did some digging, and realized he was an Abruzzo."

"And that is a bad thing because..." Duke went on.

"Janie just wanted Wolf out of jail. She went to the Grassis and told them the Abruzzos were in town, figured she would create some chaos. The Grassis don't want any other Italians stepping in on their turf, understandably enough. Marco was never heard from again, though we have no proof that they killed him. We thought that was the end of it."

"You never stopped to wonder if they were after the arms trade?" Renny asked. "Taking out Wolf seemed pretty planned. Especially over something like Lex Keith's murder. The cops wanted him put down just as badly as everyone else..."

"We considered it," Cash said, running a hand up the shaved side of his head. "But that was the end of everything. Wolf got out of jail. Things went back to normal. None of us have heard the fucking Abruzzo name since then."

"Until now," Renny said, exhaling hard.

"So they were having a meeting with the Grassis," Reign said, tone deceptively calm. "The were making a power move, trying to get in good with the importers before they took over fully. Getting connections."

"They're fucking glorified goddamn pimps on Long Island," Repo said suddenly, jaw clenched tight. "The fuck

28

makes them think they can overtake the gun trade in Jersey?"

"The fact that they obviously have almost already accomplished that goal?" I asked, realizing my mistake when all their eyes snapped to me, angry. All except Renny who was pressing his lips together like he was trying to hold back a smile.

I was not a blurter. I didn't let my mouth run away with me. Everything I said was carefully thought out and filtered to produce the reaction I wanted. And having four angry bikers pissed at me and one amused by me, was absolutely not the reaction I wanted.

What was wrong with me?

"What I am saying is," I tried, taking a breath, "that they have obviously outgrown their prostitution ring. And they must have new leadership that is hungry for bigger and better for themselves. This has been carefully orchestrated. I mean that thing with Wolf was *years* ago. I don't think I need to tell you that having an opponent as patient as that, as persistent as that is really dangerous. They are in this for the long haul. And, I know this isn't what you want to hear, but you are weak right now. You are down to five capable members. Even if you can find them and go after them... you won't be able to do it with brute force. You'll have to..."

I was cut off by the blaring of a horn outside. My eyes went to Cash and he gave me a strained smile. "That'd be my woman," he said, getting up and moving toward the door, hitting the button for the gate.

Lo came charging in two minutes later, Malcolm and L in toe. If Lo was our badass mother figure up at Hailstorm, then Malcolm was our badass father. Ex-military, skilled, capable, calm, caring, and focused, he cared for every last one of us like we were family. Which, given that he had none of his own, was likely how he felt.

L was, well, an enigma.

He had been at Hailstorm for the better part of two years and my file on him was all but blank. I had a picture where he was as obnoxiously good-looking in a candid shot of him drinking his Big Gulp full of coffee as he was in person- mid-twenties, dark, shaggy hair, dark eyes, perfect bone structure. I had a couple scribbles about the fact that he was very likely the smartest person I had ever come into contact with. He was also blunt, sarcastic, and reclusive.

What he was doing there, I had no idea. He, like me, generally preferred to work from a distance. Though I had no idea what his specialty even was.

"You guys know Malcolm," Lo said, waving her hand toward him. "This is L. They're here to help us make a plan."

Malcolm made sense. Being ex-military, he knew all about covert operations, sneaking up on the enemy, making a plan that wouldn't blow up in everyone's faces, even if they only had five able-bodied men left. Whole armies had been taken down by less.

I fell back, leaning against the wall to watch as L moved into the center of the room, pulling a pile of folders out of his black, busted-up messenger bag. "The Abruzzo family," he said, handing out the files. "Ten years ago, they were nobodies. Then Ricky Sr. died suddenly and, if you ask anyone in the know, suspiciously, and Ricky Jr. stepped up. Little Ricky, named ironically because he's about a fucking thousand pounds, wasn't happy pimping out poor women and liberally taking use of them whenever he damn well pleased anymore. He set his sights higher. And since New

York has too many established syndicates, they set their sights on Jersey."

He moved back from the group as they flipped through the pages, looking at the pictures for a second, but giving L most of their attention. "Little Ricky even had his cousin Marco go through the fucking academy and join the police force. Not, at first, to lock you guys all up, but to have someone on the inside to hide evidence when they eventually did gain power. Though, he has been missing since after Janie had Eli put him in the hospital. That thing with Wolf, that was just a smart move to bring him in."

"Why us?" Duke asked. "Got tons of crime around here. The Mallicks and their loan sharking, Breaker and Shooter with their hired muscle and contract killing, Lyon and his cocaine, Third Street and their heroin and shit, Grassis and their docks. Why us? Why the arms trade?"

"Best fucking guess," L said, shrugging, "it's easiest."

"Easy?" Reign scoffed, brows drawing together.

L held up a hand, not the kind of man who put up with overt displays of testosterone-driven anger. "It's easier. There isn't a whole hell of a lot of daily effort. You don't have to go out every day and beat the shit out of people like the Mallick family. You don't have to inspect shipping containers like the Grassi family. You don't have to find reliable contacts in South America like Lyon who can get cocaine in this country. You don't need to travel like Shooter or deal with the scum of the Earth like Breaker. As for Third Street, well, they're a pathetic force these days. Paine and Enzo held them together. They've been flailing since. There's nothing to take over there right now."

"We don't exactly sit on our fucking hands all day," Reign said, shaking his head. "The Abruzzo family thinks it wants to go off to meeting with the Russians and Irish

31

and Mexicans and Chinese all the fucking time? Do they have any fucking idea how unpredictable they all are?"

"I imagine they figure since you have had peace for so long that all your relations are solid. Who the fuck do I have to fuck to get some coffee around here?" he blurted out suddenly, making me let out a surprised laugh before pushing off the wall and walking to the kitchen.

"Don't worry about the payment," I said as I passed him, "you're not my type, L."

He was actually. Except he was too young.

"You're not my type either," he said casually, not bothering to sugarcoat it, as was his nature.

I moved into the kitchen, glad to be out of there, to be away from the almost overwhelming swirling emotions in the other room. Quiet, it had felt like forever since I got any.

At least back at Hailstorm, there was always somewhere I could sneak away to to get some peace. There wasn't a whole hell of a lot of places to escape at The Henchmen compound, especially with the kids running around.

"What's that kid's story?" Renny asked as I was scrubbing the coffee pot.

"He doesn't have one he is willing to share." I shrugged.

"And you accept that?" Renny asked, sounding surprised.

"People deserve to have their secrets at times."

"Bullshit," he shot back, making my head snap over to him, finding him watching me.

"It's not bullshit."

"It is complete and utter bullshit," he said, shaking his head. "You don't believe that at all. I'd bet you have files on every other fucking person at Hailstorm. And, for that matter, everyone who is a major player in this town." He wasn't wrong, so I just turned back and rinsed out the pot, filling it with fresh water. I went over to pour it into the machine, finding Renny standing right near it and too stubborn to move so my shoulder and arm brushed his chest as I filled the machine. "What does my file say, sweetheart?"

I felt my belly wobble at the low, intimate way he asked, his breath warm on my ear, making a shiver move through my insides.

The familiar warning alarm was going off somewhere inside, but it seemed more muffled, lost under the heavy blanket of desire.

I had been there too long. I had been around Renny and his flirting for too long. He was wearing me down. And that was not good.

I made my hand lift, hitting the button for the machine, taking a deep breath as it started to drip.

And it was right about then that his hand moved out to my hip then slid across my back, landing on the other hip and using it to turn me toward him. Already standing so close, our chests pressed into each other and my breasts forgot we were supposed to be resisting him and swelled in desire.

"You're losing those defenses..." he said, his arm tightening around my lower back. "You gonna admit you want me yet?" he asked, his voice deeper.

"Renny, I..."

"Where the hell is L's coffee?" Lo's voice called. "He's going to come to blows with Repo at this rate... oh..." she said as I sprang away from Renny, my face heating.

"It's dripping," Renny said easily, obviously not as embarrassed about being caught as I was. "If he wants, he can come in here and stick his head under it and drink it as

33

it comes out, he's welcome to. Though I don't think the insurance here covers third degree burns from idiot coffee drinkers."

"Idiot," Lo mused, pressing her lips together, her brown eyes dancing. "I think I might just tell him you called him that." Then she looked over at me, her head cocking to the side. "Mina, come take a walk with me," she invited, nodding toward the door.

What was left of The Henchmen generally didn't spend much time out on their property. They were too few and too valuable. But Lo and I could walk around freely as the Abruzzo family didn't seem overly invested in taking any of us out. Which was a smart move on their part. No matter how big their operation had gotten, they didn't want to mess with Hailstorm.

"So, Renny, huh?" she asked as soon as we stepped outside, turning and waving at the kids who were up in the DARPA glass enclosure on the roof- nothing, no firearm in the world, could penetrate that glass. They were as safe as could be up there.

"No, Lo," I objected immediately, shaking my head.

"It didn't look like a no in the kitchen," she added.

"Renny is a flirt," I brushed it off.

"He is," she agreed with a nod. "But I have seen you shatter a man's ego with a few carefully chosen words when they wouldn't back off before."

That was true enough. "Renny isn't like most guys."

"Because he is like you," she nodded. "You know, I would think it would be almost refreshing to find that- someone who gets how you are. I don't see any relief in you though. If anything, you're tense. What are you so afraid of here? That you won't be able to keep up appearances? That if he gets in, he will see that your life isn't quite as neat as it seems, that you aren't quite as perfectly controlled as you want people to believe?"

That was exactly it.

There was a legitimate reason that very few people wanted to be exposed emotionally. It made you vulnerable. It gave people with bad intentions the ability to hurt you in a more lasting way.

No one wanted to expose the hidden parts of themselves to someone unless they knew that person was trustworthy.

I didn't feel that way about Renny.

He was too unpredictable, too up and down.

And he had used information he had gained on his own people against them in the past. I didn't need that kind of uncertainty in my life.

"I can't trust him, Lo," I admitted. "It's not like you and Cash. It's not..."

"I know we're so stupidly in love that it's sick," she cut me off. "But it wasn't always that way. It certainly didn't start that way. He didn't like me because he didn't approve of what we did at Hailstorm. I had no interest in being a notch on his very, very long belt. And we butted heads and we sniped at each other and we didn't get along. But he proved himself. Sometimes you need to give men that chance."

"To prove themselves?" I asked, shaking my head. "I think their actions and lifestyle should..."

"But they don't," she cut me off again. "They don't. Sometimes men get stuck in a spiral of sport sex and responsibility-shirking and hanging out with their buddies who do the same thing, not realizing that they want more. Until more shows up."

"Right, but we're not talking about his whoring around. I don't care about that. It would be weird if he didn't, to be perfectly honest. I'm talking about the fact that he's deceptive and he is unpredictable and he..." I waved out a hand, not sure what else to say. For me, that was enough.

"You know, Mina," she said, stopping suddenly when we found ourselves under a big tree at the far end of the yard, in the field where Repo had some of his cars situated again since the garage was burned down. "Sometimes it's good to not be able to read someone, to not be able to dig around in their brains. You have been the way you are for so long that I think you forget that that is not how relationships between people work. You see what is going on inside someone because they *choose* to tell you. They put their faith to rest in you. They believe they can trust you to handle that information with care. Maybe if you gave Renny a chance to give you some of himself, he would."

"But that doesn't change the fact that I don't think I can trust him."

"You'll never know unless you give him the chance to prove that you can, babe."

She wasn't exactly wrong. And I wasn't exactly crazy about that.

"Besides," I said, shrugging, "relationships aren't in the cards for me."

"Why? Because you travel a lot? Mina, I travel a lot too. Cash is a big boy, he gets on without me when I have to go. Plus, the welcome home sex is always hot," she added with a smirk. "Don't let the job keep you from the more important things in life, honey."

I wasn't sure the last time I was with a man who I would call a boyfriend or partner or anything more than a fling or a friend with benefits. It had to have been years. Several, if I was being honest.

Most of that, I was sure, was my own damn fault. It was always just too hard for me to open up, to let down my guards, to be real with someone. And it was selfish to try to tell a guy to hang around, to let me take a year to get over my hangups. That was just unrealistic. It was easier to ignore the reality completely.

Occasionally, I would go on a date or two.

And, once in a while, I would take a man to bed, albeit somewhat rarely because it tended to only complicate things.

But as a whole, I avoided entanglements.

It made everyones' lives easier.

Why, all of a sudden, it was such a big deal, well, I was going to go ahead and blame that on the fact that I was never in the same place for so long with a guy who couldn't take a hint.

It had nothing, absolutely nothing, to do with Renny.

It could have been any guy in any city in any country around the world. It just so happened to be him I was stationed around for so long.

"It's your life and you're a grown woman, Mina, and I would be the first woman to tell you that you don't *need* a man to have a good, fulfilling life. I just don't want you to be so closed-off to the possibility on some kind of bullshit principle. Having a man isn't going to strip you of your uniqueness or your skills, babe. I don't care how good his dick is, he can't steal your spark with it," she said with a wink. "Besides," she went on, starting to move away from me, "your job here is almost done. Take a ride on that man before you're off to fucking Chicago or Boise or wherever the hell you're heading next."

At that declaration, at the realization that my time was coming to an end at The Henchmen compound, I didn't feel relief like I should have. I was almost always happy to complete a job, to be able to move on, to get back to the compound or to see a new city.

It was in my blood.

That was how I was raised- to never put down roots.

It had gotten so that, over time, I wasn't sure I could grow them if I wanted to.

I sighed, sitting down at the bottom of the tree, looking off at the compound for a long time, trying not to get too down on myself over something that wasn't my fault.

We all had our damages, our traumas, our origin stories.

Mine, thankfully, was not tragic like many of the people who ended up at Hailstorm. Mine just involved a withholding mother and a workaholic father whose job took him all over the world at a moment's notice. So I never got to learn how to make connections, how to open up to new people. It was always a wasted effort in my life. As soon as I tried to get to that point, it was time to move on.

Why bother?

But, for the first time, the idea of never bothering seemed really sad and empty.

FOUR

Renny

The L guy was like an encyclopedia of crime families. Ask him anything from fucking Lucky Luciano's shoe size to who is running the mob in Nowheresville, USA and he had an answer for you. So when everyone got their confusion and outrage out of the way, he sat down with his giant cup of coffee and gave us all the dirt he had on the Abruzzo family. And he knew a lot.

Like Little Ricky was power hungry and while he didn't often involve himself in the hands-on aspect of things, according to L because he literally couldn't walk down his driveway without having a near cardiac episode, he had his men becoming increasingly violent since he took over. Their prostitutes got knocked around a lot more, got

39

smaller cuts of the money. And, apparently, they had graduated to cold-blooded murder.

The scary part was, for all L knew and he knew a fuckuva lot, he had no idea where they were. Well, Little Ricky was sitting pretty in his mini mansion on Long Island, but there was no accounting for who the men were in Navesink Bank and where they were located.

He recommended hiring someone to do a sketch of the men Penny had seen so that we and Hailstorm, at the very fucking least, had some faces to watch out for.

Malcolm sat down with everyone and formulated some plans, all being useless until there was a location, but it was good to have an idea of what we would be doing regardless.

Sometime around dinner time, the women coming back in because the kids were getting whiny for food; Malcolm and L took off back to Hailstorm, Lo hanging back to spend the night with Cash.

And Mina was still missing.

She had come in from outside about half an hour before the food finished and disappeared again

"She likes quiet," Lo supplied as we both piled food onto plates. "It's hard to come by here."

"She likes it," I agreed, putting one plate down and grabbing another, "but it's the last fucking thing she needs."

Lo turned back to me, head ducked to the side, looking at me like she had never seen me before. "You scare her, Renny," she surprised me by saying. I knew for damn sure that Mina would never be okay with her divulging that kind of information, even though it was something I already knew.

"Good," I said, making her brows raise as I grabbed two bottles of beer and tucked them into my pockets so my hands were free to grab the plates. "Know she's your girl and you love her, but she needs to be scared. She needs to be frazzled. She needs to have someone shake up her perfect little world a bit."

"And you're the person to do that?" she asked, lips quirked up slightly.

"Might be the only person capable. Besides," I added with a grin, "I mean... just look at me..."

She laughed at that, her face lighting up. "Alright," she said, nodding. "I'm not really the 'don't hurt my girl or I'll chop off your balls' kind of friend, but you know how they supposedly pickled Rasputin's cock..."

It was my turn to laugh. "Got it, Lo," I said, saluting her with a plate as I made my way toward the hallway and down the stairs.

Fact of the matter was, the clubhouse was pretty empty these days. Even with the women and kids around, it was quieter. It was eerie. I wasn't sure I would ever get used to it. Most of the doors in the hallway, the doors that used to house our fallen brothers, were closed, were a constant reminder of what we had lost. And thanks to the constant threat, we hadn't even been able to have a proper mother fucking memorial for any of them. For the men who didn't have family, we had the remains buried or cremated according to their wishes. And we had talked Shooter and Breaker into going to the services when we couldn't so they wouldn't be fucking empty.

It wasn't right.

They were our *brothers*.

We should have been there to say words, spill liquor, toss dirt, show them the respect they deserved for their loyalty and ultimate sacrifice.

RENNY

There was a part of me, albeit an absolutely minuscule part of me, that almost felt bad for what was going to happen to those sorry sons of bitches who came in and killed our men.

An image flashed into my head, the clubhouse completely fucking saturated in blood- on the walls, the floor, the table, TV, couch, on the fucking liquor bottles, some of the beds, the bathrooms.

I closed my eyes tight, taking a slow, deep breath, pushing it away. That was all I had been doing too- pushing it away. I hadn't faced it yet. I hadn't worked through the feelings I had been denying myself. I knew it wasn't healthy, it wasn't good. It would make me even more unpredictable than usual. It was eating away at my sleep. It was keeping me on edge.

But I couldn't bring myself to relive it yet.

So it went back into the box inside to be dealt with at a better time.

I moved down the stairs to the basement that Duke had done the bulk of the remodel on, turning it into a damn fine fallout shelter. Coming from his background, it made sense. Those doomsday racist fucks.

"Feels like home down here, huh?" I asked her as I walked down, finding her on a bottom bunk, flat on her back, staring numbly at the bunk above her.

Her head turned to me, her face blank. "I came down here to be alone."

I shrugged, putting her plate down next to her hip, pulling out the beers and tossing them on the mattress then sitting down next to her feet, leaning back against the footboard so I could face her.

"In what way was that an invitation?" she asked, scooting up, careful to not touch me. She always was. It was like she knew that if we touched, shit was going to escalate.

"Your mouth might be saying 'go fuck yourself', but your eyes are saying 'please fuck me until I can't see straight anymore'. I'm fluent in eye-language," I added with a smirk as she rolled those gorgeous hazel eyes of hers and reached for her plate.

"Did you guys make a plan?"

"Not much of a plan to make until we have a number or, at the very least, a location."

"Oh my *God*," she groaned suddenly, pulling the fork out of her mouth and closing her eyes for a second.

I suddenly wished I could cook like fucking Repo.

"Yeah, sweetheart. Do that again, but maybe arch your back and..." I started and cut off on a chuckle when she kicked me with her sock-clad foot.

"Shut up," she said, shaking her head as she stabbed a piece of broccoli. "The cooks up at Hailstorm are, ah, adequate. But it's glorified military food. This, this," she said, pointing her fork toward the apple-stuffing stuffed pork loin, "is practically gourmet."

I nodded at that, acknowledging it. Repo could fine-tune an engine and do some real damage with a gun, but his cooking skills were legendary in our circle.

"So are we really not going to discuss the Pokémon socks? Like, are we going to sit here and pretend they're not right here, staring me in the face? Fucking *Pokémon*," I added with a smile as I looked over at her feet, realizing how fucking small they actually were without her clunky combat boots on them. And the socks were Pokémon-electric blue background with red and white Poké Ball on them.

To my surprise, she didn't snap that it was none of my business or tell me to get lost or claim it was some gag gift. She shrugged a shoulder slightly and looked down at her plate for a second. "We traveled a lot when I was a kid. I became really attached to my Gameboy. Flight after flight or train or car ride after train or car ride, I always had Charmander or Bulbasaur to keep me occupied."

"You don't fidget," I said and her head snapped up, brows drawn together. "Kids who grow up gaming all the time, they tend to fidget. They're used to their hands always being active so when they're still, they tap their fingers or pull their jewelry or mess with their hair. You don't fidget."

"You know how in poker, everyone has a tell?" she asked, but went on without an answer. "When you fidget, people read into it."

"And heaven fucking forbid someone gets to crack open your cover, huh?"

"Hey, Kettle, it's Pot," she said, shaking her head. "You're black."

"Alright," I said, nodding, accepting that. I couldn't expect her to spill if I didn't give her something too. "Quid pro quo, Agent Starling..."

"So in this little scenario, you're a face-eating cannibal?" she asked, brow raised.

"Play along, you pain in the ass."

She snorted at that, not able to hold back the smile. She fucking *liked* me. If she would just stop being so goddamn chicken shit all the time.

"Alright, is Renny your real name?"

"Yeah," I agreed, already uncomfortable with the line of questioning. But if I expected her to peel back a layer, I needed to as well. "It's my mother's maiden name. Renny Renolds West." That was more than I gave anyone save for

Reign and the other higher-up guys. It was more than I wanted anyone to know. Because there was only one Renny Renolds West and a search of Renny Renolds West would produce the name of two doctors named Katherine Renny-West and Roland West. From there, there would be a lot of speculation about how the son of two extremely prominent and respected shrinks from up in Maine ended up with a biker for a son. And Mina, yeah, she was every damn bit as good as she thought she was. She would dig up my dirt eventually.

Somehow, it wasn't as fucking terrifying as it usually seemed.

"Renny Renolds West," she rolled my name around on her tongue, sounding way too fucking good in that odd accent of hers. "How... distinguished. What no third or fourth attached to that?"

"My parents were a bit pretentious. They liked their appearances. It was bad enough I had copper fucking hair. They couldn't have a kid running around named Billy or Bobby or some shit like that."

"Were?"

"Are." She caught fucking everything. It was oddly sexy. Which probably said a lot about me and my odd proclivities. "Alright, you're up," I said and noticed how hard she tried to not stiffen, but she did. "Joey or Chandler?"

She jerked back at that, her perfect goddamn lips parting. "I'm sorry... what?"

"Joey or Chandler. From *Friends.*"

"I'm not sure I understand the question," she said, brows drawing together, creasing a small line between them.

"Which one do you like better?"

"You can't be serious," she said, shaking her head. "You're given a free pass to ask me anything, but you want to know my preferences on some sitcom?"

"You can tell a lot about a girl if you know her preferences on fictional sitcom characters. Pick one."

She looked up at the top bunk for a second, her head shaking. "I guess... Chandler."

"Why?"

"That's two questions."

"Yeah, but mine is trivial. Trivial questions get to have a follow up question to keep it fair."

"Are these rules written down somewhere?" she shot back. "Can I have a copy of this rule book?"

"No need, I have it all up here," I said, tapping my temple. "Answer."

She licked her lips. "His sarcasm is used to mask his deep-rooted insecurity and vulnerability brought on by a confusing and non-traditional upbringing."

"Why not Joey then? He's a simpler character."

"Who wants simple?" she shot back and it was the right fucking response. "Okay. You joined The Henchmen when you were about twenty. But you had been kicking around Navesink Bank for years before then. Why did you run away from home?"

"Why does a rat chew off his feet to escape the sticky tape?"

"Oh," she said, clearly surprised at the bluntness. Frankly, I was a little surprised myself.

"Why didn't your mother love you?" I asked, catching her off guard and her eyes went huge for a short second. "She didn't, that much is clear. But why?"

46

She swallowed a little hard at that and then exhaled slowly. "Because I wasn't a boy and because I couldn't make my father love *her.*"

"Babies never save a bad marriage," I agreed.

"Did your parents beat you?"

"Nah," I said, clicking my tongue. That wasn't their style. "When was the last time you had an orgasm?"

"What?" she shrieked, clearly thrown off her game.

"Orgasm," I repeated, trying like fuck to not grin. "You know... when your breathing catches and your body tightens and your pussy..."

"I know what an orgasm is," she cut me off.

"I was just checking. You know, in case it's been so long that you've forgotten."

She lifted her chin a little, not wanting to seem prudish about the line of questioning. "Self-inflicted or from a partner?"

"Both."

"This wasn't trivial, you don't get a backup question. Pick one."

"Fine. Self," I said, not really giving a fuck what her sexual history was, but genuinely curious how often she diddled the skittle when between partners.

"I don't know... a month..."

"A *month?*" I asked, brow raising.

"I live at Hailstorm!" she defended. "I sleep in a barracks."

"Not for nothing, sweetheart, but I don't think a goddamn man in that room would have a problem with you taking care of business right then and there."

She laughed at that, giving me a small smile and not asking me to not call her that. I had called her it earlier

47

without her objecting to it. So *sweetheart* it was. And, somehow, that was a really telling little thing.

"Why do you and Duke hate each other?"

Now there was an interesting question with no simple answer. I didn't hate Duke. I actually had a lot of respect for him until I figured out he was hiding a neo-nazi upbringing. You can't help what you're born into. I knew that better than anyone. But when I pushed that button to make sure it didn't create a spark, it set off what had been a ticking time bomb.

"We all have our things," I started, grabbing the beer and popping the top off. "I push buttons to see what they do. It's not exactly a habit that makes friends. Especially when you push a man like Duke's buttons and he fucking blows up. It's not a habit I can or even want to break and it's not something Duke can look over or forgive. We fight and we piss each other off, but he's my brother. That means something to me. Especially now."

"For what it's worth, Penny likes you. I think she'll bring him around eventually if you could maybe *try* to stop being a dick."

"Yeah, but what are the chances of that?" I asked with a smirk. "Why are you fighting this so hard?" I asked since it was my turn.

"Fighting what?" she asked, knowing damn well what I meant.

I took my plate, still mostly-full, and reached up to put it on the top bunk and put my beer on the floor, scooting forward on the mattress until our hips were lined up. My hand rose, gliding across her jaw until it cupped the side of her face. "This," I clarified. "And don't insult both of us by saying there isn't a this, because we both fucking know there is."

"Renny, it's..."

"Not complicated," I cut in. "So it's what? Scary? I scare you." Her eyes fell from mine, unable to admit that that was the truth. "Because you don't get the luxury of hiding from me. Because I can see past the shields."

"It's not that..."

"You do see that it's the same for me, right? You and me, we're two sides of the same fucking coin. No one gets to pull me apart and see how I tick. But I am letting you. It's not any easier for me to do it than it is for you to do it. But I'm willing to take the chance and see what happens. I'm just asking you to give it the same shot here. Not asking you to do something that I'm not willing to."

I had her with that.

Her eyes rose to mine, a little less guarded, a little more vulnerable. She had just given me more in ten minutes than she had given me in weeks.

The thing was, I wanted more. I wanted it all.

And judging by the fact that her eyelids were getting heavier as my finger traced up her cheek, yeah, she wanted more too.

My face lowered toward hers, watching for any sign of pulling away. Finding none, my lips pressed down to hers.

"There's someone at the gate," Cash called down the stairs. "Get your asses up here."

Mina shocked away from me, her lips parted, her eyes wide, realizing what we had been about to do.

"Move," she demanded, pressing a hand into my chest and when I didn't immediately go to comply, she shot off the other side of the bed, rushing around and slamming her feet into her shoes, obviously eager for a chance to create some distance again.

RENNY

But she was really fucking underestimating me if she thought we were going to take steps back now that we had finally taken some forward.

I got off the bed, grabbing my beer, and heading upstairs to find everyone standing around save for Summer and Maze and the kids, likely all relegated to one of the rooms.

"Who is it?"

"My guys at the gate said they don't know him. Introduced himself as Laz," Lo supplied, shrugging. "He wants to talk to Reign. They patted him down and are bringing him in."

Repo pulled the door open and in walked Lo's heavily armed guys who were on loan from Hailstorm until we could man our own gates again. Between them was a tall guy with short dark hair, dark eyes that seemed to hold a lot of depth, and a swimmer's-type body in jeans and a black tee.

He seemed completely at ease between the two armed escorts to his sides too.

Which was interesting.

"Who the hell are you?" Reign asked, brow raised, body tense, ready to react if need be.

"Lazarus Alexander," he said, his voice deeper than you'd expect.

"Alright, Lazarus Alexander," Reign said, nodding slightly. It was proof of how on-edge he was that he didn't take a second to rib him on a name like that. "What the fuck are you doing here?"

"Just figured I would give you all a heads-up that some guys were breaking into your gym."

"The fuck?" Reign asked, head jerking back. "When?"

50

"Literally right now," Lazarus said, shrugging casually. "Know you guys have been having some, ah, issues lately. Figured you might want to know about that. I was taking a walk, saw them down the side entrance in the alley so I made my way this way."

"Didn't think maybe it'd be faster to call?" Duke suggested, shaking his head. It was a good ten minute walk from the gym to the compound.

"Wow, fucking stupid on me, huh? I should have picked up the yellow pages and looked under, what? Arms dealers? Bikers? Unappreciative assholes?" he added, smirking a little.

It wasn't every day a man walked into a biker compound and insulted the men who lived there. The fact that this guy would do it was interesting. And maybe a little bit impressive.

I could tell Reign felt the same way judging by the smirk pulling on his lips. "Alright, smartass. How many?"

"I only saw two but there could be more."

"Alright. Duke, take our new friend here down to the basement until we get this sorted out. Renny, Mina, you," he said, pointing to one of the guys from the gate. They changed daily. It was impossible to learn names. "Will come with me."

"Reign," Lo tried to cut in, her voice reasoning.

"Tired of sitting behind reinforced walls while our fucking lives go to shit, Lo. I'm going. And I'll take Renny. The rest can stay behind and keep an eye on things here. And I want someone with him," he said, jerking his chin toward Lazarus, "until we get back. Let's move," he declared and we all jumped to action.

Duke led Lazarus toward the hall and basement, the man seeming completely unaffected by becoming, at least

51

temporarily, prisoner in a biker compound. Reign and I grabbed guns from behind the bar. Mina took one off of Lo. Then, as a unit, we all made our way toward the car.

Reign drove, the other Hailstorm guy in the front. Mina and I climbed in the backseat, both tense.

And while she was tense in general, she was doubly so then, her entire body ramrod straight, her hands flat on her thighs as her gaze focused out the window.

I got the distinct impression that, were it not for Reign demanding she come, she would have been much more likely to stay behind at the compound. While I was sure she had training, as all of Lo's people did, she seemed less likely to be someone who liked being in the thick of things.

And, quite frankly, I didn't like the idea of her being in the middle of a dangerous situation either. I wasn't overly protective by nature. I had been raised with a lot of fucked ideas, but true gender equality was one of the decent things my parents had instilled in me. And true gender equality acknowledged the fact that women were just as capable of handling themselves as men. Maybe most women didn't have the same amount of brute strength as men did, but with the right training, it could be made so that that didn't matter.

So it wasn't that I didn't know she was no worse off than the rest of us. I just would have preferred her back at the compound was all.

"Mother *fucker*," Reign growled as we pulled up across the street to find red and blue lights flashing outside the gym, two men being led out in handcuffs.

There went our leverage.

FIVE

Mina

Pretty much the last place in the world I wanted to be was in a car with a couple of hot-headed bikers. Our training, it generally taught us that operations were crippled by emotions. That was how you screwed up, got sloppy, made the kind of mistakes that could get you killed.

On top of that, I had extensive training, as Lo demanded, but was nowhere near as much of a natural at it as Lo was. She should have gone with them, been their voice of reason.

I was probably the only one in the car who felt relief when we first saw the police lights flashing.

Of course I also realized that it meant The Henchmen were back at square one. If they couldn't get their hands on

53

the men, they couldn't extract information, and they couldn't find where the rest of them were so they could be taken out.

"You guys hang back," Reign started, reaching for his handle and Mitch reached for his as well.

"You're not going alone. Lo's orders," Mitch said and Reign made a low, growling noise in his chest, clearly not used to not being listened to.

"Fine. We'll see how much this fuckhead will give us," Reign said, gesturing toward the tall, dark-haired, dark-eyed detective.

"Lloyd," Renny said, exhaling hard.

"He's hungry to prove himself," I offered.

"Yeah, but what are the chances that he wants to do that by catching the people who are picking off another organization in the area?" he shot back.

"He wants his cases solved. But these guys will likely plead out to breaking and entering and maybe some weapons charges if they're carrying. They'll probably get little more than time served. They'll be on the street again."

"Yeah, in half a fucking year," he scoffed. "We could all be dead by then."

I felt my stomach clench hard at those words, realizing for the first time that I would care about that. Death was as big a part of my life as anything else. After a while, you almost become immune to loss. It stops being so Earth-shaking. It doesn't make it any less tragic, but I had long since stopped crying my eyes out every time we lost someone.

But hearing Renny say that they could be dead in six months, that got to me. It shouldn't have. While I genuinely liked all the people I had met within the confines of The Henchmen compound, they weren't exactly friends. If I didn't cry over the loss of people at Hailstorm, how could I feel so worked up over veritable strangers.

I had a gut feeling that the answer had less to do with the MC as a whole and a lot more to do with a certain red-headed, tattoo-covered, blue-eyed biker.

Which was insane.

Truly.

I barely knew him.

I knew less about him than anyone else in The Henchmen compound. Granted, now that I had a full name to go on, I was about to know a hell of a lot more.

But somehow, it almost felt wrong and invasive to look into him now.

That wouldn't stop me, of course. My drive to know was perhaps just shy of as obsessive as his own drive to know things. It would drive me half-crazy to try to go to sleep at night without having at least some answers.

Like who were his parents?

What had they done to him to make him run away?

That little line about a rat and the sticky tape was telling. While they may not have beaten him, they had obviously done some kind of irreparable damage, they had left wounds that might never heal.

"What do you think of this Lazarus guy?" he asked suddenly as we both just stared out the window, watching Reign talk to the detectives, shooting a look over at the cop cars every once in a while like he was trying to memorize the faces of the guys they caught.

"What do you mean?"

"Do you think his story pans out? He was just taking a fucking *walk* and just happened to see a break-in in progress?" he asked, his voice more guarded than the usual, laid-back Renny generally was.

RENNY

"What? Do you think he was just trying to get inside? Gather more information?"

"Just think the timing is interesting. And I think his lack of concern for the guns and being taken prisoner for a while is..."

"Suspicious?" I supplied. "Maybe. Or maybe he was genuinely just doing a good deed and just so happens to come from a background in either military or crime that makes him immune to the threats you guys fed him. We'll know more when we get back."

"We?" he asked, and I could feel his gaze on me.

I knew I shouldn't have. Really, I did. But I turned my head to face him anyway and found his eyes lighter, his lips tipped up.

"Yes. That would be how you say more than one person, wouldn't it?"

"Nope. You want us to be a we. You just said it. No takes-backsies."

"What are we, five?"

"I think we should hold hands now," he went on, ignoring me. "If we're a we, I'm pretty sure we are supposed to be at the hand-holding stage."

And with that, the smooth bastard slipped his fingers between mine and gave me a squeeze and I just... couldn't seem to make myself pull away.

"Why won't you give up?" I managed to force myself to ask.

"Come on," he said, ducking his head to the side a little. "You and I both know that when this happens, not if, *when*, it is going to be fucking epic."

He wasn't wrong.

That was the sad part to me. I was denying myself something I knew would be amazing. I mean, in general, I

56

had pretty much always had good sex. What was the point
of doing it if you weren't going to do it with a partner that
knew what they were doing? But I had a feeling that, like
he told me when we first met, that two people like us,
people who were intuitive and could read a lot into even
the smallest of things, we would be explosive in bed.

I was starting to wonder if maybe I owed it to myself to
experience that before I moved on.

But, at the same time, there was this small, almost
inaudible voice telling me that once wouldn't be enough.

"You know I'm right, sweetheart."

"Don't..." I started, only to be interrupted by the opening
of the doors in the front. Reign and Mitch hauled
themselves in and slammed the door.

"Fucking Lloyd," Reign exhaled, shaking his head.
"Like talking to a goddamn wall."

"Once they get booked, Alex can find their names and
once we have their names, we can try to run their
financials," I went on, trying to pull my hand from Renny's
discreetly so the guys in the front wouldn't see. But he just
held on tighter, grinning like an idiot as I kept trying to
gently struggle. "Then from there," I went on, giving
Renny a death-glare he only chuckled at, "we can see if
they have used credit cards at hotels or restaurants around
here and maybe track down some associates. Alright,
enough," I snapped, reaching across my body and digging
my thumb into a pressure point in the crook of Renny's
elbow, making him hiss and jerk away, releasing my hand.

"Fucking ow," he said, shaking his head at me, but his
damn lips were still tipped up.

I could see Reign's eyes in the rearview, amused, and I
knew he was probably smirking too. Like he knew what
had just happened. Maybe he did.

"But what I'm saying is, we have a little more than we did. This might not be what everyone was hoping for, but it's not a setback either."

"Alright," Reign said, putting the car into reverse. "Well, you and Renny need to have a talk with the Lazarus guy anyway. So while we wait on booking and Alex, we can at least get something accomplished."

"The cops will be snooping around for another half an hour at least," Mitch piped in. "And then we need to get some people inside to check everything over too; make sure they didn't miss anything; sweep for bugs. The usual."

"Lo is gonna be pissed," Renny added, drawing my attention, head cocked to the side. "She and Janie are part owners of the gym. Actually, they have majority share over Cash. This was the first attack that didn't solely target Henchmen, but their allies as well. And that shit wasn't exactly kept under wraps; they couldn't have been blind to it. They just didn't give a fuck. That won't sit right with Lo and Hailstorm. They just fucked up."

He wasn't wrong.

Hailstorm was Lo's pride and joy. It was what she built out of the shambles of her old life. It was what was a constant for her, always there for her, always a safe haven for herself and all her little lost puppies. Me, in a way, included.

Threats in the beginning weren't rare. She was a newbie in the game; other more established organizations wanted to take her out before she got too big. She dealt with those threats, along with her small but highly trained team of ex-military and niche criminals, swiftly and mercilessly. And once she got the name on the street of a 'plain old crazy mother fucker', she branched out, expanded, made an empire that was so big that very few could or would be willing to fuck with. Sure, we lost men and women on missions. But no one came after us. Not anymore.

Really, it was a suicide mission.

Everyone knew that.

So the Abruzzos must have known that. They were either so large that they thought they could best all of The Henchmen and Hailstorm at the same time, or they maybe thought Lo was losing her edge, softening.

Which, well, yeah that wouldn't sit right with her.

No one would accuse Lo of being soft. While there was absolutely, at her core, a softness, a nurturing spirit- that was for her people at Hailstorm and her friends. When it came to enemies, she was still that younger, hungry, angry person with a point to prove, with a mission to never be fucked with again.

She was going to flip.

"And, fuck, when Janie hears about this..." Mitch added, shaking his head.

You didn't fuck with Lo because she was smart, capable, and had control over an entire lawless army.

You didn't fuck with Janie because she would, quite literally, blow your shit up.

And while she was hurting, while she was genuinely making herself sick living at the bedside of her unconscious husband, she was still Janie. She was still the most headstrong, resilient, badass woman I had ever met. She would not handle the news well that while the man she loved more than she loved the air in her lungs was laid up recovering from multiple gunshot wounds and head trauma, someone was coming after her. Even if it was inadvertently.

I wouldn't exactly put it past her to start building a bomb in the private bath in Wolf's room.

She was that level of insane when she was pissed.

"We aren't telling Janie," Reign surprised me by saying, breaking the silence in the car.

"Why the fuck not?" Mitch asked, clearly insulted that Reign thought he in any way had the right to make a decision for Hailstorm.

"Right now, Janie needs to worry about Wolf and her son. She doesn't need any more stress on top of that. In case you haven't noticed, she's not handling this fucking well. She's losing weight and she was a fucking rail to start with. Every time I see her, her eyes are red-rimmed from crying. This is fucking *Jstorm* we're talking about here, baddest bitch in the state and she's crying all the time. She doesn't need this. And we aren't going to burden her with it."

"You do realize," Renny cut in, brow raised, "that when all this blows over and Wolf wakes up and she gets briefed on this shit, that she is going to lose her ever-loving mind for being left out of the loop."

"And I'll be a fucking happy man to see her back to her normal self," Reign agreed, pulling into the garage at the compound and cutting the engine. "Because that means I have my best fucking friend back and it means that Malcolm has his father back and Janie has her protector back. So everyone is going to keep their goddamn lips shut if they see Janie, got it?" he asked, giving us all a hard look before climbing out of the car, slamming the door, and heading inside.

"You and me," Renny started when Mitch went out to follow Reign.

"There is no you and me," I cut him off, defensive, stupidly thrown-off by the whole hand-holding thing.

"Oh, there's a you and me alright," he said, smirking. "But I wasn't talking about that. Though, if you want to talk about that..." he said, jerking his head to the seat we were sitting on, "this row of seats lays down and we have the whole cargo area to prove just how much of a you and me there actually is."

An unexpected jolt of desire shot down to my core and my thighs pressed together instinctively to ease the ache as I swallowed hard before speaking. "What were you talking about then?" I asked, deciding it was safest to side-step the entire other comment. If there was one thing I had learned over the past couple of weeks, it was that Renny was capable of doing something that not many were able to- he could throw me off, surprise me, keep me on my toes. And when I was on my toes, I found that I stumbled. I lost ground. I *gave* ground to Renny.

I couldn't keep letting that happen.

Before I knew it, my back would be against a wall and there would be no escape.

"What I was going to say, sweetheart, is that we have a date with that guy you would normally be drooling all over if you weren't currently in the midst of a somewhat embarrassing attraction to a certain hot as fuck, charming as the devil, redheaded biker," he said, big grin in place.

"That ego," I said, reaching for my door handle, "something to do with your abusive upbringing?" I asked and watched as his eyes went guarded, as his smile fell and his jaw tightened. I was sure most people didn't know anything about his past and I was equally sure that those that did were not as cruel as to use it against him. I wasn't cruel by nature. And, unlike Renny, I didn't get my kicks by pushing buttons to see what they did. But I was apparently capable of being nasty when on the defensive and trying desperately to not lose the game.

I found I really didn't care for that side of me as I exited the car and made my way inside, followed the whole way by a silent, looming, angry Renny.

As I went down the stairs, I decided it was yet another reason that I needed to detach myself from the situation, I needed to get some space. In general, I tried to turn my profiling skills on myself as well as others. I wanted to know my motivations. I wanted to know what made me tick. And after so many years, I thought I knew everything about myself. I thought I knew of what I was capable.

So suddenly finding that I was capable of cruelty was not sitting well with me.

Fact of the matter was, I needed to leave.

And once we finished talking to the Lazarus guy, I was going to head out.

There was absolutely no reason for me to be there every day. I wasn't the most trained at Hailstorm. Other guys would have been much better for the job of helping to protect The Henchmen. I didn't need to oversee any more of the renovations which, yet again, I wasn't the most knowledgable about to begin with.

My specialty was specific. My skills were niche. And while I could manage well enough with the other things, why not step away and let someone else more capable take them over. Lo wanted me at the compound to get a feel for the guys, to see if they were the kind of personalities to make the kind of enemies who would come at them like someone was coming at them. Then, when I finished that, I was there to try to create a blind profile on the attackers by their actions.

Now that we had a name or, as it were, a list of names, I didn't need to be there. There was no reason. I would likely be able to make a better, more comprehensive profile back at Hailstorm working side-by-side with L who apparently was a crime encyclopedia. And maybe Alex who was currently banned from The Henchmen compound by her husband, something she railed against endlessly to the point where I almost felt bad for Breaker. But, then again, he brought that on himself. But she would be able to come up to Hailstorm and work with me.

I worked better from afar.

And I damn sure worked better when I wasn't constantly thinking about a certain redheaded, charming, impressive biker. I spent more time trying to think of ways to shoot him down and hide my ever-growing attraction to him than actually doing any kind of work.

I went to the bottom landing to find Lazarus sitting on a steel chair, ankles cuffed to the front legs, arms cuffed behind the back, making his chest widen. But he was slouched back, seeming as comfortable as you please despite the very uncomfortable position.

Repo gave us a tight nod as we walked up toward them.

"They didn't blow it up or anything did they?" Lazarus asked as soon as he saw us.

"Cops got them first," Renny supplied and Repo made a frustrated noise. "Go on up and talk to Reign. We have to have a few words with our new friend."

Repo nodded, clamping a hand on Renny's shoulder before heading up the stairs.

"If you guys are supposed to come down here to pick my brain," he started, tone casual, "let me save you some time. My name is Lazarus Alexander. I'm thirty-one. I live in Shane Mallick's apartment building because I like when

63

RENNY
people mind their own goddamn business. I've lived in
Navesink Bank for years."

"Why did you move here, of all places?" I asked, brow
raised. While Navesink Bank had its very nice areas, the
crime rate was, well, a deterrent for most people.

He shrugged a shoulder. "I was in the city. Got all kinds
of fucked up and needed to get away."

"Fucked up meaning drugs," Renny supplied, watching
the man with a quiet intensity I shouldn't have, but
absolutely did, find incredibly attractive.

"Booze to 30s to H."

"And you decided Navesink Bank was a good place to
recover?" Renny went on. "You do realize we have an
impressive drug problem here, right?"

Laz shrugged. "I've got some time in. Can't hide from
your triggers. Gotta face 'em up. So when I'm having a bad
night, I walk."

"Which was how you came across the guys breaking
into the gym," I concluded.

"Yeah, babe. I walk for hours some nights. See a lot of
shit."

"She hates being called babe," Renny supplied, not
bothering to look my way and I knew he was still ticked at
me. But that was probably for the best. "If you see a lot of
shit, why bother reporting this? And why to us and not the
cops?"

"Fact of the matter is, when you're a junkie, you get a
different perspective on the world. It's not as easy as the
cops are the good guys and the criminals are the bad guys.
It's a fuckuva lot more complicated than that. And I've been
here long enough to know that you guys don't fuck with
innocents. You keep the shit between you and who you're
having issues with. If you're overthrown and a new power

64

takes over, there's no guarantee of that being the case with them. The lesser of two evils, if you will."

I looked over to Renny, wanting to see if he came to the same conclusion as I did- he was being honest with us.

But he was stubbornly keeping his gaze away from me.

"What do you do, Laz?" Renny asked as I felt something akin to regret burrow into my belly.

Why? I wasn't sure. Because distance was what I thought I wanted. I had accomplished that goal by being a bitch. But being faced with the distance, yeah, I found I wasn't a fan.

"Why?" Lazarus surprised me by asking, snapping my attention back to him. So far, he had been nothing but forthcoming. Clamming up about his job seemed odd.

"Hands are covered in bruises and scabs," Renny said and I felt myself stiffen. I moved to the side slightly to look behind him at his hands to find he was right; Laz was covered in injuries in various stages of healing. Really, his observational skills were second to none. While everyone else was freaking out about his declaration earlier, Renny had been cataloging small, seemingly unimportant details about him.

Lazarus sighed, shaking his head. "Not a lot of employers will hire someone with my record."

"So you got inventive," Renny agreed. "Who do you work for?"

"Ross," he supplied, voice a little hollow.

"Ross Ward?" I asked, putting two and two together.

Ross Ward was a different kind of criminal. The genius of his business was that he literally employed three people-guards. And they worked on a contract business, not full-time. His overhead was low and therefore, he never had to worry about dissent in his ranks. He was smart, cold, calculated, and delivered something that no one else in the area did.

Ross Ward led an underground fighting ring.

"Guard or fighter?" Renny went on.

"Depends on the night," Laz said easily. "Someone bitches out or is too hurt to fight, one of us steps in. Either way, it's good money."

It would be very good money. While Ross took a huge cut for providing the venue and the audience to bet on such things, there was enough of a demand for it that even the fighters raked in the big bucks.

Renny gave him a nod and moved toward the stairs without saying a thing to me.

I looked at Laz who was smirking at me. "Lovers spat?" he asked, dark eyes seeming amused.

"He wishes," I countered, moving off toward the stairs as well.

"I bet he does," I heard Lazarus murmur before I was upstairs, going into the main room to listen to Renny interrupt the conversation going on there.

"We can let him go," he said with a shrug. "He works for Ross Ward. There's no way Ross would let him work with the mob and still work for him. She agrees with me," he added when eyes shifted to me as I moved in.

"I didn't say I..." I started to object, though I did agree with him. Ross Ward, as far as anyone was concerned, was the ultimate of careful. He was even picky about the associates of his fighters. He didn't take chances. He didn't get in bed with anyone because he knew that by choosing to stay neutral, that all the local bad guys could come to his little underground club and throw money around, which wouldn't be possible if, say, he picked to associate with the Russians and thereby pissed off the Italians.

"She agrees with me," he cut me off again, tone sharp. "Let him go before Ross gets pissed. We have more important things to focus on right now."

I felt my spine straighten; my shoulders pushed back. Right then.

My head turned and I found Lo watching me, head tipped to the side slightly. I moved toward her, making my way toward the hall because I had some of my things stashed in the new addition room to the back that had been used mostly as a gym space for the kids. "I'm done here," I said under my breath as I passed, feeling my guts twist slightly and trying my best to ignore it.

I wasn't going to stay around to be silenced by Renny.

And I wasn't going to stay to learn any more ugly things about myself.

I was going to do what was best for myself.

I was going to leave.

The bonus room was a mess, as it usually was. Dolls and monster trucks and blocks and bikes and puzzles were everywhere. I hadn't spent a lot of time around kids until I walked into The Henchmen compound, but I learned quickly that trying to keep a play room neat was a pipe dream. As such, I kept my things on a bookshelf way above arm's reach even for Ferryn.

I reached up and pulled down my backpack that was filled with files and a change of clothes in case I had to crash at the compound. I had just gone down on my flat feet when I realized I wasn't alone.

I didn't have to turn to know who it was, but I turned anyway to find Renny standing there- way too close.

His light eyes were penetrating and unreadable as he looked at me for a long minute.

RENNY

It happened so fast, too fast for me to think let alone react.

One hand moved out and landed in the center of my lower back, plastering my front against his, making my breath rush out of me as my neck craned up to look at him. His other hand went behind my neck, holding me there hard.

Then his lips crashed down on mine.

There was no other way, not for all the weeks of unsatisfied desire, of snapping at each other, of flirting.

It was a crash.

There would be damage in the wake.

But suddenly, I couldn't find the will to care about the consequences as my backpack fell from my hand and landed with a thump as my arms went up- one grabbing his bicep, the other digging into the shirt over his chest.

And I melted into him.

Feeling it, his head slanted, deepening the kiss until I swore I felt it everywhere, until all there was in the world was us and that moment, until my lips felt tingly and my head felt light. Until I let out a low whimper and he took the opportunity for his tongue to move forward and thrust inside my mouth to claim mine. His body curled forward, making me arch backward slightly to keep contact, leaving me fully at his mercy because if he wasn't holding me, I'd have fallen backward.

He made a low, rumbling noise in his chest that shot toward my core, making a rush of wetness meet my panties as my hips pressed into his, feeling his hard cock against my belly.

Just when the urge to rub myself against him to ease the ache growing inside became almost overwhelming, his lips released mine and he let me go back onto my own feet fully, his forehead pressing into mine.

"You're such a fucking coward," he said, voice low but full of depth.

Then, just as suddenly as it started, his arms released me, he turned, and he was gone before I could even think through the fog of desire in my brain.

I slumped backward, leaning against the wall, taking a slow, deep breath.

To be frank, I'd been kissed plenty in my life. They had ranged from absolutely no spark to fireworks. But kissing Renny, yeah, it was more like a goddamn Atomic bomb.

I should have known as much. Really, the chemistry had been strong from first introductions, even with blood in his teeth from his fight with Duke, even with an eye that was quickly blackening, even then I had felt it. It had done nothing but get stronger the longer I was around him, the more impressed I became by him, the more worn down I got from his charm.

It would have been laughable that after all that the kiss was underwhelming.

But it wasn't.

It was, well, the kind of kiss you wait a lifetime for. And I wasn't even a romantic like that. It was just the fact. He grabbed me all alpha-style and kissed me silly.

Then as if that wasn't bad enough, he had gone ahead and dropped that line and stormed off.

The worst part, though, was that he was right. I was a coward. I was running away because I knew whatever was happening between me and Renny was something epic, something big. The thing was, I wasn't prepared for that. The main reason being that I knew what it would be; it would be crazy and unpredictable and messy.

RENNY

I just wasn't ready for that.

It was easier to leave.

Cowardly? Absolutely.

But smart? Yes. At least I thought so.

Really, it was the only option.

So why there was a wobbly, uncertain feeling in my stomach as I picked up my backpack and made my way to the gates to where my car was parked on the street, yeah, I was pretending that was just the feeling of leaving a job half-finished and not the disappointment of a great opportunity lost.

SIX

Mina

"You're breathing on me," L growled, frustrated.

He wasn't wrong. I had been hovering over his shoulder as he typed up some more information he had dug up about the guys that were caught breaking into the gym three days before.

I couldn't claim he was exactly tickled to be working with me, because that would be an outright lie. I was pretty sure he almost wanted to slap me when I drank the rest of the coffee without immediately putting on a new pot. Apparently, in his workspace, there were rules. But since he was about as communicative as Wolf was on a bad day, those rules I learned mainly through trial and error.

For instance, I wasn't allowed to touch his laptop.

71

I also couldn't alphabetize his files on the Abruzzos because he had some kind of asinine system that made sense to only him.

But no offenses were as bad as the coffee one.

"Where can I set up?" Alex asked, having walked in two minutes before declaring she was 'sick and fucking tired of being in lockdown' so she decided to leave Breaker with their son, Junior, and headed up to Hailstorm for the day as a form of small rebellion. Breaker didn't seem overly convinced that the blowback from The Henchmen war wasn't going to find its way all the way up to his little house on the hill. Actually, that was the general consensus around Henchmen allies ever since Hailstorm went into the gym and found not only bugs but a small, badly built pipe bomb. Bad enough that it likely wouldn't have done much damage beyond the locked office they had placed it in.

Janie would have had a good laugh about it. You know, if we were sharing that with her. Which we weren't. Lo, to my surprise, had sided with Reign and she was getting radio silence about the whole situation.

"Back at your own goddamn house," L growled, clearly less of a team player than even I was.

Frankly, I welcomed Alex's company.

For me, Alex was an easy coworker and friend. This was mostly thanks to the fact that I never had to analyze her. She was blunt and fearless with her thoughts and opinions. If she had something to say, she said it. There was no guesswork. Which was good for two reasons. One, I didn't have to profile her. Two, she didn't have to resent me for profiling her.

"I brought you a twenty-four ounce coffee with *six* shots," Alex reminded him, slamming her laptop down *right* beside him, despite there being plenty of desk space beside me where I had set up a full arm's length away from L so I wouldn't piss him off any more than I already had with my presence. Alex wasn't exactly the sort to accommodate just because someone growled at her. That was likely thanks to having put up with Breaker's grunting and growling and demands for years. "So go ahead and pull those wadded up panties out of your ass and relax, L. You're outnumbered now. Mina and I are totally going to gang up on you now. Right Mina?"

"I ah..." I started, thrown off.

"See? She agreed. Now, the Abruzzos..."

"I don't know why you're here," L said, swiveling his chair toward her. Though, I got the impression it was less to face her and more because it pushed him a little further away from her. "In fact, I don't see why you're on this case at all. I know everything there is to know about the Abruzzo crime family."

"I got your files," Alex agreed, nodding, as she brought her laptop up.

"And?" he prompted when that was all she said.

Because her face was turned just ever-so-slightly toward me, I got to see a small smile pull at her lips before she forced them into a straight line. But it was enough for me to know that she had something up her sleeve.

"And I found it lacking."

"Lacking?" he asked, voice deceptively quiet. But with the tension in his jaw, I could tell he was barely holding onto his anger.

Being as smart as he was, it was hard for him to accept that he didn't have all the answers, especially about his specialty.

"See, I really liked knowing how Mack takes his coffee and all, don't get me wrong," Alex said in a dry voice. "But

I was a hell of a lot more interested in the fact that he has a weakness for girls. Meaning, young ones."

"What?" L exploded, almost sending his chair flying he jerked upright so fast. "Young girls? There's been no record of that."

"On the books," she nodded, "you're right. Hell, you can't even find any *suggestions* of that kind of thing. But then you find him in the dark web and you see that he has this SN and that that SN has been used to view kiddie porn on a website that just received a very malicious form of malware that may or may not be funneling money out of the subscribers' accounts and into a non-profit that helps survivors of child sexual abuse."

Alex, since joining forces with Janie years back, had grown a lot in her skills. And because the two had their own connection to the shithead who ruined good chunks of their lives, the man Wolf eventually killed after Janie's botched plan to blow him to kingdom come, they had joined forces to become a sort of police force on the dark web. They trolled the worst sites and attacked the members, brought down the sites themselves. They were a duo of vigilante cyber do-gooders. There was even a fan page for them on the dark web somewhere. They would both pretend that they didn't know that that fan page existed, but they both absolutely knew.

So Alex stealing from rich pedophiles and giving to victims, that was just the work of any Tuesday.

"That wasn't even in your profile," L shot at me, wanting to spread blame around, though it didn't exactly matter to the case that he was a sick whack job.

"I can't catch everything, L," I reasoned, shrugging.

"If there is any justice in the world," Alex went on, typing something on her laptop, "while he's in jail, he will be getting a little taste of what it feels like to be a victim."

As someone who didn't subscribe to a common belief in the psych community that sex offenders could be reformed, I had to agree with Alex. There was no fixing that kind of sick. Sexual recidivism was at about forty-percent. And that was only what was reported. The thing about child sexual predators is that they target children, they can manipulate and scare them into silence. Most experts would put that number more at sixty to seventy percent.

And yet they kept putting those fucking sickos back on the streets.

"You know, I'm with George Carlin," Alex said randomly. When we all gave her blank looks, she shrugged. "In one of his stand-ups, he said something about how all criminals should be sectioned off in some of the useless flyover states based off their crimes. Murderers here, sex offenders there. Load them up with weapons and drugs and every month, open a door between each of the camps and let people sneak through. Let them suck and fuck and shoot up and torture and kill until there are none of them left. And, yes, I know this is weird coming from a criminal who is married to a criminal and is good friends with mostly criminals. But you know what I mean. This is all kinds of fucked up that these bastards walk free."

"Do any of the others have his particular brand of fucked-up?" L asked and I could tell it was killing him to do so.

"Not that I can find. I mean, El Jefe himself, Little Ricky, sure likes his teen girl with old disgusting fat man porn. But the girls are all legal. Can I call him El Jefe?" she

RENNY

asked, looking between us. "I mean they're Italian mob and that's a Spanish term..."

"Il Capo," L supplied, surprising me. "That would be the Italian way of saying 'the chief'."

"Right, well Il Capo likes to entertain the idea that *any* pretty young woman would be willing to suck and fuck his disgusting ass despite the only reason the girls doing it in porn is for the payout. But, you know, guys are stupid that way. Them and their twisted porn..." she trailed off, shaking her head. She swirled her chair then, head tucked to the side, looking at L. "What kind of twisted porn are *you* into, L?" she asked, then went right ahead and laughed. "I'll bet it's women who suck you off while you drink gallons of coffee or some shit like that. Anyway, yeah, I can't get a drop on a location for these guys. Their purchases and shit were all over the map. Has Janie made any progress on... what?" she trailed off when L and I shared a look.

"Jstorm isn't on this case," L said carefully.

"What do you mean Janie isn't on this case?" she asked, brows drawing together. "These are the people who got Wolf locked up and gave her a world of worry years back. And they're the same fuckheads who put several bullets in his body and made him crack his head on the car on the way down which has put him in a goddamn coma. Of course she's in on this."

"Lo and Reign decided," I started, only to be cut off by her.

"Oh fuck," she said, shaking her head. "Reign is going to be in the market for a new set of balls when she hears that. And, Lo, well, I know she and Janie have this mother-daughter thing, but I'm not sure that won't stop Janie from flipping shit on her either."

76

RENNY

"Regardless," I cut in, agreeing, but knowing better than to interfere, "we have all agreed to leave her out of this because she doesn't need the stress."

"Right," she said, nodding. "Of course you guys did."

See, I didn't see it right then.

I should have. It was right there in my face, flashing like a neon warning sign.

But I was off my game. I was in a fog that I was pretending had nothing to do with the sex dreams I had been having about Renny that left me refusing to sleep and therefore a bone-deep kind of tired.

I never would have missed it otherwise.

Because Alex didn't say she agreed.

She said of course *we all* did.

That little oversight on my part would lead to a pinnacle point that none of us would see coming.

But I had no idea at the time. So we all just sat down and got to work until a couple hours later, Lo walked in with a refill for L and Alex who was every bit the addict L was, though she picked on him about it.

"Mina, come take a walk with me," she suggested in a way that wasn't a suggestion, but an order.

"I am pretty much useless here anyway," I said, looking over at L and Alex as they click-click-clicked away on their respective laptops as they had been doing for hours, occasionally mumbling something to the other, but mostly leaving me out of the loop. Three people used to working by themselves being forced to work together was an interesting dynamic.

"You haven't been sleeping," she observed as we walked the halls that would eventually lead outside.

"I've been having bad dreams," I supplied, not letting her in on the fact that they were bad because they were so damn good. And Lo, having had her own nightmares, having dealt with Janie's downright crippling ones, and the ones of half the men and women in the barracks, didn't question it. We all saw some evil, awful stuff in our lines of work. It wouldn't be normal if we could always rest easily.

"And I've caught you on that Gameboy pretty much daily," she added. We all had our tells, our habits that pointed to times of distress. Malcolm paced. Lo sprang into furious action even if she didn't have a way to fix the problem. Ashley hummed a song from her childhood. Me, I played my Gameboy- a leftover habit from childhood that I never could shake. I had tried other ways of distracting myself- music, reading, meditating. Nothing worked half as well as my old video games.

"Lo, it's just a..."

"I know that you're not one who shares your feelings easily, Mina. I respect that. But you have to be able to confront them yourself, not distract yourself from them."

I had been successfully distracting myself from various feelings for my entire life. Healthy? No. But I had always gotten by.

"I'm fine, Lo."

"You're always fine," she agreed, nodding. "The thing is, I want more for you than *fine*. Fine sucks. No one wants to die knowing they lived a *fine* life."

She wasn't wrong. She rarely was. So, not having anything to say to that, I stayed silent.

"Alright," she sighed when we walked out onto the grounds, making two of the new dogs in training run over, wagging their tails happily, knowing who the boss was. She reached out and pet them then sent them off back to the other dogs protecting the perimeter. "I have a new job for you."

Thank God.

Really, I was losing my mind.

I found I actually kind of liked L, eccentricities not aside because I found them intriguing, but despite the fact that he resented my presence and made it clear I was unwelcome. But I was floundering. I wasn't bringing anything to the table. They would be better off with just L and Alex on it.

It would be good for me to move on, to pack a bag and head in a new direction, to be able to lose myself in a new profile. Maybe I would be able to sleep again with some distance between us.

See, I was underestimating Lo in that moment.

Again, I should have known better.

"Where are you sending me?"

"Not far," she hedged, refusing to make eye-contact as she looked around the grounds. "See, something came up last night. One of our allies needs profiles on three guys."

"Three?" I asked, getting excited. Talk about a good distraction.

"Mhmm," she said, tucking her hands into her back pockets as she finally stopped walking and turned to face me.

"Where am I heading?"

"Back to The Henchmen compound."

The words landed with impact, making me feel like my shoulders slumped under the weight. "What? No. Absolutely not, Lo."

"Mina, there have been some new developments and they need profiles."

"So send me the names. I will do them from here. Or, you know, they have their own profiler there too, you know."

Lo nodded. "They do. And Renny is good, but Reign wants you too. He thinks you're more objective in this situation and he thinks you both seem to catch different things about people. You profile differently and this is a really important job that he can't have fucking up. He wants you and he is willing to pay three times your usual salary for it."

Three times.

Three times?

Fact of the matter was, there weren't a whole hell of a lot of me and there definitely weren't many with as positive a track record as mine. So, because of that, I made a killing. Really, it was ostentatious. Granted, I worked for Hailstorm, so it was a sixty-forty deal with the larger chunk to me. But even with forty percent gone, it was more money than I needed. Especially seeing as I lived at Hailstorm. We could, and often did, move on and get our own places outside the compound. But since I traveled as much as I did, that was impractical. Instead, I spent too much money on nice hotels and first class flights, figuring there was no reason to not enjoy my income a bit.

But three times my salary was, honestly, a bit too much.

"Is he out of his mind?" I asked. "I am asking that genuinely. Is he crazy? Has the stress gotten to him?"

"He is just being careful, Mina. He can't afford to be careless right now, to make mistakes. So he is paying enough so that you can't, in good conscience, turn the job down."

Really, for three times my salary, could I? As much as I wanted to say no, to save myself the confusion and stress, I really didn't think it was possible to turn down that kind of money. Hell, I could buy a house with it if I wanted to.

"There is a catch though," she added, getting my full attention.

"Of course there is," I snorted. I should have known there was. "What is it?"

"You're kind of going undercover," she hedged.

"Undercover as what at an MC compound? I love you and Hailstorm, Lo," I said with a smirk, "but I don't care how much he pays me, I'm not going to be a clubwhore."

She laughed at that. "Could you imagine?" she asked, shaking her head. "I think the clubwhores are in semi-retirement right now. No, I would never literally pimp you out, babe."

"What then? I think Maze was a prime example of them being a bit backward in the female equality among members thing."

"Here's the deal," she said, finally getting to it. "The Henchmen have some new prospects. They want to start taking on probates and bolstering up their numbers again. But they want to be careful. They need someone inside to pay close, but unobtrusive, attention on the new guys. And to be there full time, well..."

"No," I said, shaking my head.

"You would need to be someone's old lady. And since everyone already has..."

"Nope. Not a snowball's chance in hell. Not for a *million* dollars, Lo."

"No one is saying you have to *be* a couple. You'd be playing a part. You'd be acting."

No, we wouldn't.

Fact of the matter was, if Renny and I started pretending to be biker and old lady, well, the inevitable would happen.

"It's not going to happen. I'm sorry. I can't."

"Why?" she asked and I knew to be wary of the look in her eye. "Because you don't trust yourself around Renny? Really, babe, I thought we trained you better than that."

That was a low blow and she knew it.

But I wasn't tapping out.

I had my pride, sure, and that comment bruised it. But I wasn't going to be ruined by an ego. I was smarter than that.

"Nice try. But no."

"Mina," she said, her voice going softer, more reasonable, "what if one of them is a plant? What if they are going to take them out? You know these guys and women and kids. Do you want that on your head if it goes south?"

She was right; I had spent enough time there to get to know all of them personally. Reign with his gruffness and ability to put everyone ahead of himself. Cash with his sweetness, his good humor, his capacity for love. Repo with his bone-deep loyalty. Duke and his resilience. And Renny, well, with his various positive qualities that I didn't even want to think on.

Then there was Summer with her sweet toughness. There was Maze and her badassery. And there was Penny with her innocent goodness.

The kids, well, it went without saying that I never wanted anything to happen to them. They were as innocent as innocent could get.

"Why do this now? Why do this at the compound? Have the guys be external until the profiles are done so no one is at risk."

"Because, despite shit hitting the fan, there are traditions. This is how it is done, how it has always been done, how it will continue to be done in the future. It is, above all, a brotherhood. The prospects need to be brought in and trained around that mentality. And, maybe a little part of it is the guys wanting to torture the new guys with menial tasks. They could use some fun after all the stress."

"You don't understand what you're asking of me, Lo," I said, emotion slipping into my words.

"Babe, it's not torture. You sit on your ass around the clubhouse most of the day. You pretend to be..."

"In love with *Renny*," I filled in. "In *lust* with Renny."

"Put your big girl panties on, Mina," she offered a little gruffly. Then to soften the blow because while we both knew she was the boss and I ultimately did have to do what she said or risk being out on my ass, we were still friends and she didn't like to pull the boss-card if she didn't have to, she added, "And maybe Renny will pull them off you. Or maybe he won't. Your personal life is your personal life. What you do or don't want to do while over there is up to you. No one is forcing you to do anything you don't want to do."

She was right.

No one was *forcing* me.

I had a feeling, though, that I would end up doing something that better sense would tell me I absolutely did not want to do.

Torn, I looked back at Lo and she dealt the death blow. Granted, she did it with a wince and her voice was nowhere near as strong as it usually was when she spoke, but she still said it- the words that would change everything.

"It's an order, Mina. Do this job or pack your bags and leave Hailstorm."

SEVEN

Renny

Lazarus simply didn't leave.

After the meeting with the guys about what happened at the gym and what that meant and then confronting a Mina who decided to be a chicken shit and run, we had gone down and uncuffed him. We hadn't apologized since we weren't sorry about trying to protect our own, but he didn't seem bothered by the whole ordeal anyway.

Reign offered him a drink since we were all having one thanks to a shitty day. He refused seeing as he was clean, but hung back anyway. Repo and Duke seemed to take to him instantly and I had to admit his somewhat laid-back ease about being in a biker compound in the middle of an underground war was intriguing and welcome seeing as no one else would dare step foot anywhere near us right then- not even close friends. We couldn't blame them either. They had women and kids to worry about.

When everyone was ready to turn in and he didn't seem to take the hint to leave, Reign shrugged and decided to lock him into the extra room that had been built on during renovations for the sole purpose of housing new prospects. Numbers decimated, Reign knew we couldn't and wouldn't survive past the year, even if the war was over, with our numbers as low as they were. And as much as it was too soon, our brothers not even cold in the ground yet, it was a necessary evil.

Starting in the morning, all the kid stuff would have to move to the basement and we would set to building the bunks in the new barracks room. The reason they would be out there instead of in the basement where all prospects, including myself, had slept, was because the barracks room had shipping container walls and a heavily locked security door. Reign was literally planning on locking the guys in when no one was awake or around to keep an eye on them.

He wasn't taking any chances.

Then, I swear to fuck, it was straight out of goddamn *Field Of Dreams*. The next night, the guys at the gate came in to tell us as we sat bullshitting with Laz that there were two guys at the gates... with duffle bags.

"The fuck you mean they have duffle bags?" Reign scoffed.

"They each have a bag filled with clothes and personal shit," Mitch supplied. "We went through it all. There are no weapons and we patted them down. They each had a switchblade but readily told us about them in their boots."

"What? Are we running a fucking hotel now?" Cash laughed.

"They said you'd want to see them."

Reign looked around at us, knowing we each were carrying and knowing we were on-edge and alert. Then he nodded. "Alright. Send them in."

Then he did.

And in walked two guys. Both were blond. One had longish hair and a full blond beard. The other was clean shaven. The bearded one was thinner, but strong. The clean shaven one was more solid. Both had blue eyes and the same carriage- set shoulders, lazy gait.

"And why the fuck would I want to see you guys? Never seen you before in my life."

"See now," the bearded one said, smirking, "that's where you're wrong. You've seen us. Actually, you taught me how to put a curve on my fastball."

Everyone seemed to straighten at once, curious.

Reign's brows drew together. "Who the fuck are you guys?"

"Cyrus," the bearded one said, meaning himself. "And Reeve Harris. Our pops was..."

"Gus," Reign said, remembering suddenly though the rest of us were in the dark.

"Yup," Cyrus agreed, nodding. "Died in that shitty deal with the Irish some ten years back."

"And your mom wanted nothing to do with us after. Refused the widow money and everything," Cash nodded.

"So what the fuck you doing back here?" Reign asked, blunt as ever.

"Know that shit when you go to college to rush and they have to let you because you're a legacy?" Cyrus asked, lips twitching.

"You want me to let you prospect because your pops was a member," Reign nodded, understanding. "Why?"

"Pops always wanted us to join. He would go on and fucking on about brotherhood and loyalty," Reeve piped in for the first time.

"We've seen all the shit going down the past few months. Then to hear you lost almost all your men. Pops would be rolling in his fucking grave to know we sat on our hands and didn't do right by his memory."

"What about your mother?" I asked.

"Stroke five years back," Reeve answered just as bluntly as I asked, piquing my interest. He was the older brother-more serious if his manner was anything to go by. His brother seemed a little more open and forthcoming.

"Jobs?" Repo prompted.

"Reeve is an electrician. I have disappointed my family by playing guitar at that new coffee lounge they opened up down the street."

Reign looked around at us, trying to get a read on our opinions. Fact of the matter was, we needed men. Granted these guys were no hardened criminals, but they had grown up around Henchmen. They understood how things worked. They could be toughened up.

Finding a mutual understanding between all of us, Reign looked back at the brothers. "Things are a little bit different this time around. We have to be careful right now. So when you guys aren't at work or there isn't someone around to babysit you, you'll be locked up in the barracks room with Laz," he said, waving a hand toward the guy sitting next to Duke who both the men jerked their chins at, "and any other new probates we might bring on. That a problem?"

"Whatever it takes," Reeve shrugged.

Reign nodded. "Same rules that have always applied with my leadership still apply. Drink, fuck, fight, I don't

care. But there are no drugs in this building and you show
our women and kids respect. You take whatever order is
passed down to you from us and you fucking do it without
complaint. Even if that means you're waxing our fucking
bikes with the shirt off your back."

"So what you're saying is I should be shirtless all the
time?" Cyrus asked, making Lo who had just walked in
laugh.

"Can't say that's a terrible idea," she agreed, giving him
a smile as she passed him and moved to sit on Cash's lap.

"That's Lo," Reign said, nodding his chin toward her.
"She runs Hailstorm. Those are some of her men you see
around, helping keep a perimeter until we can neutralize
the threat and have you fucks do that for us again. Wolf's
woman is also from Hailstorm. Janie. She's with Wolf at
the hospital, but she'll be back eventually and trying to boss
you fucks around. In fact," he went on, looking over at Lo
with a look that seemed to say 'play along'. "Renny's
woman is from Hailstorm too," he said, sliding his gaze to
me as I felt my stomach drop.

I knew it then. I knew what the plan was. And I couldn't
say I was put-off by it. No, in fact, inside I was doing a
mother fucking victory dance. She was coming back. Not
only was she coming back, but she was going to have to
play my woman? Hell fucking yeah. There would be no
running back to Hailstorm, no putting a professional barrier
up. In fact, she would have to let me put my hands on her
and she would have to pretend to like it. Actually, there'd
be no damn pretending. It would be a genuine reaction.

Because the woman wanted me for fuck's sake.

She was just too scared to feel it.

I mean, granted, there would be some work involved,
but for the most part, it was proving we were in a

relationship. And, well, I planned on putting on a convincing show.

You know, for appearances sake.

My eyes moved over to Lo, finding her already watching me, likely taking in my excitement and amusement and maybe even the determination as well.

Why was I so fucking set on Mina? Yeah, that'd be a good question. And I didn't exactly have an answer that seemed satisfactory to me. Maybe it was because she was like me- she could analyze herself and her actions and the motivations behind them until she was blue in the face and yet she still couldn't fix herself. Just like I couldn't fix myself either. Or maybe it was because I wanted to see the real her, the one she kept hidden under the outward appearance of cool, calm, collected, and capable. Underneath the uptightness.

I wanted to peel away the layers and find what was inside.

Judging by the look Lo was giving me, she knew exactly what I had planned. And, maybe because Lo was a hopeless romantic or maybe because she knew her girl needed some messiness in her life, seemed to be fully behind the plan.

"So they're allies," Cyrus nodded.

"We don't really have any enemies except the current threat. So don't be starting any shit on your personal time with any of the local groups from 3ʳᵈ Street to Shooter to the Grassis and Lyon. Last fucking thing we need is another enemy because some fucking probies couldn't keep their mouths shut or their hands to themselves."

"I don't have any enemies, man," Cyrus said, giving him a fun-loving smile. "No one would want to mess up a face as nice as mine."

89

"Lo, Renny," Reign said, standing, jerking his head toward the door to the garage.

Lo slapped a hand on Cash's thigh then got off his lap to follow. When I stepped into the garage, I heard Lo talking.

"I agree," she said, nodding.

"Just to cover bases."

"Exactly."

"They see things differently," Reign added.

"And it's the only way to explain her presence here," Lo added. "Now you," she said, as the door closed behind me.

"Me?" I asked, rocking back on my heels. "What about me?"

"You're not going to be a dick to her," she told me, giving me a hard look. "I know you want her and I know this is a golden opportunity for you to make a move, but you need to keep in mind that she isn't signing up for this. This is her job. She has to do this. Don't make her uncomfortable. Don't back her into a corner. Don't make her..."

"Lo," I cut her off, shaking my head. "I know you want to protect your girl, but don't insult me. I have no intentions of trying to force her into fucking anything."

"Okay," Lo nodded. "I know you're a good guy, Renny. But I also know you have this drive to get under someone's skin. I just want to make sure that you don't fucking flay her, okay?"

"Got it," I agreed.

"I'm most interested in Reeve right now," Reign said. "Cyrus is pretty up-front. We've spent some time with Laz now so we have a little bit of a feel for him. Reeve is tight-lipped so I want some focus on him. But, they're all priority. You can fuck around with Mina until your heart is content, but this needs to be your main focus."

"Got it," I agreed, nodding. "Now, if you'll excuse me, I have some sprucing up to do on my honeymoon suite," I grinned, turning and going back into the clubhouse then down the hall to my room.

It wasn't exactly an impressive space. None of the rooms were. But it was home. I had four dark green walls and a private bath with a shower, tub, and double vanity. My bed was a queen because I liked having some room on the sides and opted out of the king like most of the other guys. The sheets were tossed and everything needed a fresh wash if she was going to be staying so I stripped the bed.

Then I did what any fully-patched MC member would do.

I called the probates in and made them do the laundry, scrub the bathroom, sweep the floors, and wipe all the surfaces.

I forgot how nice it was to have probates around. Granted, it wasn't that long ago that I had forgotten what it was like to be the lowest man on the totem pole. But I had done it back when there were half a dozen fucking assholes still around from Reign's father's days as the president who came up with the shittiest, most demeaning tasks possible to try to break us. These new guys, they had it easy. And the grunt work would remind them that they had people to answer to, that they weren't individuals completely in charge of their own lives anymore. They were part of a brotherhood and there was a hierarchy and they had to respect that. No better way to learn that than having to wash your superior's fucking underwear.

There was a soft knock on my door a couple minutes later. "Come on in, blondie," I called knowing there was only one person in the whole compound who didn't bang on the door like a parent who knew their teenage daughter had a boy in there without permission. Or, just as often, entered without knocking at all.

"Hey Renny," Penny said, giving me a smile as she looked into the bathroom to see Cyrus standing inside my shower stall with a squirt bottle of bleach and a scrub brush. "You put them to work already?" she asked, shaking her head. "You know, I could have helped you straighten the place up..."

"It's their job," I shrugged, sitting on the foot of my bed.

"They're not getting paid for it," she countered. "And they're sort of being treated like dogs who can't stop chewing the furniture by being locked up when the owners aren't home."

"They knew what they were signing up for, Pen. Besides, me and Duke and Maze went through a lot worse than they will. It's all good. What brings you down to my neck of the woods?"

She moved over toward the bathroom, closing the door. "I like Mina," she started oddly.

"I like Mina too," I agreed, smiling, patting the bed so she sat down and we could talk more quietly.

"So, I guess what I am saying is- don't scare her off."

"Trying not to. Seeing as that works against my end game here, honey."

"What *is* the end game here?" she asked. "Just to sleep with her? Or just to see what makes her tick and then toss her in the trash all pulled apart? Do you want something serious out of it?"

Those were good questions. Especially seeing as I hadn't exactly been Mr. Relationship in the past. What could I say? I was younger than most of the guys in the club and I liked to go out and sow my oats still. I wasn't a dick and I didn't make promises, but I enjoyed the company of many women on a temporary basis.

But most women simply didn't pique my interest. I found them easy to read, to understand, to put my finger on. And, quite frankly, I got too bored too fast to consider anything more than a short fling.

Mina wasn't boring. She was far from actually. And the tiny little snippets I had dug out of her only made me want to uncover more. But there would come a day when there would be nothing left to find. What then? Would I be bored and want to move on? Or would I be in so deep by then that there was no going back?

I wasn't the kind of man who got scared by that idea. Relationships could and should be a healthy part of most peoples' experiences. They were important. You found out some things about yourself within relationships. So the idea of giving up whoring around and enjoying coming home to the same woman? Yeah, it was appealing in a lot of ways. But it had to be the right woman.

"Can't tell you that I have a ring on deposit and plans to marry her, Penny. But I don't have plans to fuck her over either."

"Okay. That's the best you can offer right now," she said, giving me a smile. "Oh, clear out a drawer for her and about two-thirds your closet," she told me as she walked to the door. "And a drawer or three or four in the bathroom. Trust me," she added as she walked out.

So then I did just that.

And I went to bed.

And then I waited for my old lady to arrive.

Smiling the whole fucking time.

EIGHT

Mina

"I'm not dressing like a whore, Ash," I scoffed as she sat on her bunk one set over from mine and nixed all the clothes I took out of my trunk.

"I didn't say a whore. I'm just saying that you can't be hanging out at the compound dressed like you're about to go dig a well or do covert ops."

"Lo hangs out there in cargo pants and tank tops all the time," I countered.

"Yeah, but Lo is Lo," she shrugged it off. "You're you. You can't pull it off."

"Gee, thanks," I said, rolling my eyes. "I have only been dressing this way almost every day of my life for years. Nice to find out now that it doesn't suit me." I dropped down on my bunk atop a giant pile of my clothes and exhaled hard. "That's like all the clothes I have, Ash. Since you already said I can't wear the clothes I wear on business trips."

"No one is going to buy a Henchmen shacked up with a woman in a fucking pantsuit, Mina," she laughed, shaking her head. "Don't you have any jeans and girly tees or girly tanks?"

I had *one* pair of jeans. There was still a tag on the waistband from the store.

As if sensing my response, she hopped up. "Alright, well, we're pretty close in size. You have a slightly bigger ass than me, but I have some leggings that are forgiving."

"Leggings aren't pants," I objected immediately.

"They are if the material is thick and you can't see through them when you bend over," she shot back. "Here-black, gray, and galaxy-print. Now all you need is some basic tanks and tees. And you have a shitload of them. What about sweaters and shrugs or... right," she smiled when I gave her a blank look.

What the hell was a *shrug*?

I never gave much thought to my clothes. Not that I was clueless. I was just out of the loop. I grew up with a mother who kept me dressed very femininely and very modestly. Then I came across Lo who threw me in utility pants and tanks and combat boots and I just rarely ever looked back. There was no need. Most of the people I associated with, associated *me* with Hailstorm. There was no reason to dress any other way.

"Alright, here, I have a heather gray sweater and a wine-colored shrug and... oh, flats. You can't wear combat boots all the time."

RENNY

Ashley was a favorite of mine if I were being honest. A lot of the women around Hailstorm were so incredibly over-trained and skilled that it was scary and intimidating and I felt lost when they started talking about operations and bomb-building and how to put together a gun faster. Ashley was ex-military and nurse who managed to be more... average than most of the others.

I wasn't sure there was another woman around who would give me fashion advice. "Actually, keep this one. Sandy gave it to me," she said, tossing the wine-colored 'shrug' at me.

Sandy was her most recent girlfriend. "That went south already?" I asked, realizing I had done the 'sympathy voice' when she raised a brow at me.

"Apparently it was a deal-breaker that I don't like cats," she said, rolling her eyes.

"Well, I'm with you on that. I hate being covered in hair."

"Right?" she agreed, dropping down on her bunk. "So, I am going to slip into nurse-mode here for a quick second. Are you on the Pill?"

"What? Ah, no," I said, shaking my head, thrown off a little by the abrupt change in conversation.

"Shots? IUD?" she went on.

I shook my head. "No, I ah, had a implant put in last year," I said, rolling up my sleeve to show her the matchstick-size piece of plastic just under the surface of my skin.

"Why isn't that in your file?" she demanded and I could tell she was genuinely unhappy with me for not providing that information. It was her, among others, job to keep track of our medical records. "I did your last pap," she went on.

96

"I had it done in Canada last winter. I was due for a checkup and the doctor recommended it to me since I can't do the Pill."

"You should have told me. It alters things in small ways when you're on hormones."

"Well, you can put in my file that for the next five years, I have hormones in me."

"Alrighty, well, I don't have any seeing as I don't get involved with cocks of the real variety," she said, giving me a small smile. "But I know the reputations of those Henchmen. If you plan to hook up, or," she cut me off as I started to object, "even if you don't plan to hook up, please buy a box of condoms and keep them in your bag. Better to be prepared."

"Okay, Mom," I smiled. I didn't tell her that I always had condoms because, implant aside, I had made it into my mid-late twenties without ever having had sex without a condom. I'd like to say it was just genuinely being overly careful, and there was that, but I was sure that a bigger part of it had to do with that level of intimacy and the fact that I was never fully comfortable with it.

"Okay, so I think you're all set," she said suddenly, jumping up and shoving a bunch of things into my bag so fast that I couldn't even make out what the items were and before I could complete a full breath, she was zipping up the bag and picking it up. "Let's get you to your redheaded biker man."

I felt my stomach do a flip that I wasn't entirely sure was dread. In fact, it felt a lot like excitement to be perfectly honest. But as I tossed my bag in the back of the car and drove down the hill toward town, I tried like hell to convince myself otherwise.

If I was going to survive this job, I needed my wits about me and my guards up. Even if I would be wearing galaxy-printed leggings and a wine-colored shrug. Even if I didn't fully feel like myself because I was playing a part. I still needed to be careful.

Because a part of me recognized that Renny was dangerous to me. Not because he *would* hurt me, but because he had that power. No one had that power. Not since I was a kid.

I walked into the compound a complete bundle of nerves, every inch of skin seeming to spark off, my belly in tight knots. The common room had two new faces I didn't recognize, obviously brothers if the eyes and noses were anything to go by. The one without the beard also had a nice jaw to show off as well.

"Well now, who do we have here?" the bearded one asked, slowly getting out of his seat with a charming smile.

"Sit," Lazarus demanded casually, looking over at me. "She's taken."

As if on cue, I felt strong arms wrap themselves around my belly from behind and a warm chest curving around my back, a face ducking into my neck. "She's taken alright," Renny's voice said close to my ear, his breath warm, sending a shiver across my skin as my sex did an unexpected tightening. "Welcome home, baby cakes," he said and I had to bite my lower lip to keep from telling him to not call me that. I was supposed to be a woman in love who wanted pet names, no matter how ridiculous they were. "Aw, you're all tense from work," he said, giving my belly a squeeze. "Well, why don't we go to our room and I can... relax you?" he suggested and the bearded guy whistled, Laz chuckled, and the other one did his best to look like he hadn't overheard though he absolutely had.

With that, his arms slid from my stomach and around my lower back as he pulled me down the hall and toward his door.

"Home sweet home, honey," Renny said behind me as he shut the door.

It was a nice room. Private. After so many years at Hailstorm, it was easy to forget what a normal bedroom was like. He had a giant (to me, used to a twin bunk) queen bed covered in a green and brown comforter with the white sheets fresh and tucked down over the top. The walls were a deep green with various framed sketches in graphite or even full color. There was a deep brown dresser inside the door with a TV on top and a door beside that to the bath.

Really, were it not for the towering form of Renny, it was practically a vacation.

"Don't call me honey," I reminded him as he fought to pull my bag from my hand.

He ignored that as he tapped the dresser behind me. "I cleared out a drawer here, half the closet, and two drawers in the bathroom."

"Why?" I asked, turning to look at him, brows drawn together.

"Because you're supposed to be my woman and that means you need to look like you live here. They bought that you were away on a work trip, but you need to settle in."

"Alright," I agreed, but moved to the closet and put my bag at the bottom. I wasn't ready to settle in. A part of me was sure I might run at any minute. "So, I know Laz..."

"The bearded one is Cyrus. He plays guitar at a coffee shop. Charming. Laid-back. Reeve is his older brother. He's an electrician. More tight-lipped."

"And there here because..."

RENNY

"Their pops was a member before he was killed."

"So, this is a legacy thing?" I asked, brows drawing together.

"Cyrus made the same argument," he nodded.

An awkward silence fell then as we both just stood there- me by the closet, him near the door. "Let me just clear this up right now, Renny. I'm here to work."

"You go ahead and do that, Mina. And I will work on breaking down those walls of yours."

"Renny," I sighed, shaking my head. "Give up."

"Can't do that, sweetheart. But what I can do is say I sleep on the left side of the bed and I have to have the TV on or every fucking thing wakes me up."

"I sleep with headphones on at Hailstorm," I commiserated.

"I will remember to put the seat down but I leave my shoes every fucking where."

"Why are you..."

"I don't snore, but I sometimes have entire conversations in my sleep. It's weird as fuck. Oh, and blanket stealing will not be tolerated."

Damn him. I felt my lips curve up at the end of his little speech. "Good to know," I said, realizing for the first time that I would have to share a bed with him. I thought he would be considerate enough to bring in a cot or something. But of course not. Why would he do that when all he had wanted for months was to get me into a bed?

"Your turn," he prompted.

"My turn?"

"Tell me your little life secrets. You know, so I know what to expect. Do you leave the toothpaste in the sink? 'Cause that's fucking disgusting."

RENNY

"I don't leave the toothpaste in the sink. And, um, I don't snore or talk in my sleep. I clean up after myself because that is what Lo expects at Hailstorm. I like to sleep in mostly because I don't sleep well."

"Alright, so we got that handled," he said as I moved to the door, figuring now was the best time to get to work. The sooner the better. "Ah, I think not," he said, slamming his hand on the door as I reached for it.

"What? Why not? They're all out there. It's the perfect time to catch them, when they're all at-ease."

"Yeah, babe, but we've only been in here five minutes."

"Don't call me babe. And so what?"

"So, I might be cool with a fifteen minute quickie, but you're not walking out of her in under five looking like I didn't even muss your fucking hair. In fact," he said, smile wicked, "maybe you can throw in some throaty 'yes, yes, yeses' or some 'just like that' or, if you're feeling naughty, 'yeah, fuck my pussy!'."

Oh, good lord.

I wasn't exactly shy about sex. And nothing about what he actually said offended me, but I felt my face getting warm as I stood there.

"You *blush?* No fucking way," he said, grinning huge. "Look at that, it gets redder when you bring attention to it!" he added, clearly delighted by my discomfort. "Do you think they'll turn beet if I maybe," he started, hands raising and framing my face, "said I wonder what you taste like. Sweet? I bet you have the sweetest fucking pussy. There," he said, but his voice wasn't teasing anymore; it was heated; it was low and sexy and promising as his thumbs moved out to stroke over the apples of my cheeks.

"Do you flush when you're turned on too?" he asked, mostly himself, as one of his hands left my jaw and slid

101

down my neck, snagging the collar of my shirt and pulling it down to expose some of my chest, looking for proof of his theory. "I can just imagine," he went on, leaning forward, his nose moving up my jaw toward my ear, making me shiver involuntarily again, "stripped bare on my bed- your chest, belly, thighs all warm and red as I run my tongue up your inner thighs, biting hard once," he said and his teeth snagged my earlobe unexpectedly, making me let out a surprised groan, the sound loud even to my own ears. "Then feeling your entire body tremble as my tongue slides up your wet pussy and my lips close around your clit and sucks hard."

Desire was a pulsing, overwhelming thing coursing through my whole body. It was loud and strong enough to push away the rational voice in the back of my mind telling me to raise my hands and push him away.

My arms did raise, but my hands landed on him- one low by his hip, the other on his arm just under his shoulder, and they curved and dug in as my hips pressed into his, as my body tried to get closer, get a relief from the need overtaking me.

My back arched backward as his lips kissed down the column of my neck and down to my chest where he was still holding my shirt down several inches.

"I'd let you come," he told me, his tongue moving out to trace under my clavicle. "But then before your pussy even stops spasming, I'd slam deep inside you and fuck you hard and fast, make that one orgasm roll right into another one. Then just because you've made me wait so long for it, I'd give you another one. Until you're so come-drunk that you can't even fucking move afterward."

My air sighed out of me as his tongue traced back up my throat until his mouth was by my ear again.

"But not just yet," he told me, pulling back suddenly, leaving me embarrassingly unsteady, grabbing him tighter for a second as my heavy lids fluttered open to find his light eyes watching me intensely. As soon as my gaze found his, he released me, reaching up toward my hair, slipping his hands in, and mussing it up. "There we go, that's better," he said, sexy as all get out to teasing and light in the span of a *blink*. I would have found it impressive if I wasn't so thrown off by it. "Let's go," he said, reaching down, grabbing my hand, opening the door, and pulling me out.

I reached up self-consciously to flatten my hair as we walked out into the main room, feeling a blush creep up again as Renny threw himself down in an armchair and I moved to go sit on the arm of the couch next to the guys.

"Pumpkin cheeks," Renny called, making my eyes bug. *Pumpkin cheeks?* "I have your seat right here," he said, patting his thigh.

And, well, we were supposedly post-coital. It made sense for me to sit with him. The jerk.

"Right," I said, forcing a smile as I moved back to him, sitting carefully down right above his knees.

I should have known better. He was never going to let me get away with that. He reached for my hips, sank in, and dragged me upward until I was on his lap. And it was right then that I realized he hadn't been able to completely cool his desire as quickly as he pretended to. Because his hard-on was pressing into my ass as I sat there.

My gaze went to his face without me realizing and I found him already watching me, eyes a little heated. He reached out, tucking some of my hair behind my ear. "Bet you're just as wet as I am hard," he said in a low, audible only to us, rumble.

103

He would win that bet.

But I needed to focus.

This was a *job*.

And I had known he was going to make a move. I thought I was prepared. I obviously underestimated Renny. I had him pegged for sweet and charming and boyishly flirtatious.

But Renny was a man.

And Renny could dirty-talk any man under the table.

And I was a woman and I reacted.

Now that I knew what he was capable of, I would be better prepared.

Or so I was telling myself.

Because if I really thought about it instead of making unfounded declarations, I would realize that there was no preparing for it. Anytime he got that close to me, talked that dirty to me, put his hands and mouth and tongue on me, I was going to melt.

"So, this is Mina," Renny declared, making me shake my head, realizing I had totally been starting at him. Feeling me jump and to squash any hopes I had that maybe he hadn't noticed, his fingers dug into my hipbone and his lips tipped up. I turned back to the others in the room and gave them a smile. "Mina, this is Reeve and Cyrus and, of course you already know Laz."

"Nice to see you without the cuffs on, Laz," I said, and he smiled at me. He was a somewhat serious kind of man. Seeing him smile was almost off-putting.

"Cuffs?" Cyrus perked up, brows raised. "Angel, did you cuff this man and have your dirty way with him?"

I was in the process of laughing when Renny's voice cut me off. "Just so we're clear- when we have an old lady, that means we don't fucking share. Mina is *mine*. Look at her all you want. Can't fucking blame you and it's a compliment to me seeing as I'm the one she crawls into bed with at night. But keep your hands off and don't insinuate she is anything but loyal."

Chastened, Cyrus slumped just ever so slightly. He wasn't used to a firm male presence which probably had a lot to do with losing his father young. "Got it," he said, his voice having lost a little of its levity.

"It's nice to meet you Cyrus," I offered, making my voice a little softer, a little sweeter than usual. "Don't mind Renny. He's a neanderthal," I offered, figuring it would be good to create a different dynamic with the guys than Renny had. If he was a boss, a man to take orders from, someone who maybe couldn't take a joke because it said he wasn't being authoritative, then I could be the one who made fun of that. Because as an old lady, that was in my power. And maybe it would make the guys, especially Cyrus, flock to me and open up to me. "I hear you play guitar."

"Picked it up because it seemed like all the musicians got all the pussy," he offered, smirking.

"He is leaving off the fact that he first picked up a guitar at eleven," Reeve added, smiling slightly.

"What can I say? I was an early bloomer in the ladykiller department. Don't get your dick all bent out of shape because I always get all the chicks." He tempered the comment with a wink that would have been ridiculous on anyone else, but he managed to pull it off.

"And Reeve, you're..."

"An electrician. While some of us were singing fucking John Mayer songs, the rest of us were doing actual work."

"I played a John Mayer song once. Fucking *once*," Cyrus defended. "And it was a request. *'Your Body is a*

Wonderland'," he explained to me. "And, well, her body was a mother fucking wonderland which I got to experience because I sang that song, you fuck."

"You still *knew* that fucking song, man," Reeve said, shaking his head.

They were close.

If I was right, they likely moved out together when they were old enough. Reeve, being the more responsible and serious one, got a job that would make up for the fact that his brother was a bit of a slacker.

Really, none of this was groundbreaking. And all of it could have been ascertained by Renny and Renny alone. He knew what he was doing. I wasn't needed there.

"Got a four inch scar across his throat," Renny said, only loud enough for me to hear.

"What? Who?"

"Reeve," he offered and I turned back to Reeve, squinting a little and sure enough, there it was. I had completely missed that.

A scar across his throat?

"Suicide?" I asked, barely letting my lips move.

"Not a chance," he answered back, reaching up to pull me so my head was on his shoulder.

"How do you know that?" I shot back, trying my best to not nuzzle in. He smelled good. How had I never realized that before? It was something clean and unobtrusive. So not likely cologne. Maybe it was just his soap.

"Just do," he said, his hand moving absentmindedly down my arm, making the skin goosebump in a delicious way.

"So what is he hiding?" I mumbled.

"Exactly," he agreed, leaning over and planting a kiss to my forehead. And it was so unexpected and so sweet that my belly did a weird little flip flop.

"And if he is hiding something, so is Cyrus."

"Yep. See?" he asked, reaching up to boop my nose, "we make a good team."

As I sat there and listened half-heartedly to the guys talk, knowing Reign was paying me an obnoxious sum to give them my *full* attention, I couldn't help but, for the first time in my career, start to doubt myself. I missed Laz's knuckles. I missed Reeve's throat. Granted, I never claimed to be hyper-observant; my specialty was figuring out what was being said between the actual lines of dialogue, what motivated people, what made them who they are. But still, those were some pretty huge things for me to have completely missed.

"Sugar lips," Renny said, his voice amused.

Sugar lips?

He was just screwing with me.

"Yeah?" I asked anyway, tilting my head up to look at him.

"Asked if would whip us up something to eat," he said, clearly enjoying himself.

"I, ah..." was a pretty awful cook.

"Anything will do, hop to," he demanded, pushing me off his lap and I took my feet in a weird little daze.

Hop to?

Hop to?

He would pay for that later. I gave him a look that told him just that. "Fine," I snapped, making my way toward the kitchen.

"Trained her pretty good," Renny said, just to goad me. "She couldn't follow an order for shit when she showed up."

I was pretty sure an actual growl escaped me as I turned into the kitchen and went for the fridge that Repo always kept well-stocked. It was full, of course, but I didn't know any recipes.

But I grabbed about half the contents of the fridge and dropped them on the counter anyway. I was leaning down trying to drag a giant pot out of a cabinet when I heard a male voice from above me. "Not much of a cook, huh?" Laz's voice asked, making me straighten, pot between my hands.

I put it down on the stove. "Why would you say that?"

"Honey, you took out a bottle of maple syrup along with the butter, hot sauce, and all the meat and fruit in the fridge."

Okay, so maybe I wondered if maybe you made dishes a little sweet when you added a little syrup. And apparently that was wholly wrong.

"He knows I don't cook," I let him in on. "He's just flashing around his peacock feathers so he looks like a badass around you new guys."

Lazarus chuckled, putting the hot sauce, butter, and maple syrup away. "So the pot," he said, jerking his chin toward it. "Were you thinking soup or stew or chili?"

"I was thinking of throwing everything in it and see what happens."

"A fire, most likely," he smiled, making little crows feet form next to his eyes. I found them endearing. "My ma, growing up, we didn't have a whole fuck of a lot of money, not even for food. So she used to make what she called

Kitchen Sink Soup when we had just little bits left of a bunch of shit. She hated wasting anything."

"Kitchen Sink Soup?"

"Yeah, meaning everything but the kitchen sink," he let me in on, reaching for the spinach and ripping it with his hands and dropping it into the pot. "Funny thing, no matter what she threw in, it was always good. Not even you can fuck it up," he said with a smirk that I found I really liked.

"So what can I do?" I asked, looking at the pile of food.

"Peel carrots and then slice them."

"I can handle that," I agreed, looking through all the drawers before I finally found the peeler.

Then we set to work, talking occasionally.

"Your mom didn't cook?" he asked as I dropped some of the onions I had been chopping into the pot.

"My mom was into appearances. So she would order in and plate the food then toss the take-away containers and pretend she cooked."

"Why the fuck would she do that?"

"Because she was looking for any way to make her husband love her," Renny supplied, making me jump hard, jerking my head over to find him leaning in the doorway, looking like he had been there a good long time.

He was right, damn him.

And that was *personal*.

"Don't worry, Mina," Laz said, as if sensing the tension between me and Renny, "there are other ways to a man's heart than through his stomach."

"Laz, the back bar needs to be cleaned," Renny said dismissively.

Lazarus stiffened at the same time I did. Because Laz was in recovery. Renny knew that. And he was making him go clean the back bar? For no reason?

"Not a problem is it?" he went on, his tone dead.

And there he was- cold, unpredictable Renny.

I had started to forget he existed.

"Nope, not a problem," Laz said, shaking his head as he went to the sink to wash his hands. "Just let it simmer and don't touch it," he told me, giving me a small smile. "It should pull through just fine."

"Thanks for your help," I called to his retreating form as Renny pushed off the doorway and moved in. I advanced on him immediately, shoving my finger into his chest. My voice when I spoke was low and livid. "What the fuck was that about?" I hissed.

"He does what he's told to do. I told him to clean the back bar."

"He's a recovering alcoholic, you ass!"

"And now we will see if he has self-control around those bottles," he shrugged.

I exhaled hard. Anger wasn't going to work on this version of Renny. I had seen him and Duke go at it several times and it never changed anything. Better to approach him with calm.

"Why are you being a dick right now?" I asked, tone even.

"I'm doing my job. You're supposed to be doing your job too. Or did you forget that?"

"I believe I just stood here and listened to a long part of Laz's back story. So, no, I haven't friggen forgotten to do my job. What is with the attitude?"

"No attitude. Just making sure you're earning your paycheck."

My blood was boiling. *Boiling.* I didn't do anger often so when it coursed through me, I was ill-equipped to handle it properly.

So I lashed out.

"I don't know who the *fuck* you think you're talking to right now," I started, advancing him, pleased when he actually went back a step. "But I am *not* one of your probates. I am *not* beneath you. I have a job to do and I have to do it while you are grab-assing and insulting and demeaning me to the men around here. I am not going to put up with you turning into a goddamn jackass to boot. Check your fucking attitude when you speak to me."

"Careful, Mina," he warned, his voice even colder.

"Careful or... what, Renny? You might be a genuine ass when you're in one of these moods of yours, but you won't put your hands on me. So, what? You'll make comments about my unhappy upbringing? Oh, wait, you already did that. You have *nothing* on me. So keep your threats to yourself and do your damn job and leave me the hell alone."

"You're right. I don't have much on you. Funny, that. Seeing as I have known you for months, have been trying to get to know you for months and you won't give me shit. You barely even give me a smile. But five minutes in the kitchen with some nobody fighter and you are spilling all kinds of shit to him."

"Seriously?" I asked, mouth falling open slightly. "You can't be serious right now. You're... jealous?"

"You went from soaking your panties for me in my room to melting into me as we sat in the main room and you zoned out to spilling all your secrets to a guy you don't know from Adam? So, what? I'm good for a fuck but not some background information?"

"So this is insecurity," I concluded. "That's interesting." If he wanted to play cold, well, he was out of his depth.

Because women, yeah, we could freeze your dick off when we wanted to.

"Oh fuck off with that," he said as I turned to go stir the soup.

"Fuck off with what? A taste of your own medicine? It's bitter isn't it? And I bet no one else is willing to shove it down your throat. I'll be happy to freaking gag you with it."

"You're being..."

"An ass?" I supplied, brow raised. "Cold? Detached? Insulting? Hey, Kettle, it's Pot again... and you're still fucking black."

To my surprise, he froze for a long second, watching me. It happened gradually. I would have missed it if I hadn't been watching him so closely. But the skin around his eyes softened. His jaw stopped being so clenched. Then a slow, familiar smirk tugged at his lips.

"You curse a lot more when you're riled," he observed, clearly enjoying that little tidbit.

Really, it was unsettling how he switched back and forth between the two versions of himself. And, being that I wasn't used to it, I was finding it hard to let go of the anger I felt, the offense I took to everything he had said. It wasn't exactly fair of me. I knew he had some issues and I knew that, in a way, his moods like that weren't really him. They were his monsters, his damage, his scars all wearing his face and talking with his mouth.

But that knowledge didn't make it easier to accept the cruelty he was capable of.

Because, fact of the matter was, one afternoon when I was sitting with L feeling useless, I had finally looked into him.

And a search of Renny Renolds West led me pretty immediately to a Roland West and a Katherine Renny-

West. And the scary thing about that, going in knowing he ran away and he was dealing with some psychological issues, was the fact that Roland West and Katherine Renny-West were both shrinks.

You would think that two people in the mental health field could easily produce a very well-rounded and stable child. But, more often than not, in my career, I had found just the opposite to be true. Especially when *both* parents were in the mental health field.

As I read through all the articles and accolades for the power couple, I got a sick, twisting, God-awful feeling of dread in my stomach. I could find no proof of it, but I *knew* I just knew they had somehow used that innocent little boy of theirs as a guinea pig. They poked his buttons to see if he screamed or laughed or raged or peed himself.

And they created a monster that did the exact same thing.

Circles, vicious, awful circles.

We were all seemingly doomed to them.

Even people like me and Renny who made our lives figuring out why people were the way they were, who understood human frailty, who knew how to take those predispositions and use them against people or use them to try to help people understand them too.

We were still caught in our own circles.

"See, now you know something about me," I said, turning away to the soup again, knowing I didn't want to mess with it, but stirring it to distract myself.

"So what did you find out about him then?" he asked, all easy charm again, leaning against the counter beside the other side of the stove.

I took a breath and turned my head to him. "You're allowed to have your dark moods, Renny. And I'm allowed to be resentful about what you said when you were in one."

"Sweetheart..." he said, eyes going just a little sad and I found I didn't like that look there, but that didn't change anything either.

"No," I said, shaking my head. "I understand that you maybe can't help it, Renny, but it doesn't make that behavior okay. I know you can turn it off like a light switch, but I don't work that way."

"So what you're saying is..." he prompted, tone cautious. Worried, he was worried.

Maybe that was a good thing.

"I am saying you need to walk away and leave me alone and I will talk to you again when I want to talk to you again."

"Mina, I don't want..."

"Too bad," I cut him off. "You don't get to have what you want when you want it all the time. And right now you don't get my forgiveness. You'll get it eventually. When I am ready to give it. Until then, a wide berth would be appreciated."

I said it.

I even sounded like I meant it.

But the last thing I truly wanted was a wide berth.

In fact, a strange, prominent part of me actually wanted to walk over to him, curl into his chest, and feel his arms wrap around me.

But that wouldn't work.

Because if things progressed with me and him, as they seemed like they would be doing, despite my better judgement, then there needed to be ground rules and there needed to be an understanding about what was and was not acceptable. Then there needed to be consequences to actions outside of those boundaries.

If I gave in, if I forgave him like it was no big deal over something small like the confrontation we just had, then it would give him permission to keep doing it, to let it escalate.

And that wasn't okay.

So as much as I felt like I was choking on my own tongue when I said it, I got the words out.

Renny watched me for a long minute, looking for a fracture he could dig into and use to collapse my anger.

But he found none.

So he nodded, eyes even sadder. And his tone when he spoke was almost defeated. "Whatever you need, sweetheart."

With that, he was gone.

And I tried to convince myself that that was what I wanted.

RENNY

NINE

Mina

I went to bed early.
But only in the literal sense.
I brought myself into the room and climbed into the bed early.
I didn't sleep.
Of course I didn't. Because after Renny left and Lazarus came back into the kitchen and declared that I hadn't fucked up the Kitchen Sink Soup, we called everyone to dinner and everyone took their bowls to various spots to eat.
Renny respected my wishes. He took his bowl and sat with Reeve and Lazarus on the couch, watching some kind

116

of survival show on TV and all having strong opinions on the survival methods used by the contestants.

I sat with Cyrus who was, as one would expect, and easy conversationalist. He went on and on about the new coffeeshop, *She's Bean Around,* and the 'crazy ass chicks' who owned it. He told me some stories about growing up around The Henchmen compound, though unlike Reign, Cash, and Wolf's mothers, Cyrus and Reeve's mother tried to keep them as far away from the place as possible. From what I heard about the way Reign's father ran things in his day, I didn't blame her. And once her husband was gone, she took them as far as fast as she could.

"Why didn't you guys come back to prospect sooner?" I asked, taking my last spoonful of soup and deciding it was my favorite recipe. And I was even pretty sure I could make it again.

"Eh, you know how it is. Reeve had moved out when he was eighteen, got an apartment, started training and working. As soon as I aged up, I just showed up at his door. We were young and liked the independence and lack of rules. Our ma was a real hardass. We had ten o'clock curfews even on Friday nights in senior year. We were just having fun. We would see the guys around from time to time and talk about 'maybe one day' but it never felt right."

"But it felt right now? When there's a real danger involved? And when, for all intents and purposes, you guys have a good, crime-free life going?"

It wasn't normal for grown men with decent jobs and their shit together who had grown up with a strong and law-abiding mother to just suddenly decide to become arms dealers.

"Our little sis just moved off on her own about a year ago so we didn't have to worry about her anymore. It just seemed like a sign, y'know? And we did some research and found out that Reign had kinda turned shit around to be less twisted. Figured it was now or never. A bucket list kinda thing, I guess? Besides, I work at a damn coffee shop. Not like I am giving up a whole hell of a lot by prospecting here."

"You guys have a sister?" I asked, surprised it was the first I was hearing of it.

"Yeah, Wasp is a little..."

"Wasp?" I cut him off, smiling. Granted, Reeve and Cyrus weren't common names, but they're weren't off-the-wall either.

"Nickname," he explained. "She's a hellion. My mom once told her she acted like a queen bee and she objected and said she wasn't a bee because bees died after they stung you and that she was a wasp instead, because they just kept on stinging all they fucking wanted. It just stuck."

"She sounds like a character."

"Yeah, she took after Pops earlier than we did."

"Meaning?"

"Meaning she got herself a fucking converted school bus and some female friends and she runs fucking cons across the country. She'll likely drop in sometime now that she knows we finally bit the bullet. She's been encouraging this since we were teens, said if it wasn't a sexist place, she would prospect herself. She would have too. And her ass would have gotten in. In a weird way, she'll be proud of us."

Seeing as I worked in a criminal organization, I could understand that. It was always a big deal to get accepted. Especially when the organization was as old as The Henchmen MC.

RENNY

"Have you ever done anything even remotely illegal? Or are you just jumping in?"

"Does all the typical teenage shit count?"

"What typical teenage shit?"

"Smoking, fighting, illegally downloading shit, drinking, maybe even a B&E or two, but nothing got taken. It was just to fuck with these assholes that were always yelling at us to stop hanging out on the street."

"No rap sheet, no crime," I offered.

"Then I'm a regular mother fucking boy scout. Think that works against me here?"

"I think it's important to not have the law looking too close at you. If you had already had a bunch of charges for arms, they would start looking at you closer. Clean slate might be just what they need around here."

"Good to know. Where is everyone?" he asked, gesturing around to the mostly-empty room.

"Reign went to see Wolf and Janie. Cash and Repo are entertaining the kids with some kind of hoverboard thing he ordered. The women are likely taking a much-needed nap."

"And Duke?"

I felt my lips curve up a little wickedly at that. "He and Penny just met a couple months back so whenever they get the chance..."

"Gotcha," Cyrus said with a smile that was leaps and bounds more devilish than mine. "So you and Renny. That's an interesting matchup."

"Why's that?"

"Because you both have this lightswitch thing."

I felt myself stiffening at that. Renny was the one with a lightswitch. Not me.

"How so?"

119

RENNY

"You both turn hot and cold in a blink. He's warm, you're usually cold. He's cold, you're warm. Both of you walking outta that kitchen a bit ago, it was like the fucking North Pole up in here. But, I guess that must mean when you're both warm, it's fucking hot as hell, right?"

"Right," I agreed, sitting there a little dumbstruck by his declaration.

I had never considered myself a hot and cold person. Mostly because I generally accepted that I was mostly cool most of the time.

But either I had been wrong about myself my whole life, or I was suddenly becoming warmer at times.

And, really, I knew exactly what and who caused that.

Which put me excusing myself with a supposed headache and going back to our room, remembering right then that I was going to have to share a bed with him. But there was nothing I could do about that at that point. So I grabbed my duffle bag and made my way to the bathroom to realize that there was a reason Ashley had been in such a rush to pack my bag.

Because she left out some essentials.

Namely, anything that could be worn as pajamas.

I suddenly got the impression that everyone in my life was on some kind of mission to push me and Renny together. When the hell did I become that pathetic friend that everyone wanted to set up?

On a sigh, I walked back out into the bedroom and snagged one of Renny's t-shirts out of his drawer. He was taller than me, but not by that much. So the t-shirt was not a dress on me; it came down maybe two inches past my crotch, covering my hot pink pantie-covered ass. It wouldn't matter anyway; I would be under the covers, pretending to be asleep.

120

So I brushed my teeth, washed off my makeup, turned down the lights, and climbed in the bed, laying as close to the edge as was possible without falling off, curling up, closing my eyes, and spending the next two hours overthinking.

Sometime around midnight, the door opened and closed quietly and Renny walked around to his side of the bed, picking up the remote and turning the TV on before grabbing some things out of the dresser and going into the bathroom to shower.

He came back smelling even stronger of that scent that always clung to his skin. I didn't dare look. The room had a glow from the TV that I could see even with my eyes closed. He would know I was awake. So I stayed as still as possible as he climbed under the sheets, shifted around for a couple minutes, then fell asleep.

And I knew he was asleep because he was right, he talked.

I moved slowly, sitting up, watching him for a long minute, his face almost seeming more severe in sleep-likely because it was lacking his frequent easy smile. The fact that his dream must have been a dark one probably didn't help. His voice was low and dark, most the words coming out mumbled, but I could make out curses here and there and the occasional deep, pained growl of "no".

I reached into the nightstand and pulled out my old Gameboy, climbing under the sheets like a tent to muffle the sound, and played as Renny tossed and turned.

"You catch anything good?" his sleep-groggy voice asked, making me start so hard that I actually dropped the Gameboy onto my lap. My head jerked over to find him under the sheet with me, his light eyes shining even in the dark.

RENNY

Feeling oddly caught, I yanked the sheets down until they fell down to my hips. Renny appeared in the television light too, still watching me.

"Forgot something," he murmured a second before I felt his fingers tracing near the inside of my knee and slowly start gliding up, making my belly go liquid immediately.

"I, ah, yeah, Ash packed me. She obviously forgot to... Renny," I warned as his fingertips whispered up and slid in toward my inner thighs.

"Not what I meant, but it's a nice fucking bonus," he said as his finger touched the edge of my panties where it met my hip then slid across the waistband then down just slightly. I expected to feel him press between my lips, to stroke his finger up and find my clit and put an end to the throbbing sensation there. Instead, he snagged the Gameboy I had utterly forgotten about and lifted the weight off of me, pulling it up and turning it off.

"Oh, right," I said, my voice a little airy.

He arched up, balancing on one arm and moving over my chest to put the thing down on the top of my nightstand, taking his sweet time about it. Then, just as slowly, his head turned to look at me looking, I was sure, for some sign of objection.

As much as I wanted to muster some, I couldn't.

"Forgive me yet?" he asked, voice a low rumble.

"I..." I started, swallowing hard against my dry mouth.

"Not yet, huh?" he asked, lips twitching slightly as he moved back to my side, but closer, his whole front against my whole side. "Let's see what I can do about that then," he said, promise in his eyes.

His hand reached out and brushed my hair off to the side, touching the logo on the front of the tee. "I like you in my shirt," he told me as his hand flattened and moved to

122

the side, completely covering my breast and squeezing with perfect pressure, making me arch up slightly as my air rushed out of me.

God, it had been so long since I had been touched. And I had wanted him from the first time he smiled at me with blood in his mouth, as crazy as that was.

His thumb and forefinger found the gently hardened bud of my nipple and rolled it, sending a jolt of need so strong between my legs that I had to press my thighs together to try to ease the desire.

"Sensitive," he murmured as his fingers pinched the point slightly before his hand moved across my chest to give my other breast the same attention.

By the time his hand slid down my belly, I was pretty sure I had never been more turned on in my life. Every nerve ending was poised, was receptive to even the slightest of touches. His hand pressed down hard on my lower stomach that already felt oddly heavy.

"Look at me," he demanded and my head shifted on the pillow to find his face.

It happened simultaneously.

His lips crashed down on mine.

And his hand pressed between my legs.

I cried out against his lips, the sound muffled by his mouth, as my hips shifted slightly toward him. There was no teasing. No hinting at touching the sweet spot but not actually doing it. His fingers landed on my clit and immediately started working it in hard, slow circles.

"How about now?" he asked, lifting his head slightly, eyelids heavy.

But words weren't exactly something I was capable of at that moment.

"No?" he asked, smile wicked. I lost his fingers for a second before they slid up and then under my panties, stroking up my wet slit and finding my clit again. "Let's try this then."

He worked me for a long minute, eyes watching me intensely, as he drove me upward. And then his lips pressed down on mine again.

Again, it was simultaneous.

His tongue thrust into my mouth.

And his fingers thrust inside me.

I jolted, turning onto my side, my leg hooking over his hips as his fingers curled inside me, raking over the top wall and making gentle, perfect, relentless strokes over my G-spot as he kissed me hard, hard enough to bruise.

Hard and soft at the same time and it was an overwhelming sensation as he forced me to feel them simultaneously until I felt like I was teetering on the edge of something that threatened a pleasure that bordered on pain.

And I felt myself instinctively recoil from it, to pull away, to avoid the things that might be impossible to protect myself from.

"Shh," Renny whispered as his lips left mine. His breath was warm on my face, and my eyes fluttered open. "Just let it happen, sweetheart. I got you."

Somehow, in that moment, I found myself putting my faith to rest in that. I found myself trusting him.

So when he pushed me back to the edge again, I didn't try to plant my feet, to fight it, to pull away.

The orgasm tore through me- a deep, hard throbbing that made my entire body shudder once as Renny pressed his forehead to mine and I cried out loudly, fingers digging into his arm and back hard enough that there were sure to be marks after.

As the shocks subsided, his free arm slid under me and curled up, grabbing me at the base of my skull, and pressing my head into his chest as his fingers continued a slow, lazy thrusting, bringing me back down.

But even when the orgasm was done, his fingers stayed inside me, a kind of intimacy I would have recoiled from normally.

Sex was sex.

Intimacy was a different animal entirely.

And I had never been comfortable with it before.

But somehow, in that room, in that bed, in the arms of a man I knew was as unpredictable as the weather, it not only felt comfortable. It somehow felt right.

Right in that moment, I couldn't seem to stop myself from blurting out what had been on my mind, and the subsequent insecurity that went along with it.

"Do I blow hot and cold?"

"What?" he asked, slowly pulling back slightly, eyes landing on mine.

"Cyrus said we're weird together because we both blow so hot and cold."

"Cyrus is an idiot."

"Cyrus is an objective third party," I countered.

"Alright, fine. He's not an idiot," he conceded.

"You didn't answer my question."

He sighed a little. "Fine. You pretend to be cold. I think the longer you're stuck around the same group of people, the harder it is for you to keep up that pretense. So you warm up. And that makes you seem hot and cold. Happy?"

It wasn't exactly the kind of news that made you happy. As much as I had absolutely worked to become cooler, more detached, guarded, it hurt in a strange way to be called on that. It shouldn't have. Logically, it should have made me happy. Maybe if I wasn't post-orgasm contented and Renny's fingers weren't *still* inside me, I could have found the determination to be that woman I had worked to be my whole life.

"No," I admitted, looking into his eyes and seeing understanding there.

"You like pretending to be cool, Mina," he said, his fingers sliding out of me then out of my panties to settle on the material covering my ass. "But I see underneath the ice. It's not as thick as you want it to seem. Just a small puddle really. Bet you I can melt it without much effort."

I had a sneaking suspicion that he would win that bet. I had just been in a bed with him for a couple hours and I was pretty sure I was already thawing.

"That scare you?" he asked, his hand behind my neck moving down to whisper across my shoulders.

I took a breath and gave him the truth. "It would scare me less if I knew you well enough to trust you."

His face went just a little guarded at that. "What do you want to know?"

"Everything," I said honestly. "I want to know everything. I mean... I know you have had something dark happen in your life and I understand that it might not be..."

"You gonna shut it so I can tell you everything or what?" he asked, lips tipping up at one corner, but the motion didn't make it to his eyes.

"What?"

"Well, if you want to know all my dark and twisted, doodle-bug, you need to hush so I can give it to you."

"Doodle-bug?" I objected with a snort.

126

"You like it," he said, ducking his head a little. "In fact, you like all the pet names. You just don't want to admit it, snuggle-puss."

I laughed at that, shaking my head at him.

"Alright, I'll shut up. Give it to me."

Then he gave it to me.

TEN

Renny

No one got everything.

Everyone who needed to, got bits and pieces, got the *Cliffsnotes* version. That meant the guys in the club had a generalized idea of what I came from and what motivated me to be a dick at times. But they didn't get the ugly details.

Some things weren't meant for sharing.

But the fact of the matter was, shit changed in that kitchen a few hours before. Why? I wasn't sure. But after the argument with Mina, I had felt remorse for my usual dickishness.

I *never* felt remorse for it before.

I figured maybe that was a sign. What it was a sign of was a bit foggy, but as I thought shit through, I came to the conclusion that, at the very least, it was a sign to dig deeper into it.

But Mina had trust issues and if I wanted more from her, I had to give her more from me.

"My parents were always brilliant," I started, holding her tighter when she went to pull away, to put space between us. But that was the last goddamn thing I needed. As a whole, I tried to not even think about my upbringing, let alone dissect it. But it was time. "So much so that they were cold and clinical in their outlook on life, in their interactions with everyone. Scientists to the core, in a way."

"Smart, hm?" she asked. "You fell way, way far from that tree, huh?" she teased and I know she was just trying to lighten my mood.

I was smart as fuck and she knew it.

"They didn't believe in things like guilt and love and affection. How the fuck I was even conceived is a goddamn mystery. I half believe it involved test tubes because there's no way those two fucked. Anyway, I think the purpose of having me was purely clinical."

"They wanted to test different parenting theories on you," she guessed.

"In a way, yes. The problem was, they wanted to test them fucking all on me. Had they maybe tried some attachment parenting or French-style parenting on me and stuck with the method, maybe I wouldn't have gotten as fucked in the head as I did. But one night as a baby, I was made to cry it out and self-soothe. The next, I was coddled. The next, crying it out again. Then as I got older, they would test out the Marshmallow Experiment on me- see if I was a kid more into instant gratification with a small reward or one with self-restraint who could wait for the bigger payout later."

"Which were you?"

"I'd still take the mother fucking marshmallow now over the cookie later," I admitted with a humorless smile.

"What else?" she prompted when I went silent.

I shrugged. "They tested out negative reinforcement over positive. I was apparently more receptive to negative because that was the one they stuck with. There was hardly a day when I wasn't 'naughty', 'silly', 'bad', or 'stupid'. There was no malice in their words, mind you. They weren't programmed that way. They just knew that when they called me stupid, I worked harder. And when they called me bad, I cleaned up my mess or settled down. So when I did something bad, I got belittled, but when I did something good, figured out some kind of puzzle they threw at me, I got whatever small little token of approval they were capable of."

"What about as you got older?"

"That's where they had more fun with me in a way. I didn't play Monopoly or Life. My games were more like 'that man in the red hat is a bad guy, tell me why' variety. I was observant by nature and they worked to exploit that. I was taught to make snap judgements, to create chains out of small links. If I couldn't figure out why the half moon cuts on his forearms meant that he was a rapist, then there would be bare walls and cold floors in my future. I learned quick to not miss anything."

"You said they never hit you," she started, slipping slightly into profiler mode which I would normally find sexy, but in that moment, with her magnifying glass focused on me, I only found it unsettling.

"No hitting."

"But it wasn't just psychological, right?"

"For the most part, yes. But there was some EST in my teens when I was becoming 'defiant'. Really, I was just able to see how fucked up it was that I wasn't allowed to have a TV, video games, music, or toys."

"You weren't allowed to have toys?"

"They figured I would learn to entertain myself better if I had to find ways to amuse myself. I had a lot of pet potato bugs," I said with a head shake.

"So... nothing? Not even simple wooden toys?"

"Do matchsticks count? I used to build fucking cities out of those things."

"Did you have friends?"

"We lived out in the boonies and most of the kids were put off by how I would analyze everything they did or tell them how I knew they had hotdogs for lunch because of the grease stain on their pants and the mustard on their cheek. As if the red hair wasn't bad enough, I was a freak."

"Were you always prone to the... ah... flipswitch thing? When you go dark and obsessive?"

"My father was a flip-switcher when he couldn't figure something out. It was night and day when things were going well versus when things were being more complicated than he felt they should be. Because, you know, humans aren't rational and predictable like he liked them. He was a bear for a week once when some agoraphobic patient of his wouldn't respond to exposure therapy. That was the week he decided to cure me of my fear of bears."

"By?" she asked, tone guarded, likely knowing she wasn't going to like what was to follow.

"By chaining me to a tree like a fucking dog all night," I recalled, remembering how sick I had been. Literally sick with fear. I vomited over and over until there was nothing left to throw up. Then, terrified the meat I had from dinner, even regurgitated, might be appealing to the bears, I had dug a hole in the half-frozen ground with my bare hands and buried the sick.

"How old were you?"

"Seven? I think. Hard to tell. Somewhere around then. Fucking crazy thing was- it wasn't some irrational fear. We *had* bears. I could wake up most mornings to see one out back. But he was in a mood about the patient he couldn't fix so he figured he'd fix me."

"Did he?"

"Do I seem fixed, baby?" I asked. "I mean, I wasn't mauled to death that night and it wasn't as big a concern after that. But I became obsessed with phobias and motivators after that. It wasn't good enough if some kid told me he was afraid of the dark. I needed to know what he thought was in the dark to be afraid of and then I needed to know where he got the idea of what was in the dark. Eventually, somewhere in my teens, I became a lot more like him. When I couldn't figure something out, be it school work or some study I was doing on someone without them knowing, I would shut down and get either cold or cruel, I would become obsessed with stabbing my fingers in the wounds to see if they squealed."

"Why does Duke's past bother you so much?"

"Duke's past doesn't bother me, aside from being disgusted that skinheads still exist. It interests me that he has so much guilt about it when it was beyond his control. I wanted to see what kind of power his family still had over him. I wanted to know if his motivator was obligation."

132

"Was it?"

"It was shame," I said, shaking my head. "He's so fucking convinced that he's covered in scum because of them that it is hard for him to accept that he deserves more than to be covered in shit the rest of his life."

"What is your motivator?" she pressed.

"Good question," I said, shrugging. "Fuck if I know. I'm too all over the place to figure mine out."

"Why did you run away?" she asked.

"*Raising Renny*," I supplied.

"I'm sorry?"

"*Raising Renny*," I repeated. "When I was seventeen, they brought me down to their office in the basement where they had stacks of paper laid across the table. Seventeen of them."

She nodded them, understanding. "One for each year of your life."

"Exactly. Had they maybe not been batshit fucking crazy, it wouldn't have been so unsettling. But they chronicled everything. How many times I wet the bed and what that said about my mental capacities. What my nightmares were. When, how often, and speculations on *why* I started getting hard-ons around eleven. The embarrassing and fumbling stories of my first crush. I sat there and read it from first to last page, finding they somehow knew about how I lost my virginity and what it said about me that I chose the girl I chose to do that with. I flipped shit."

"Understandably," she said, turning her head slightly to plant a kiss on my shoulder.

"I crashed the computer and I burned the pages. I told them exactly how fucked up I thought they were."

"What did they do?"

"They sat there and wrote down fucking notes. And seeing that, seeing that no matter what I did or said, it would never elicit any kind of genuine reaction out of them, that there would be no changing them, I left."

"You couldn't have had much..."

"I didn't have shit. Not even a change of clothes. I grabbed their car keys and hit the road. Didn't stop driving until I hit here."

"And?"

"And I kicked around town for a few years. I drank, I fucked, I got into a shitload of fucking fights. I was young and mad at the world and couldn't turn off my foot-in-mouth tendencies. It never even occurred to me to not tell a girl that her boyfriend was clearly cheating on her. Or tell some random guy that his repressed homosexual drive was making him a bully."

"You never did learn, huh?" she teased.

"Nah. I just found people who didn't mind it so much. And people who found it useful. Reign likes me tagging along and telling him why the Russians are refusing to do business all a sudden or what is motivating the Mexicans to demand the guns for half the price."

"Or tell him why the new probates should or shouldn't be in the MC."

"Exactly."

"Have you ever tried to talk to someone about it?"

"I'm talking to you."

"I meant a professional."

"You know as much as any shrink. Analyze me, Doc."

She considered me a for a long moment, those fucking amazing eyes of hers a little sad. "Fear of failure and need of approval."

"What?" I asked.

RENNY

"Your motivators. You have a fear of failure and a need of approval. Like it or not, that's why you do what you do. If you didn't do this, if you didn't read people and poke and prod at them, what would you have to feel pride about? What do you bring to the table?"

"You mean aside from my devilish good looks and world-class pussy-eating abilities?" I asked, trying to lighten the mood, uncomfortable that she was maybe uncovering something I didn't want to know about myself.

She laughed at that, looking away for a second. "Yes, aside from that."

She was right.

I didn't have much to bring to the table outside of my small subset of skills. I was a decent shot. I was cool under pressure, as I should have been having grown up in a pressure cooker. But I wasn't a practical sniper like Repo. I didn't have Reign's experience. I didn't have brute force like Wolf or training like Duke.

"See, I think you dig and you poke at sore spots because you can, in a way, bring the rat home to your owner and get a pat on the head. And you are afraid that, if you stop bringing home the rats, even if your owner is getting kind of sick of cleaning up the bodies, that you will in some way have failed." She paused there for a second. "The thing is, you belong here now, Renny. You don't have to work at this so hard."

"Easier said than done, lamb chop. It comes and goes as it comes and goes."

"Have you ever maybe just... tried though?"

"Tried what? Tried not being myself?"

"I'm not saying to not be yourself. I'm not even saying to stop analyzing people because, in some ways, it can be a good skill. But try to stop from going so dark and cold.

You're not a victim of your impulses, Renny. You're supposed to be the master of them."

She wasn't wrong.

I usually just went with it, got obsessed with it, when there was something I wanted to figure out or a reaction I wanted to try to bring about. I had convinced myself it was for the greater good of the MC to dig up everyone's skeletons, to dust them off, to dangle them in front of their faces and see how they spooked.

And, in some situations, like vetting the prospects, it was useful. I would even go ahead and defend the first incident with Duke. Was it shitty? Sure. But did I get to see that his loyalty was squarely set where it belonged? Yes.

But it didn't need to be a continuing cycle. If you kept jabbing your finger into a healing bruise, it would never go away.

I was, in some situations, causing more harm than good.

That being said, it was so ingrained, it was such a part of my life from such a young age, I wasn't entirely sure it would be something I could always control. If the impulse was small, just a curiosity that could go rogue and become an obsession, yeah, I probably could hold off and think clearly about it. But if it was one of the situations when I went zero to one-hundred in a blink... I didn't think I possessed enough restraint to handle that.

But she was right; I could fucking *try*.

That shit in the kitchen earlier, that could have been avoided. It was jealousy gone rogue.

I had been working my long game on Mina for months, tried every goddamn thing I could think of to try to get her to take a chance on me. But she had pushed me away at every opportunity.

Then in walked Lazarus.

And, see, I was secure enough to call the man what he was- he was fucking good looking. He was the bastard most heroes are written to look like- tall, dark, handsome, and just dangerous *enough.*

He didn't even need to flirt with her and she was standing in that kitchen, working side-by-side with him when she had always done everything she could to keep space between us, and she told him shit. It wasn't epic, life-changing shit, but it was pieces to the puzzle. She told him about how much she hated Dutch food, much to her father's never-ending amazement. She told him that of all the places she saw as a kid, there was nothing like Russia. She liked the architecture. She thought it looked like it was out of a storybook. She told him a silly story about the one time Lo made her pitch in making dinner at Hailstorm once and she managed to screw up minute rice.

I lashed out at Laz because it was easier.

Then I accused her of not doing her job because I knew it would get a rise out of her. I hadn't expected, though, that she would call me on my bullshit, that she wouldn't rise to the bait and defend herself, but attack me instead. And the craziest fucking thing happened while she ranted and raved- the switch flipped off all on its own.

And I felt bad about it having been on in the first place. That was new for me.

A 'breakthrough' as my parents would have called it.

I was curious to see if it was something that could happen regularly with anyone, or if it only worked because it was her, because she just intrinsically got it, because she wasn't the type to take offense to it or back down from putting me in my place.

I wasn't going to get my hopes up too high. After twenty-someodd years, I didn't see myself changing much. But anything was possible I guess.

I could, as she suggested, *try.*

"Hey Renny," she said, voice sweet, sweeter than I was used to hearing it, sweet as it sounded when my fingers were inside her and she was whimpering and crying out.

"Yeah, sweetheart?" I asked, looking back at her to find her lips slightly parted, her eyes a little heavy-lidded.

"I think maybe I know enough to trust you now," she declared, voice still smaller than usual.

"Yeah?" I asked, knowing what that meant. It didn't just mean she was going to stop keeping me at a distance. It didn't only mean, either, that she was going to give me a chance to prove myself.

It meant she was finally going to stop fighting the attraction between us.

She wanted to take things to the next level.

"Mmhmm," she murmured, pushing forward so I rolled onto my back and she rolled onto my chest. Her arms planted beside my chest and she pushed up slightly to look down at me. "So about these world-class pussy eating skills..."

I smiled then, bigger than I had in a long fucking time.

"Oh, babycakes, you're in for a treat."

RENNY

ELEVEN

Janie

I was a mess.

Really, that was the kindest way to put it.

I mean my eyes actually *hurt.* Every time I blinked, it felt like sandpaper scraping across my eyeballs. This was thanks to the crying I had been completely unable to stop the past several weeks.

I hated crying.

But when the person you trusted most in the world, the person who knew all your dark and twisted and ugly, the person who taught you that you could be loved because of them, was laid up in a hospital bed for an extended time, showing no signs of getting better, well, you fucking cried.

RENNY

They told me to be patient. The doctors, that is. Yes, plural. I wasn't about to trust some two-bit emergency room doctor with Wolf's wellbeing. So I took his advice and that of the cranial specialist and the neurologist and the dean of medicine. And, then when I still wasn't sure, I had Lo find me the leading specialist in head trauma and had him flown down to Navesink Bank to give me his opinion as well.

They all pretty much said the same thing.

The bullets did damage, sure, but they got them out and he was healing. The real problem was the force with which his head whacked off the ground.

I had tried to be light about it at first; I even made a joke about how hard-headed he was. Because, quite frankly, in my head, there was no way he wasn't waking right up. There was no way he was going to be laid up in bed for weeks, wasting away.

But that was exactly what happened.

The brain swelled, they told me. You had to give it time to go back down. Then and only then would we know if he could wake up. They told me to not get my hopes up for the first few weeks, that it was rare for someone to wake up that soon. Give it three months, the specialist told me. If he showed no signs of consciousness, he would come back then for a follow-up.

It was a waiting game.

And, well, anyone who had ever met me knew that I was not, in any shape or form or stretch of the definition... a patient person. And being a person of action, I was having a really hard time sitting on my hands and doing nothing.

Well, not nothing. I bossed the nurses and doctors around. I gave Wolf his sponge baths because no one fucking else was going to do that. After the first few days of shock and devastation passed, I tracked down our son and I made it a point to spend time with him, even though a huge part of me was still wanting nothing more than to spend every single second beside or on that bed with him.

Malcolm needed me.

He was a good, strong, adaptable kid and he had all of The Henchmen and their women and their kids for company, but he needed his parents and being down one, he needed me more than ever. Whether he'd admit that or not. Malc had, in many ways, taken after both of us. He was often quiet, a silent observer, a thinker, like his father. But just as often, he was loud and opinionated and a bit headstrong like me. He looked like Wolf too- broad, stocky, rugged, even at his age. He would be bigger than me by his first year in middle school.

So every afternoon, I would leave Wolf for an hour or two and would meet up with Malcolm and, usually, Lo at a playground or restaurant or movie. Whatever he wanted to do that day. He never asked about Wolf, because even though he seemed too young to know, he knew, he understood.

And maybe a part of him wanted to protect me from having to explain.

Again, so much like his father it was almost painful at times.

But all the rest of the time, when I was usually on my laptop or on a mission or training, I was holed up in a sterile hospital room listening to the beeps on Wolf's machines and getting more hopeless by the day.

"A coffee and three energy drinks," Alex's voice said, making me jerk out of my thoughts, turning away from where I had been staring out the window at the river.

"Hey, what are you doing here?" I asked, not bothering to force a smile like I did for Summer or Maze or Lo when they visited. Or even the men for that matter. Alex knew better. Alex knew me best.

"I was actually supposed to be here yesterday but Breaker got all growly on me and I, ah, well... we got distracted and lost track of time. Anyway, here," she said, handing me the coffee and putting the bag of energy drinks down on the windowsill.

"Supposed to be?" I prompted, flipping the tab on my coffee and taking a long drink, making a small moaning sound. "Where the hell is this from? It's amazing." I had been drinking so much hospital coffee that it was almost starting to taste alright to me.

"It's from some new place in town called *She's Bean Around*. When Wolf is back on his feet, we are so bringing the girls club there from now on. The girls who own it are fucking hysterical. Anyway, yeah. So... I was called in on this whole Henchmen thing. Lo brought me up to Hailstorm to work with Mina and L on this new lead."

Right then, right that very second, I got the first surge of emotion that wasn't frustration or bone-deep sadness.

Because that was all it took.

I *knew*.

I fucking knew they were all in on a plan to keep me out of the loop.

Poor little heartbroken Janie, we can't tell her what is really going on.

"Those mother fuckers," I hissed, every muscle in my body going tense.

"Reign's idea, from what I understand."

"But Lo and everyone else just went along with it," I bit out, my jaw so tight that it was hurting. "What is the lead?"

"This is some kind of long-planned, premeditated attack from the Abruzzo family."

I felt my stomach drop then, falling onto the edge of Wolf's bed near his feet.

"The Abruzzo family? The *Abruzzo* family? As in Marco and Long Island and pimping out prostitutes?"

"As in Little Ricky, ironically named, getting too big for his britches, that's also a bad pun..."

"The guy is fat is what you're saying," I said, feeling a small smile tease my lips.

"No. No. He's not fat. He, ah, well he might break whatever scale they use to weigh blue whales. He's a planet to himself. Anyway, yeah, he took over and he for whatever reason set his sights on the arms trade here. I guess he thought The Henchmen were an easy target."

To be perfectly honest, that wasn't an unfair conclusion. The Henchmen, before they did all the renovations I had only heard about, were a little lax security-wise. The gates were manned, but hardly ever closed. Anyone could prospect. Anyone with tits or a familiar face could get into the club on a party night. They had people watch the grounds, but the grounds themselves were too easily penetrated. As proven the night someone took Summer.

And, well, they were a relatively small operation. Granted, they certainly had more numbers than, say, The Mallick family or even the Grassis, but there was no going after the mob and while there was money to be made in loan sharking and Charlie and his sons lived good lives, it wasn't quick or easy money.

If they could come in, kill off the competition, then just move right in and take over, yeah, it would be a big payout in a short period of time.

RENNY

The Henchmen, for all their street-like roughness and almost cheap look to their clubhouse, had bank. They had a fucking boatload of money. So much so that Reign didn't even blink when Lo gave him the totals for expensive, rare shit like DARPA glass.

There was a lot of money to be made in guns. Small militias and criminal organizations all over the world needed guns. And it wasn't as easy as one might think to get connections that could supply that many guns. But Reign had them. And half the eastern United States syndicates used weapons bought directly from The Henchmen MC.

"You haven't been watching TV, have you?" Alex asked, jerking her head toward the small thing hanging in the corner from the ceiling.

I waved my hand to the pile of books on the windowsill. There was an endless supply always coming in from the people at Hailstorm who knew that was how I generally preferred to spend my time. It was useful too, because I hadn't been sleeping.

Apparently, even though he was still alive and I could crawl into the bed with him, him not being able to wake up meant that I started getting the nightmares again. Worse, more often, and much more vivid. It got to the point where nurses would come running from the screaming I had started to do again and I just got a mix of frustrated with my memories and embarrassed by the open display of them that I stopped sleeping.

Alex came in on my third full day of no sleep.

"No, why?" I asked, brows drawing together.

"The Henchmen had a visitor a few nights ago from this guy named Lazarus who said he saw people breaking into the gym..."

144

"The gym?" I exploded, jumping up onto my feet. "*My* gym!"

"Yeah. But by the time Reign and the others got there, someone must have tipped off the cops because they already had two of Little Ricky's guys in custody. Lo had some guys go in once the cops were done and they found bugs and..."

"And?" I prompted, impatient.

"And a very badly made bomb," Alex supplied, tone cautious.

"How badly made?"

"Like a teenager finding plans online bad."

I felt myself snort at that, finding it equal parts insulting and amusing. You don't hire amateurs to build bombs. And you don't plant bullshit baby bombs at a place partially owned by a bomb expert.

What the actual fuck?

"Janie," Alex said, lips tipped up slightly, "tell me I didn't just fuck up by telling you."

"Fuck up?" I asked, smiling humorlessly. "No. You did the smart thing. I can finally... help out now. No disrespect to L, but he's clueless dark web-wise. And I know you know what you're doing, Al, but you don't have the kind of time I currently do," I said as I went over to my messenger bag in the corner and dragged out my laptop and a charging cord. "I will find these fuckers."

"Alright, doll, I gave you ten. We gotta go get Junior from Paine's before he breaks anymore of Elsie's expensive shit," Breaker said, stepping into the doorway, all tall, blond-bearded handsomeness. "Hey, Jstorm, how you holding up?" he asked, giving me a sympathetic smile with sad eyes.

RENNY

I was getting really sick of that look. And that whining-type voice people used when they asked how I was.

So long as I wasn't rocking in a corner, I was fucking fine. Even if I was a mess. Even if I was raging. Even if I was crying. Even if I was yelling at Wolf to wake up.

Even then... I was fucking fine.

I wasn't a goddamn China doll.

"I'm holding up," I said, giving him a small smile, already half-distracted with all the work I needed to do. "Malc is really excited for the sleepover this weekend. Thanks again for having him."

"He keeps Junior from driving us up a wall," he said as his wife walked over toward him. "We're happy to have him."

"We'll drop in again in a day or two," Alex said, giving me a smile. "Text me if you want me to drop anything off for you."

"Will do. And thanks, Al. For being the only one who didn't think I was too weak to handle the truth."

"You? Weak? Never," she said, jerking her chin at me and walking out.

I dropped down on the window seat, put my laptop on my lap, the coffee and the energy drinks at my side, and got down to work.

Really, it didn't take as long as one would think. But maybe that was only because I was personally invested, determined, hyped up on way too much caffeine, and with a desperate need to put an end to the chaos.

Because while personally, for me, it was all about Wolf. He wasn't the only victim. In fact, he was the luckiest so far. He was the only one who had been targeted who was still alive. There was over a dozen dead.

146

RENNY

And they weren't going to stop, not when the strongest members were still alive and willing to fight it out to protect them and theirs.

It needed to end.

By early the next morning, I had been able to track them via traffic cams.

"Where you going?" Digger asked from the doorway, him being Wolf's guard for the day. He also knew me well enough to know I was too wound up to just be running for coffee.

"Malc has a school slip I forgot to sign," I lied, internally cringing at using my own kid as a cover, but it was for the greater good.

He was the son of a Henchmen.

He would never be safe until the situation was settled.

So mama had some business to handle.

I left the hospital, hopping in Digger's car, and driving to the outskirts of town, up the obnoxious hill toward mine and Wolf's cabin, expanded from where it used to be a small one-room structure. It currently had two bedrooms, since we had no plans on more children, and a goddamn ever-loving laundry room. *In* the house, not in that freaking shed a mile away. That shed was a clubhouse for the kids when they came to play.

I parked, climbed out, and grabbed a pair of gloves out of the house that almost felt unfamiliar it had been so long since I had been there, then went back outside and started walking.

Wolf was maybe the only person who knew the exact location of where I went when I needed to do some building. And he only knew because he helped me build it—ten feet under ground with reinforced walls, a hidden door, and several booby traps to keep anyone from stumbling upon it.

Because I wasn't the kind of woman to build dollhouses or model ships.

No.

I built bombs.

And when there were times that I couldn't work at the place Hailstorm had set up for me, like back when I blew Lex's place to kingdom come and didn't want anyone to know I was in on it. And like right then.

Because if Hailstorm knew I was there, they would know why, and then the calvary would come to stop me.

And fuck that.

I wasn't poor little heartbroken Janie. I was mother fucking Jstorm and someone was coming after half of the people I held near and dear and that shit would never fly.

I was not going to be *that* girl. I wasn't going to break. I wasn't going to sit around and woe-is-me and wring my hands and bemoan how unfair the world was.

I was going to right the wrongs.

I was going to make them pay for thinking we were weak, that we would lie down and take the fucking, that we weren't going to fight back.

Because, for all the fanfare, for all the carefully plotted attacks, Little Ricky's organization wasn't as bulletproof as he thought it was. At least not to me, not to someone hellbent on finding them.

Little Ricky himself, who was every bit as gigantic as Alex had said, was still in Long Island. Because just like he was power and money hungry, he was a coward. He sent others to do his dirty work.

I would leave him be.

RENNY

First, because a vindictive part of me wanted him to suffer, wanted him to know what it felt like to lose his organization, to worry for his own life, for a while.

Second, because The Henchmen would never forgive me for stealing the chance for them to get their vengeance.

I was just thinning the herd, culling the sheep.

They would get to land the final, devastating blow.

I opened the door, the joints whining from disuse, and made my way down, flicking on the battery-powered lights, and closing the door.

I wasn't a fan of small, dark, underground spaces, but when it came to things as dangerous as the ingredients in a good bomb, it was safety-wise to be as far underground as possible, to prevent any collateral damage if something went wrong.

But nothing was going to go wrong.

I could build a bomb in my sleep I had been tinkering at it for so long.

They always underestimate in shows and movies how long it takes to make a bomb. They sit a guy at a table, have him throw some pipes together and sprinkle some powder inside them and they're done.

Truth be told, it was a long, tedious, painstaking process that you needed to get absolutely perfect or you had a bomb that didn't detonate or only detonated partially. You only got one chance to create the impact you wanted so you needed to do it right.

So while I was impatient and I wanted to get things handled, I took a deep breath, I compiled all the working parts from the stopwatch to the ammonium nitrate, I sat down at the table, and I slowly set to work.

Hours later, I sat back, rolling the tension out of my neck and shoulders. It was probably the longest I had gone without sick to my stomach worry about Wolf since the bullets ripped into his body.

Even remembering it, even just having the quick flash move across my mind, I had to get up and move, I had to try to take slow, deep breaths.

Nothing had ever compared to that moment.

I had lived through a lot, a sickening, disgusting lot in my time with Lex, but Wolf had been the one to finally show me a good side of life again. He had helped me sleep. He had brought me back to life. And to stand beside him, a smile still on my face because he was home finally, and hear the bullets break out, to feel him push me behind his solid form, to watch as he went down, as the blood bloomed from the holes in his body, as he slowly slipped unconscious...

I had felt gutted.

I had felt like someone had reached into my chest and ripped my heart out of my ribcage.

I had felt like my world had crashed down around me.

I had felt truly and utterly devastated.

I didn't even understand the meaning of that word until that moment.

I just... lost it.

And I didn't stop losing it for a long time.

Hell, I was pretty sure I was still a little lost.

But at least I wasn't useless anymore. Wolf wasn't the kind of man who would have wanted me at his bedside, tending to him like a baby. He would have much preferred I was getting shit done, getting justice, protecting his people. What was left of them.

I didn't even want to think about having to tell him what had happened since he was shot- how many men he would have to mourn while he recovered.

But if I could at least help eliminate the threat, I hoped it would mean he would take it easy and give his body time to heal. If he woke up while things were still crazy and up in the air, I could see him ripping out his IVs and trying to take off on a one-man mission to put an end to it all, likely making himself worse in the process.

I carefully boxed it up and made my way back to the car, keeping the gloves on even as I drove one town over where the idiots had luckily rented a very secluded three bedroom home on a cul-de-sac. Technically, there were two neighbors, but they were bank-owned and vacant. They didn't want to be seen. And, luckily for me, that meant I wouldn't be either when I parked on the street behind and cut through the woods, the night falling giving me perfect cover with my dark hoodie as I made my way across the backyard and toward the Bilco doors and greased the joints before pulling them open and slipping unseen inside.

It wasn't the kind of basement you wanted to be in. Me, I never really liked being in any basements, but this one was dirt-floored and spider-infested with old, forgotten rusted hoes and rakes leaning on the walls beside festering buckets of lord-knew what. Well, one smelled strongly of gasoline so, hey, that worked in my favor. Who the hell left buckets of gasoline laying about? That was just asking for an explosion.

A floor above me, I could hear the scrape of a chair, the thump of footsteps, and the muffled, low register of male voices talking.

My heart was a frantic, sickening thing, lodged up near my throat as I set the bomb down in the most central location then went back to drag the bucket of gasoline over as well, carefully pouring it on the floor as I set the timer

151

then as quickly as I could while being silent as possible, I made my way back out, closed the doors, and booked it.

The timer was set for thirty minutes and I wanted to be back at the hospital like nothing happened by then. It was a believable alibi. The staff knew I pretty much never left and certainly never for extended periods of time. They would see me walking back up onto the floor with a vending machine coffee and assume they just happened to miss me walking past a couple minutes before.

On that note, I got my coffee that I desperately needed. Adrenaline drained, I was feeling the lack of sleep. Four days strong. I was going to need to crash, nightmares be damned. My body would only take so much.

I slipped Digger's keys into his pocket and went to move past him. But he snagged my arm. "What'd you do?"

"You'll know in about ten minutes. Tell Lo that I don't appreciate being left out of the loop."

With that, I pulled away, closed the door, and took my first deep breath in over an hour.

I kicked out of my shoes, took a long pull of my coffee, then put it down and climbed into bed with Wolf.

I really wasn't supposed to. There were rules.

But those rules flew out the window when they saw exactly the kind of fit I was capable of.

No one even mentioned it anymore.

Wolf was colder unconscious than he usually was. In bed at any other time, he was like a furnace; I barely ever needed a blanket. But in that hospital bed, he was almost cool to the touch, something I found unnerving no matter how many nights I curled up with him and felt it. So I kicked up the covers and pulled them up to my shoulders as I nestled my face into his neck, breathing in a smell that wasn't his own because it was all hospital soap and sanitizer and plastic and wrong.

But it was still Wolf.

He was still mine.

Even if he didn't feel and smell like himself.

Even if he didn't even know I was there.

I felt the tears well up at that and the hopeless feeling it brought with it, but fought them off until exhaustion finally took a hold of me.

--

"You smell like bombs."

I had been teeter-tottering between sleep and awake for what had to have been twenty minutes, my body knowing it needed more sleep, but my brain saying it was better not to risk a nightmare by allowing that.

But at those words, at those four, beautiful words coming from a rough, horse voice that was so, so incredibly familiar, I jolted fully awake, shooting upward, not realizing that by doing so, I had slammed my hand into Wolf's stomach until he let out a grunt.

Another sound that was genuinely music to my ears.

As soon as I looked down and I saw those amazing, beautiful honey eyes on me, well, I lost it again.

I thought I had sobbed hard when they first brought him in and, well, pretty much every single night that followed, but none of that even came close. Apparently relieved crying was even more uncontrollable than sad crying.

"Shh," he said as I planted my face into his chest to muffle the noise.

But I couldn't. I couldn't stop and I couldn't be quiet and I didn't even try until I felt the last of the tears slip out,

153

until I felt bone dry inside. Then and only then did I wipe my eyes, press up, and look at him again.

"How long?" he asked, hand moving almost comically slow off the bed to touch the side of my face. He must have been weak. He had been wasting away little by little every day.

I swallowed hard, knowing there was no way to sugarcoat the truth. "About nine weeks."

"Nine?" he growled, trying to push up, but I scooted back and placed my hands on his shoulder, pressing him back.

"You still have stitches," I warned him. "No moving until the doctor looks you over."

"Fuck the doctor," he hissed. "Details, Janie."

"Can you at least get..."

"Details," he ground out and, well, I didn't blame him. I would have felt the same way after waking up and realizing that much time was gone.

"Alright, um. We got you here. You went into surgery. Reign and all the guys came back from their pointless trips. Then, ah..."

"Janie..." his voice had warning and I looked up into his eyes and saw the need to know there.

"Reign, Cash, Repo, Duke, and Renny are okay. The rest..." I trailed off, shaking my head.

"Fuck. Mother *fuckers*. Who?"

I exhaled hard. "They just figured it out a couple days ago thanks to a mix of Penny and the Grassis. It's the Abruzzo family. No," I hissed, pushing him back down again. "I smell like bombs, remember?" I said, voice low in case there was any chance of someone overhearing. "Reign and Lo conspired to keep me out of the loop because, apparently, I'm so damn fragile."

154

"Lost weight," he observed, pinching my upper arm.

"So did you," I countered. "Hell of a diet, multiple gunshot wounds and major head trauma."

"Missed me," he said, reaching up to touch the swollen mess that my eyes must have been.

"Of course I fucking missed you, you idiot," I said, smiling. "I haven't been able to sleep right in nine weeks. You don't smell like you and you're cold and," I swallowed as another sob rose up in my throat. So much for thinking I was done. "And I didn't know if you were going to wake back up."

"I'm up," he said, shrugging one of his massive shoulders.

I felt myself smile at that- big, goofy. Because he wouldn't say something sappy like 'I would never leave you' or 'I'll always come back to you'. Because he was a realist. He couldn't make those promises.

"Malcolm is going to be so happy to see you," I smiled. "He's been holding up and being all stalwart, but I know he's been worried. He's been staying at the compound. No, wait," I said when he went to shoot up again. "It's okay. They were at Hailstorm for a long time while they redid the compound. New fences and security and walls and this really nifty DARPA glass room. It's practically impenetrable now. He's as safe as can be. Reign would never bring the kids back if he didn't believe that. You know that."

"He okay?"

"He's... Reign," I offered, knowing he understood. Reign was a lot of things, but above all- he was a man of his people. It didn't matter what went down, he held it together for all of them.

"Hey, Janie, we just want to check... oh!" the nurse started, stopping halfway across the room.

"He woke up," I supplied stupidly, unable to stop the big grin splitting my face.

"I can see that," she said, giving me just as big a smile back. I think the staff, after a while, started to lose hope. Not that I blamed them. It seemed hopeless. And they felt bad for me because I couldn't resign myself to the seemingly inevitable.

She was happy for me.

"Let me just go call for the doctor and tell him the good news. He is going to want to look you over."

She left with that and I turned back to Wolf. "Don't worry. I've been doing most of the... looking over. None of those nurses were going to get to wash you up."

"Washed me up, huh?" he asked, eyes getting a little heated.

"Oh, no you don't," I laughed, shaking my head at him. "You don't want the doctor coming in here to you with a hard-on, do you?"

"Fuck the doctor," was his very typical response and I laughed. God, it felt so good to laugh again. And not the kind of laugh I gave to friends who told a joke or Malc when he tried to lighten the mood- a laugh followed by a bone-deep guilt for feeling even the tiniest bit happy when Wolf's fate was unknown. It was a full, guilt-free laugh. "Didn't know I was gone," he said, his hand sliding to the back of my neck, pulling me forward. "Missed you anyway."

And with that, he pulled me close and sealed his lips to mine.

I wanted to be soft and gentle and keep him from getting too worked up. But the second I felt him beneath me, lips claiming mine again, there was no restraint. I kissed him with every second of uncertainty, every shed tear, every knot my stomach had been twisted in, every bit of fear and defeat and frustration and what was at the root of all those feelings- the seemingly bottomless pool of love I had for him.

"Alright, alright," a voice said from behind us, making me jump, but Wolf held me for a second more, giving me soft for a bit before pulling back. And when he did, my lips felt swollen, sensitive. I pressed them together and turned to see the doctor standing there, smile understanding, eyes as kind as I remembered them. "So, look who finally put his wife out of her misery," he said, coming closer as I slowly climbed off the bed, feeling my heart fly up in my chest when Wolf reached for my hand, held onto it, and gave it a reassuring squeeze. "That is quite the woman you have there. Thought half the staff was going to quit that first week," he added, looking at Wolf's monitors. "Do you have any pain anywhere?"

A minute or two later, still in the middle of a barrage of questions, the door flew open and there was Lo. "Jstorm, I swear on all that is holy, if I didn't love you so much I would... oh my God," she stopped, her jaw going slack, her eyes going wide.

"'Sup, Lo?"

Her mouth opened and closed twice before she shook her head as if to clear it. "'Sup Lo?" she repeated scoffing. "Got ten hours?" she asked.

"Take her," Wolf said, squeezing my hand again before releasing me. "Go on. Got enough sleep," he added when I stubbornly planted my feet.

To that, I gave him a small smile and followed Lo out of the room.

"Why didn't you call me?"

"He just woke up. Like... just. I didn't even get that far," I added as she reached for her phone to, no doubt, call Cash.

"Wolf is up," she said, then clicked the call off. "Bathroom," she said to me, leading me down the hall until we found the public one. We went in and she looked around before taking up guard just inside the door. "What the fuck, Janie?"

"I was upset, Lo," I snapped. "I wasn't broken. I wasn't weak. I wasn't too fucking fragile to be able to handle what was going on. I had nothing to do up here but sit and worry and wonder who might be next, who I would be mourning over, why we couldn't get a drop on anyone. And meanwhile, you've known for *days* who it was and that they were in town and you did nothing?"

"We didn't do nothing. We had everyone we could on it."

"You had everyone but *me* on it!" I snapped. "I love the people at Hailstorm and I love Alex but you and I both know that none of them hold a fucking candle to me, Lo. And you just got lucky that nothing else bad happened between you finding out and me handling it. How could you and Reign put everyone at risk like that? My *son* is in that compound."

"Janie, I know you think you were handling it, but you weren't handling it. You were a shell. You weren't eating or sleeping and you were always crying. We didn't think you had what it would take to power through and get answers."

"That wasn't your decision to make. And it wasn't Reign's either. This was not okay. And I am pissed at you for this. But right now, I'd rather go ahead and be happy that my husband is awake after two and a half months and

158

RENNY

that my son has his father again and that most of the bastards who did this to him and to me and to the rest of The Henchmen are in pieces right fucking now."

"I have to say," she said, calm, almost eerily calm despite the crazy situation and the fact that I was mad at her, something that hadn't happened in our friendship in many years, "for someone with no sleep and tear-swollen eyes... that was some fucking epic work, my little Jstorm."

"Was there collateral damage?" I asked.

"It was perfectly controlled. Eight bodies. It was a good hit to their organization."

"So what now?"

"Well, now... most of the men are on their way to Long Island right now. Renny stayed behind to watch the probates and the women and kids."

"Wait... probates?" I asked, stiffening.

It seemed so soon, but I guessed, it was necessary.

"Long story," Lo said, smiling. "And wait till you hear about Renny and Mina..."

"*Renny and Mina?*" I asked, face scrunched up. "No fucking way."

But her very distinctive, romance-obsessed smile was all that I needed to know to realize that yes, yes fucking way.

Apparently there was a new power couple in Navesink Bank.

RENNY

TWELVE

Mina

His story didn't shock me.

That was probably the worst part about the whole ordeal. It spoke a lot to the darkness I had seen in my line of work that genuine psychological and emotional abuse toward a child by their parents who were even professionals in the field didn't phase me anymore.

It didn't mean I wasn't horrified by it. I was. It was despicable. It was absolutely unforgivable that someone would use their child like a lab rat. It was even more troubling to know that they were highly trained and must have known that detachment parenting and using negative reinforcement and withholding affection were possibly the *worst* methods they could have used for rearing a child.

160

But, then again, they themselves sounded genuinely cold. Maybe they didn't think anything of it. Which was just sad.

Really, it was amazing Renny was as warm as he was the vast majority of the time. I guess a lot of that was thanks to him getting out as early as he did. Seventeen with the world at his feet; he must have gone buck wild. He must have indulged in women and booze and lawlessness. And, eventually, he made real connections. He learned how to interact appropriately. For the most part.

I understood why he was the way he was.

Though, like I told him earlier, it didn't make it okay and he should try to not go so dark, but it was better to know there wasn't true maliciousness there. He was just raised that way and he hadn't been able to break the pattern.

I knew a thing or two about that myself.

And maybe that was the tipping point for me- maybe seeing a bit of my own shortcomings and insecurities within his, in knowing that there were very few people who could ever understand me the way Renny was capable of.

Whatever it was, by the time he stopped speaking, the decision had already been made somewhere deep inside.

It was going to happen with us.

I understood that, by making that choice, I was signing myself up for the good along with the bad. And Renny's bad could be very bad. But if he tried to control it at least a bit, if he didn't go dark over something as silly as me talking to Laz about our pasts, if he could make an effort to not deliberately use my flaws against me, I was okay with taking that chance.

Because, quite frankly, Renny when he was good, was *really* good. He was sweet and flirty and funny and silly and all the things I wasn't. I found myself almost insanely drawn to those parts of him- the warm he was capable of.

Apparently, he was also sexy as all hell to boot.

Always a plus.

So when the decision was made and I let my guard down most of the way, what I felt was connection and a desire so strong you would swear it was a need.

I didn't fight it.

I was done fighting.

"Oh, baby cakes," he said with a smile that threatened to split his face- open, boyish, contagious, "you're in for a real treat."

My sex tightened in response, already knowing he was going to make good on his promise.

He curled upward, coming chest to chest with me, his hands sliding down my sides until he snagged the tee and slowly slid it up over my skin, so slowly that my skin had a chance to goosebump in response before it finally fell from my wrists and was discarded to the end of the bed.

"Know how many nights I sat up thinking about these," he asked, his hands moving up my belly, touching the sensitive undersides of my breasts, then completely covering them with his palms. "Didn't even do justice to the reality," he went on, his fingers sliding to the sides and stroking his thumbs over the hardened buds.

My hips moved against his, feeling his hardness press against my heat and letting out a hard breath.

"Remind me to send Ashley flowers," he murmured, hands pressing into my sides slightly to anchor me as he bent me backward. "Have a feeling you normally wear goddamn flannel pajamas," he added but took away the insult by sealing his warm mouth over my nipple and sucking hard.

RENNY

Besides, I couldn't even be mad, I totally did sleep in flannel pajamas.

His lips released me and his teeth snagged me instead, biting in just hard enough to make me let out a low moan before moving across my chest to continue the torment.

Then he was bending me further back until my shoulders hit the mattress, until I unhooked my legs and planted my feet and settled back. His face shifted to the middle of my chest, his tongue moving out and tracing a slow line down the center of my belly, not pausing, not stopping to lavish over anywhere.

Because he had a destination in mind and a point to prove.

His lips sucked my clit inward, making my hips buck upward at the shot of desire. My hand slammed down on the crown of his head, holding him to me as his tongue moved out and started lavishing over the sensitive point.

His hands slid up and under my thighs, grabbing my ass, and hauling me slightly up, giving him more access as he sucked, licked, then thrust his tongue inside me until my thighs were shaking, until my breath was a strangled nothing in my chest, until I felt my walls tightening hard and his tongue moved out and his lips closed around my clit and sucked in quick pulses until I completely shattered apart.

My entire body went taut as my fingers practically ripped out his hair and his name came almost screaming from my lips.

My weight crashed back down on the bed after, my skin feeling like it was humming, my breathing frantic and shallow, as Renny kissed back up my belly, stopping between my breasts where he rested his chin to smile up at me.

"How'd I do? Legendary?"

I did something right then that I didn't think I was truly capable of until that moment. I freaking giggled. Giggled, like a teenaged girl. Even *as* a teenaged girl, I was pretty sure I never did such a thing.

"I'll take that as a yes," he said, planting his hands near my shoulders and moving over me. "I was right too."

"Right?" I asked, brows drawing together.

"Yep," he agreed, but didn't elaborate.

"What were you right about?"

"Sweet fucking pussy," he said, smirk going devilish. "Think I'll have to have a little bit of that for breakfast every goddamn morning."

My cheeks heated at that, both turned on by but slightly embarrassed by his openness.

But before I could let myself really analyze those feelings, as I was bound to do, his hips ground into mine, making his hard cock slip up my slit and make a delicious pass over my oversensitive clit.

"Yeah, we're nowhere near done," he said, smile full of promise before his lips crashed down on mine again- harder, hungrier, reminding me that while a bit of my need was sated, his was raging strong through his system.

He rolled, pulling me with him until I was on top again, his hands running down my back and grabbing my ass.

His lips pulled from mine as his fingers whispered up my spine then over my shoulders. His fingers of one hand moved inward on my arm, just above my elbow and rubbed his fingers over the small matchstick under my skin.

"Got my papers for you when you're ready to take that step," he informed me, once again almost scaring me with his ability to see things everyone else missed.

164

And as much as I didn't want to throw ice water on what was one of the hottest moments in my life, I went ahead and said it because I was told once that if you didn't have communication with a partner, you had nothing. "I don't have sex without condoms."

His head tilted to the side at that, light eyes penetrating and it took a lot of willpower to not squirm or fumble to find an explanation. "I showed you mine," he said oddly a moment later. "Eventually, you're going to have to show me yours."

"My what?"

"Scars, sweetheart," he explained, folding up toward me, arms crossing over my lower back, holding me tight where I might have pulled away. "Why you're so terrified of intimacy and all the mess it brings with it." I must have stiffened, because he squeezed me tighter. "But that's for another time. Right now, you need to see more of my glorious body," he said unexpectedly, making me let out a surprised laugh as he flipped me onto my back, straddling my hips, and making a ridiculous, adorably cocky show of sliding his hands down his chest and stomach before snagging the waistband of his pajama pants and slowly dragging them down. "This is the part where you'd be throwing money at me normally," he informed me just before the waistband got low enough for me to finally see him bare to me- his cock hard and straining and promising to fill me perfectly.

At that thought, there even seemed to be a genuine hollowness deep inside, begging for fulfillment.

My eyes slid slowly back up, catching the outlines of some of his tattoos before they found his face, his smile gone, his eyes heated. My fingers slid up his thigh and his lips parted as my palm curled around his cock and stroked him to the base. His air hissed out of him, urging me on, and I stroked upward again, sliding my thumb over the head and moving his wetness around.

He took a slow, deep breath, seeking control as he reached outward toward the nightstand and pulled open the top drawer. He took out the condom and ripped it open with his teeth. His hand covered mine for a second, squeezing tighter, doing one last stroke with me before pushing my hand away and protecting us.

I reached up, pulling him down toward me, my back arching into his chest as it brushed mine. But I barely felt the pressure before his head cocked to the side and he declared oddly, "Nope."

"Nope?" I asked, slow-blinking twice.

"Yup, nope," he declared, lifting up and pulling me with him until we were both sitting, me straddling him. "Missionary is for love making. You and me, we're fucking tonight," he declared as his hand went to his cock and the other went to my hip, digging in hard and pulling downward, his cock gliding deep inside me. I dropped my hips, taking him in fully on a throaty moan. "Fuck me, Mina," he demanded, moving backward, his hands settling halfway up my thighs.

And, well, with the desire a sharp, painful need deep inside, there was hardly even a pause before I started riding him- fast, but not overly rough. I half folded over him, planting my hands near his shoulders as one of his hands slid between us and pressed into my clit- just a firm pressure, but with my riding him, there was a perfect friction.

And when my orgasm started building, making my movements more frantic and erratic, I lost his fingers as both his hands grabbed my arms right above the elbows and yanked them backward hard and fast, making my shoulders object, as he pinned them behind my back, planted his feet on the bed, and started thrusting upward into me- hard, rough, making me take him as deep as my body would allow at a pace that was so demanding that my breath got strangled in my throat for a long minute before the orgasm tore through me almost violently.

He didn't come with me though.

I was still whimpering through the pulsations when he suddenly threw me onto my back and jumped off to the side of the bed, grabbing my ankles and dragging me until I was hanging off the end, then slamming back inside me as his arms hooked under my knees, holding them in the air as he pistoned into me with the same borderline brutal pace that had shattered me a mere moment before.

His light eyes were on my face the entire time, his jaw tighter than usual, his lips parted slightly and there was the occasional hiss from between, a sound I found entirely too sexy.

"No," he said when I felt my walls start to get tight again. Soon, way too soon. I wasn't the kind of woman who had orgasms that tripped into one another. I knew they existed, but was pretty sure they were about as common as men with eight-inch long cocks that were so thick that you couldn't close your hand around.

But my body in that moment was trying to tell me that maybe, just maybe, the absence of it in the past possibly had less to do with me and more to do with my partners.

But Renny, while capable of making it happen, wasn't going to allow it.

Because right after he felt me tighten, he pulled out of me, dropped my legs, reached down to grab my hips, and rolled me onto my belly, then slammed in deep from behind and made me let out a loud moan that was, thankfully, muffled slightly by the sheets.

But that, apparently, was not what Renny wanted. He wanted to hear me.

Because his hands reached out and grabbed my wrists, yanked backward until I was standing, hanging forward, my arms pinned back by his sides as he kept slamming into me. I bit into my lip, trying to keep the moans inside, but as his thrusts got harder, I was helpless to keep them in.

"One more time," he ground out and I could hear the need for his own release heavy in his voice. "There," he said, slamming into me even harder as my walls tightened around him, as the orgasm started to crest. "Come," he demanded and then I did, crying out his name loudly enough to wake whoever might be in the rooms on either side of ours.

My legs went wobbly and I would have collapsed forward had he not been holding my arms.

He slammed deep on a growl, jerking his hips upward. One of his hands released my wrist and moved around my belly, pulling me upward until my back pressed into his front. His forehead hit my shoulder as he struggled to even out his breathing.

"Fuck," he said a minute later, nipping my shoulder before he slowly slid out of me.

Body spent and without him holding me up, I turned and collapsed down onto the edge of the bed, taking slow breaths as he disappeared into the bathroom for a long minute.

I wasn't aware he had come back up until he was kneeling in front of me, his hand landing on my knee. The other moved up to my chin, snagging it and using it to pull my head up.

"Don't you fucking dare be putting those guards back up," he demanded, eyes almost a little sad at the idea.

I felt my lips tease up slightly, shaking my head. "I can't think clearly enough to do that," I admitted.

He let out a low chuckle. "Halle-fucking-lujah," he said, slowly standing and sliding behind me onto the bed. "Come on," he demanded as I slowly turned and went to reach for the tee I had been wearing. He folded up quickly, yanking it out of my hand, and tossing it hard enough for it to land halfway across the bathroom floor. "You won't need that."

I let out a half-laugh, suddenly feeling the urge to wrap my arm across my breasts, but fighting it. "I get cold at night," I tried, shaking my head at him.

"Ninety-eight point six degrees over here," he said, cocking one arm behind his neck, the other hand patting his chest. "I'll keep you warm and toasty and if that isn't quite enough, I can think of other ways to warm you up."

I scooted up the bed and over the covers and moved toward him, shaking my head. "I think I'm good for a week. Or month," I said, letting out a yawn as I settled on his chest.

"Hate to break it to you, but now that the lid is off the honey pot, I got a taste for the goods. You might want to start power napping because I plan to fuck you silly at least twice a day from here until eternity."

There was an undercurrent of seriousness to that that I felt thrill through my body, but I let out a small, quiet laugh as his arms slid around me. His lips pressed into the top of my head as he gave me a squeeze.

"Sounds good," I admitted, smiling a little at the idea.

"Rest up," he warned and my eyes slowly drifted closed, body beat, and mind, for once, not racing around and making it impossible to sleep.

But I was startled awake all of an hour later, completely unsure what had caused my heart to slam into my throat as I shot up off Renny who shot up into a seated position.

"The fuck was that?"

"What was what?" I asked, hand over my heart that was slamming so hard it was starting to worry me.

"Loud bang, honey," he said, scooting away from me and grabbing his pajama pants off the floor then moving across the room to grab a tee out of his dresser. "Get dressed," he said as he went into another drawer and pulled out a gun.

I shot off the bed, more alert than I had ever been over the course of maybe ten seconds as I dragged the shirt onto my body and grabbed the leggings I had discarded earlier, yanking them up my legs as I went to my bag and found my own gun.

When I turned back, Renny was pulling the door open, looking out into the hall and I could hear Lo's voice. "It's not here," she said, making my belly stop doing the twisting it had been. I put my gun on the bed and followed Renny into the hall as everyone seemed to be convening in the common room.

Lo's phone rang as Repo flicked on the TV. Everyone was in various stages of dress- all the men in pajama pants and nothing else. Lo had on one of Cash's shirts and a pair of panties. Penny was in short shorts and a shirt that had obviously been hastily thrown on because it was backward and inside out. Summer and Maze were, I imagined, quieting whatever kids might have been woken from the sound.

"Shit," Repo said as the news station reported an explosion. There wasn't anything for a long couple of minutes other than that report as the news, I imagined, scrambled to get someone on the scene. But the reporter in the studio held a finger to her ear as she claimed the police reported it was a controlled explosion in a residential neighborhood.

"What, Mina?" Renny asked and I hadn't even noticed he had been staring at me.

My gaze slid to his as it finally clicked, what Alex had said at Hailstorm, about how we all had agreed to keep Janie out of the loop.

She, however, obviously had her own ideas on the matter.

Because, though I had not the smallest bit of proof, I knew, I just *knew* who was behind the explosion.

"I guess Janie found out about the Abruzzos," I told him and heard the conversation around us fall off at my declaration.

"No fucking way," Reign said, shaking his head. "We all agreed."

"Well, someone must not have," Lo said, waving her phone. "Digger said Jstorm disappeared earlier under the guise of Malcolm needing her for something and just came back about fifteen minutes ago and told him to tell me that she didn't appreciate being left out of the loop."

"Shit," Reign said, shaking his head. "Anyone got a cup? Something to protect my balls? Bet she plans to fucking roast them on a hibachi."

It was a weird, tense moment, but almost in unison, we all felt smiles pull at our lips, knowing it was the damn truth.

Lo's phone started screaming again and she lifted it up to her ear. "Yeah? What did she... okay... yeah," she said, looking at Cash and then Reign. "Address? Got it."

"Who was that?" Cash asked.

"L. He said he got an email from Janie. It had Little Ricky's name and an address."

Reign visibly tensed, prepared. It was the moment they had all been waiting for for months, but now that it was here, it was clear the weight of the meaning was pressing on them all- most especially Reign and Repo who had pregnant women to think of. But it didn't change anything. At the end of the day, they had a business and life to protect.

They had to do what they had to do.

"Me, Repo, Cash," he said, rattling off who he knew he could never keep at the compound even if he commanded it.

"I have personal stake here," Duke reminded him, meaning the God-awful beating Penny had gone through.

Reign looked around, torn, not wanting to leave the women and kids. "I'll take care of them," Renny said, voice firm. "And Mina is here and Lo. We can have half of Hailstorm here in half an hour too. Besides," he reasoned, "They won't even know who the so-called victims are for hours or even days. There's no way Ricky will even know what happened. And even if he did, there's no way he could get guys here faster than you can get there and take care of him once and for all. Don't worry about here. Worry about making those fuckers pay for what they did to us."

I had never really gotten to see Renny the hot kind of angry. When he was lost in his head, it was a cold, detached sort of rage. This was not that. This was what it was like to see him enraged over the loss of his men, to be wild with the thirst for retribution, for blood. Even if he couldn't have it on his own hands.

He didn't want to stay behind any more than the others did. But there was no way Reign would leave the

172

compound without at least one of the men there. And he also knew that Duke had a grudge to settle and, perhaps, a better skill set for the job as well.

I looked over at Lo, seeing something in her eyes that was all but foreign to her- worry. She had been running Hailstorm for a long time. She sent people off onto dangerous missions all the time, knowing damn well there was always a chance that someone might not come back.

But this was different.

She was watching Cash go on such a mission.

And as hard as Lo could be at times, everyone knew that Cash was her sun and moon and universe. He was her happily ever after, her alpha hero from all the romances she had been devouring for ages.

Even the chance of losing him was scaring the hell out of her.

As if sensing that, Cash moved forward, snagging her arms and backing her up against the wall, dipping his head down toward her ear and whispering something.

Reign and Repo shared a knowing look, the two being the only ones with pregnant women and young kids to worry about, then they moved almost in unison down into the hallway to give their wives the news.

Penny slid down from her perch on the arm of the couch and onto Duke's lap, tucking her head under his chin as his arms wrapped her up tight.

It was a heady mix of emotions in the room- the strong, vibrating adrenaline, the thirst for revenge, and the almost oppressive weight of sadness and worry.

My gaze slid to Renny to find him already looking at me, his eyes knowing, like he knew exactly what I was feeling.

There was a strong, almost overpowering urge to go to him, to feel his arms slide around me. He wasn't leaving and we were new, but I could only imagine how Summer, Lo, Maze, and Penny felt. And my heart hurt for them.

But just when the urge was almost too overpowering to fight anymore, there was a loud slamming sound from the back of the building.

Renny's lips quirked up. "Puppies got spooked," he said, sounding amused. "Guess we gotta go let them out so they don't pee the floor."

With that, he moved to go to do just that.

Feeling like I was intruding on private moments going on in the common room, I followed him, stepping inside the room as he did.

"What's going on?" Reeve asked.

"What's with the gun?" Cyrus said almost at the same time.

"What do you need from us?" was what came from Lazarus, making my gaze slide to him, finding him a little more tense than usual, his hands curled into fists at his side- ready, prepared. It must have been how he looked right before a fight.

"There was an explosion across town. We're fine here. No threats. Go back to bed."

"Renny," I said, raising a brow at him. From what I understood, probates were the low men on the totem pole and subject to crazy or demeaning jobs, but they were still members of the club for all intents and purposes. They were supposed to be in the loop.

He looked at me, likely reading all that on my face and sighing.

"Fine," he said, shaking his head at me. "Apparently my woman here thinks you need to be in the loop."

My woman.

I felt my belly go a little liquid at that.

Granted, I was *supposed* to be his woman in front of the probates, to keep up appearances and keep them from realizing we were vetting them, but it was more than that now. I was, in a way, his.

Normally, I would recoil from that.

Fear of intimacy was my thing after all.

But somehow, it almost felt right to be claimed. Back in that bed, he had claimed my body. And whether I fought it or not, prolonging the process, I knew it was only a matter of time before he claimed other parts of me- most notably, my heart.

"We'd appreciate that," Reeve said carefully, his eyes unreadable and I realized again how much we needed to look deeper into him.

"We figured out who the threat is and Reign, Cash, Repo, and Duke are heading to deal with it once and for all. Me, Mina, Lo, the women, kids, and a huge army of men and women from Hailstorm will be by to keep an eye on things around here. That means that Laz will be on kitchen duty and all of you better put your thinking caps on and come up with ideas on how to keep the kids occupied and the women calm. It's going to be a long couple of days. Get dressed and come out."

With that, he reached his free hand down to take mine and pull me with him out of the room and down the hall to our room.

He slammed the door, put his gun down, and turned to me, his hand going behind my neck. "You alright?"

I felt my brows draw together. "I think that's my line in this situation. None of my people are going off to exact vengeance and leaving the whole safety of the club on my shoulders."

"Who are you kidding," he asked, smiling a little humorlessly. "I might be the last standing Henchmen here, but as soon as Lo is done yelling at Janie about going off without her, she's going to be back here and barking orders. She's more of a leader than I am. I'm just here to keep an eye on the probies and be a familiar face for the kids."

"I think you underestimate yourself," I said, not liking that he somehow thought he was less than the rest of them. From my understanding, he had taken out a threat the night that Shredder and Vin were killed, saving Duke's life. That was no small thing.

His head cocked to the side, watching me. "Think I like having a woman trying to defend my honor," he said, moving to grab clothes then kissing me on my cheek as he made his way to the bathroom.

I took a deep breath, going into the closet and digging for some clothes, settling on the jeans Ash had packed and slipping into a bra, but throwing Renny's shirt back on over it. He came back out a minute later in jeans, a black tee, and his leather cut, his hair a little damp from where he must have wet it to get it back in order.

I scooted in while he sat down to slip into socks and boots, quickly brushing my teeth and tying my hair up.

When I came back out, he was still sitting off the edge of the bed. He looked up and held an arm out in invitation. I didn't overthink it. In fact, I didn't think about it at all. I just went to him. As soon as I was close, he grabbed my hips and pulled me down until I moved to straddle him.

"You alright?" I asked when he said nothing and I couldn't read anything from his expression.

His smile curved slowly upward, meeting his eyes and making his whole face look devilish. "I didn't get my breakfast."

"What?" I asked, confused. "Laz hasn't even made it yet."

"Not what I meant, sweetheart."

"What did you... oh," I said, feeling my cheeks heat as I remember what he said he wanted to have for breakfast every morning- me. "Well," I said, my own smile moving to match his, "you know they generally recommend three meals a day and two snacks..."

"Meet you for lunch then. Can't say that lunch won't roll into dinner... and maybe dessert," he said, his hand going behind my head and pulling me to him, kissing me long and hard and deep until my lips felt electric.

Then, before I could even fully open my eyes, he was standing, an arm around my lower back. "I'd be happy to walk out there like this sugarlips, but I don't know if you want the new puppies to see you clinging to me," he offered and I finally snapped out of it, realizing he was walking across the room with me wrapped around him, and settling my feet on the ground.

"Right," I agreed, reaching down to make sure my clothes were straightened.

"Hey Mina," he called, stopping half in the hall.

"Yeah?"

"Have I mentioned how fucking worth the wait this was?" he asked, turning and walking away without waiting for a response.

I followed behind him agreeing whole-heartedly.

Except, unlike him, the wait hadn't just been a couple months.

RENNY

I had been waiting to open up for my entire freaking life.

And I had the gut feeling that he was absolutely right; it was so worth the wait.

THIRTEEN

Renny

Lo left shortly after the guys filed out, no doubt going to see what was going on with Janie, how much she was going to suffer for keeping the notoriously mercurial and volatile Janie out of the loop.

Two of the Hailstorm guys were with Summer, Maze, and Penny along with Cyrus in the basement. Cyrus was apparently a big hit once he brought the guitar out and luckily had the laid-back, fun-loving personality to be able to handle children without getting flustered, something that was bound to get him a seal of approval from the women. Fact of the matter was, the kids were a very present part of the group suddenly and that wasn't something that was going to change until the numbers were bolstered and the members trustworthy.

Things would be too up in the air for a while.

Even if Lazarus, Reeve, and Cyrus worked out and became patched, the process was just starting. Three new men would hardly be enough. We needed a dozen new men within two years if we wanted to survive. And knowing Reign, he would continue to be as selective as he had always been. He wanted men with their own particular skill sets, men who would be loyal, and men who would respect the way he ran his club.

"Damn it," Mina hissed, snapping my attention back to where she was standing next to Laz at the stove. Reeve was making a pot of coffee, looking over at her exclamation as well.

"The first two always come out like shit," Laz consoled as she swiped the very pale, very doughy-looking pancakes into the garbage.

I liked Laz for a new addition. He was young enough to be capable but old and experienced enough to bring his particular knowledge to the club. Repo would likely pick him too seeing as Laz would give him a break from doing all the fucking cooking.

The fact that Mina took to him, my initial jealousy aside, was also another thing working for him. She wasn't exactly the type of woman who willingly set herself up for failure. She was too tight, too controlled for that. But she had signed up to cook with Lazarus twice, an act that pretty much guaranteed some screw ups as she learned what she was doing. And had it been just about anyone else teaching her, she probably would have concluded that it wasn't her thing and that she would leave it up to people who knew what they were doing. But because it was Laz and because he seemed as perpetually laid back as a mother fucking sloth but also the ability to encourage you without being condescending, had her reaching for the batter again, dropping a couple dollops down, and trusting in his words.

I wondered right about then how the ever loving hell he worked as a fighter. Even if the fighting was just on occasion, when it was needed. Maybe, if Ross wasn't in a snit about Laz joining our team and fired him, I would show up and see him in action- just to better understand him.

I'd bring Mina along too.

Because, quite frankly, now that I had her, I had no fucking plans on letting her go. Maybe that made me sound like a neanderthal, but the fact of the matter was, when a man who had been so committed to non-commitment found a woman who made him want to lock her down, well, he fucking locked her down.

So we were going to have a date at a goddamn underground fight club because that was about as romantic as a guy from an arms-dealing MC and a girl from a lawless army got.

"Hey Lo, what's up?" Mina asked, bumping Laz's shoulder and pointing to her pancakes. He nodded his head at her as she moved away, stopping short a foot to my side. "What?" she asked, her mouth falling open. "Really?"

Then she looked at me and her face split into the biggest smile I had ever seen her have.

She reached out, grabbing my bicep. "Wolf is awake," she told me and there was really no good way to describe what that kind of relief felt like.

Where Reign was the spine of the club and Cash was the heart, Wolf, yeah, Wolf was the fucking soul.

We had been walking around missing a chunk of ourselves for months, no one willing to admit it, but every one of us terrified we would have to learn to live with that absence in our lives forever.

"Yeah. Thanks. Of course. Tell Janie how happy I am for her," she said, ending the call and pushing it into her back pocket.

And her first instinct right then?

It was to wrap her arms around me and squeeze me tight.

She didn't really even know Wolf, couldn't have shared more than a few words with him ever, so her gesture was entirely for me, not herself.

That, well, it was fucking telling.

She was thawing.

And my theory on her was right. She was every bit as warm as I suspected.

"How is he doing?" I asked, only loosening my arms enough to let her pull back to look up at me.

"Lo said he's pissed and wants out of the bed and doesn't want to hear shit about needing more time to heal, that he has spent 'enough fucking time healing' and that he wants to sign out and come back here."

"Of course he does," I said, smiling at the image.

While Reign, Cash, and Repo were known to drop in and visit, try to console Janie, I hadn't been able to get to the hospital much. The last time I had seen him had been two weeks before and he had lost a lot of weight and, to me, just seemed like he was fading.

I had almost resigned myself to the seeming inevitable.

I was never more happy to be wrong in my life.

"He's not leaving yet, obviously," Mina added. "Janie won't hear of it until the stitches are all out and they are sure the swelling in the brain is better. So he has at least a week or two more there unless he gets stubborn and signs himself out when Janie isn't paying attention. Which, well, sounds like him."

"Yeah it does," I agreed, giving her a squeeze. "Does Janie want to tell Malc herself or one of us to do it?"

"Tell Malc what?" Maze asked, walking in, purple hair tied in a careless knot on top of her head, her belly hinting that she wasn't too far from delivery.

"Wolf woke up," Mina told her, making Maze stop halfway inside the kitchen, frozen in shock for a long second before letting out a sob loud enough to startle both Laz and Reeve who looked over at her like they were terrified she had gone into labor and they might have to assist in delivery.

"Get over here, Violet," I said, tucking Mina to one side and holding the other arm open for her.

And Maze, hardass, badass, ex-probate she was, was a complete emotional mess when she was pregnant. And, given that she and I had prospected together, we had a bond and she didn't even pause before she flew at me, burying her face in my neck, and started crying almost uncontrollably.

When I chanced a look over at Mina, she quickly jerked her head away, but not before I saw the unmistakable glimmer in her eyes.

Oh yeah, big warm, softy alright.

"Lo said to tell him, that he has been as worried as she has and that she doesn't want him to have to wait another minute."

"Think you should do it, sweetheart," I told her, making her jerk back, brows drawing together.

"I think I'm the last person who should tell him."

183

RENNY

"It's gotta be one of you women. He's been raised in an MC. He does the stiff-upper lip thing really well and if I tell him, he's going to hold it all in which isn't good. He's gotta cry it out and..."

"I can..." Maze started to offer, but stopped immediately when I gave her a hard squeeze. "Yeah, you know what," she said, sniffling once and wiping her eyes, "Renny is right. You should tell him."

"I know him the least," she objected. "I work with Janie and I see Malc all the time around Hailstorm, but I haven't really bonded with him."

"Well, nothing like telling him the dad he's been worried is going to die...isn't, to bond you guys. Come on, you got this."

She opened her mouth to object again, but must have picked up on the united front of me and Maze and known that Summer would easily jump on our side and that Penny wouldn't pick a side because she was too new, too unsure of her place still. "Alright," she said, nodding and pulling away from me. "I'll go tell him," she added as she turned and went out of the room.

"Is this some kind of test?" Maze asked once she was gone.

"Test?"

"Yeah, a test. You know... you being an asshole and poking at people. What are you trying to prove here?"

"I'm not..." I started to object, but Maze maybe knew me a little better than that. "She avoids the kids as much as possible," I said with a shrug.

"You know how they say that a maternal instinct is ingrained?" Maze asked. "Well, it's not. Some women have to work at it and some women won't show any signs of it until they have a kid of their own. We don't all want to pick

184

up a crying baby or make funny faces at them for hours.
And many of us don't have a ticking clock or that uterus-
squeeze thing when we see a cute kid. We have shit to do
and a life to live. Until one bursts its way into that life,
sometimes they just aren't something we are drawn to."

"I get that, Violet, but I also think that Mina steers clear
because she doesn't understand kids. And for someone like
her, that is unsettling."

"So what? You're going to force exposure therapy on
her every time you think she needs to get over something?
Hate to tell you this, Renny, but she's going to catch on and
she's going to get pissed about it." She wasn't wrong. It
hadn't even occurred to me that what I was doing was
pushy until she brought it up. That was something I had to
work on obviously. "For a smart, observant guy, you can
be a little dense and clueless. Hone your conversation
skills, Renny. You're going to scare her away if you don't."

And with that sage little bit of advice, she moved away
from me and over toward Laz who she promised to name
her baby after if he gave her the first couple pancakes.

I didn't bother to mention that the baby was a girl and
they already had a name picked out.

I heard Mina walk back down the hall toward our room
a couple minutes later and gave her a few minutes alone
before I called one of the Hailstorm guys in to watch the
probates as I went to see why she was hiding.

I barely got the door closed before she was charging at
me, jamming her finger into my chest hard enough to make
me slam back against the door.

"That was *bullshit,* Renny. I didn't want to make a scene
in front of Maze and the new guys, but don't you ever
fucking try to *test* me like that again. I get it. I'm not all
sunshine and roses and I don't sit for hours and play Barbie

with Ferryn or watch cartoons with Malcolm, Seth, and Fallon. I *get* that I am not Susie freaking Homemaker. But that doesn't mean something is wrong with me and it doesn't mean you get to try to push me into being something I am not."

"Mina, I didn't realize I was testing you until Maze called me on it," I said, shaking my head. "Hand to fucking God. I didn't even think it was fucked up. I'm not saying that it's okay that I didn't see that it was wrong, but I'm asking if maybe you can understand that I didn't know."

Her finger stopped bruising into my chest as she took a deep breath. "I like kids."

"Okay," I said, shrugging. "And if you didn't, okay too."

"I like them," she said again, almost a little desperately. "They just..."

"They scare the shit out of you," I supplied, smiling a little.

Her shoulders dropped at that, exhaling. "Yeah," she said, nodding, looking relieved that she didn't have to say it.

"Because they don't have hidden agendas and they don't have motivators you can pick apart and use to predict their behavior."

"It must be terrifying to be a parent," she said, shaking her head. "You get this thing that you made or you adopted or whatever and it's... blank. It has nothing but basic human urges and only the two innate fears of falling and loud noises. That's it. That's all they are. You *turn them into* who they become. Every word you say, every word you *don't* say, every look you give and every touch you offer them and everything you do as a person... it shapes them. That is... that is so crazy that anyone takes that on. I mean you are genuinely to blame if they come out to be little psychopathic narcissists or well-rounded individuals. And no one really has all the answers to tell you how to mold them right. You can screw it up so easily. Don't smile at me like I'm being silly," she said, crossing her arms over her chest and small-eyeing me.

"It's not silly. Actually, it's a fucking shame that people don't consider those things."

"Then why are you smiling like that?" she asked, still wary.

"Because, I gotta be honest here, pumpkin, you're the cutest fucking thing when you're having a near panic attack over something that isn't even a factor in your life."

"Well," she said, clearly thrown off, "you brought it up."

"And you gave me a little piece of yourself without me having to pry it out of you," I said, pushing off the door and moving toward her.

"What are you doing?" she asked, brows drawing together, backing up as I advanced.

"Know what's a good meal?" I asked as she hit the bed and couldn't retreat any farther. "Brunch. And I am fucking *famished*."

"Renny," she tried to object, "we are supposed to be watching the..."

"Lo's guys are keeping an eye and making sure the puppies don't chew the furniture."

"Well, we should really be..."

The rest of her sentence got cut off when I reached down and pressed my hand between her thighs, making her breath whoosh out of her.

"What should we really be doing?" I asked, smirking slightly as my finger pressed against her clit and her head tilted back slightly.

RENNY

"I, ah," she started, shaking her head. "I don't remember."

"Well then, it can't be all that important, right?" I asked, my hand sliding up to undo her button and zip then shoving my hand down them and inside her panties, stroking up her already slick slit and finding the small, swollen bud of her clit and moving over it in circles.

"Right," she agreed, her hands going to my arms and digging in hard.

"And you wouldn't keep a man from a meal over some unimportant shit, would you?" I asked as my middle finger slid down her pussy and pressed inside as my thumb kept working her clit. Her entire body jolted and she let out a low whimper that I swear I felt in my cock.

She opened her mouth twice and closed it again before she finally got the words out. "No, I wouldn't do that."

"Didn't think so," I agreed, pulling my finger out of her then before she could even object, reached up and dragged the jeans and panties down her legs. Then, before she even pulled another breath in, my hands pressed into her shoulders and sent her flying backward onto the mattress, landing with a bounce as I grabbed her jeans and panties and ripped them free of her feet and lowered myself down by the edge of the bed.

My fingers slid up the soft skin of her calves, moved inward at her knees, and pressed her legs wide against the mattress, giving me a perfect view of her sweet, wet pussy.

I wasn't one of the guys who ate pussy because they wanted a girl to suck dick. It wasn't an obligation or a exchange. It wasn't a thing I did to get something else I wanted more.

No.

188

RENNY

I was one of those guys who just genuinely liked eating pussy.

Especially when said pussy tasted sweeter than any fucking fruit I had ever had in my life. Mina, yeah, she tasted like a fucking treat. And I wanted to feast on her, to gorge myself and, in the process, feel her writhe beneath me, whimper, moan, and scream, have her fingers pull my hair or scratch bloody marks across my back.

So I kissed my way up her inner thigh and sucked her sweet little clit into my mouth, sucking it in pulses until her breathing went erratic, until her hips started rising and begging for fulfillment, until she couldn't hold back the sounds anymore and started moaning helplessly, knowing every drop of her pleasure was at my goddamn mercy.

If a man had his priorities straight, that was the only kind a power he needed to get drunk off of.

As such, when her thighs started shaking and her body went taut and her moans went silent because her air got caught in her throat, I licked her faster, with a little more pressure, until she cried out, her palm slamming down on my shoulder, her leg kicking out straight, a rush of her sweet wetness coating my tongue.

Then I licked her some more, just for good measure. Until her body was spent and her fingers started sifting gently through my hair. Then and only then did I lift up and look down at her.

I had to say, I really liked the look of her spread fucking eagle on my bed. I got a distinct, strong feeling that that was exactly where she belonged, whether she realized it yet or not.

She didn't move, but watched me for a long moment as I planted my knees at the edge of the bed. Then, her hands

RENNY

slowly raised, sliding up my thighs toward the fly of my pants.

"Nuh-uh," I said, shaking my head at her, not wanting her to think it was anything other than it was- me wanting to get her off.

But then she smiled- slow, a little wicked. "But I'm hungry too," she said and I swear to fuck I almost came right then and there.

"Well, we can't have that, can we?" I asked as she pushed the button and moved the zip, her body slowly folding up toward me.

Her hands went inside and pulled my pants and boxer briefs down. Her head tilted up to look at me as her hand reached out and held my cock at the base. And eyes still on me, she moved her tongue out and traced it across the head, licking off the pre-cum and sending a bolt of desire through my system, making my cock harder, my balls painfully full.

Her free hand slid up my thigh and rested just under my hipbone as she ducked her head and let me slide in her velvety soft mouth. My hand landed on the crown of her head, slipping into her silky hair- just a pressure, not guiding her.

She didn't need any fucking guidance.

She knew exactly what she was doing.

She had perfect suction, perfect speed, perfect tongue, perfect fucking everything.

But long before I could come down her pretty throat, she slowly released me, putting her arms straight up in the air.

There wasn't even a second of disappointment. I would have her mouth again. But right then, she was offering me her body. There was no fucking way in hell I was going to

190

RENNY

refuse that. I reached down and pulled the shirt up and off, reaching behind her back and unclasping her bra, leaving her gloriously naked before me.

She slowly started backing up on the bed toward the headboard and I kicked out of my pants and followed her up, covering her body with mine as my lips went down to hers.

This time, though, they weren't hard and hungry and desperate.

The kiss was slow, deep, sweet.

She whimpered as my tongue moved forward to claim hers, her legs going up and folding across my lower back, pulling me fully down on her. My cock pressed against her cleft and she ground up against me, her wetness coating my dick and making me need to take a slow breath and fight the urge to slam inside her.

It felt like hours and could have gone on for hours still before my lips pulled from hers and drifted down the column of her neck, between her breasts, toying gently over her hardened nipples with my tongue.

I was starting a path lower again when her hands grabbed me and pulled me upward over her again. When my eyes found hers, I found something there I never expected to see- utter openness. Her hands slipped around my back and held me as her hips started thrusting gently against me, sharing her hot wetness with me and I had to grit my teeth and bury my face in her neck to keep control as she took what she needed from me.

But I pushed back up when her hand slid between us and I felt her hand close around my cock and move it downward until the head pressed against her tight opening.

191

"Mina, it's okay," I said, shaking my head, knowing she was the one who insisted condoms were an absolute hard-limit for her.

She tensed beneath me. "You said you were clea..."

"I am," I agreed, leaning down to kiss her lips softly. "I have the papers to prove it, but you didn't want..."

"I changed my mind," she said, her hand releasing my cock and her legs putting pressure on my lower back until I could do nothing but slowly slip inside her hot, wet, tight pussy.

"Fuck," I groaned when I was buried deep, pressing my forehead to hers, taking a minute to hold myself together.

I had maybe fucked without a condom twice in my life and it was back when I was too young and stupid to consider consequences. Since then, condoms were always a thing and twice-yearly checkups were done regardless of that. In my humble opinion, sex was only fun if the sex was consequence-free.

I knew Lo ran a tight ship and everyone was subject to in-depth physicals several times a year. That and Mina's reluctance to not use condoms for her own reasons were all the proof I really needed that she was clean. And with her implant, we were about as safe as we could get.

That being said, it had been so fucking long since I felt a woman wrapped around me- raw and hot and wet and tight, that I had all but forgotten how fucking good it felt.

Control, I fucking needed to find some.

"Renny, please," she whimpered, her hips thrusting up against mine, trying to get relief from her need.

I lifted up, looking down at her as I slowly slid out almost completely then pressed back in- slow, sweet, unhurried. We had all the fucking time in the world. And there was nowhere else I'd rather be than buried inside her.

RENNY

So I kept that pace as she writhed under me, as her hands clawed into my back, as her moans became almost pained whimpers and her walls got impossibly tight around me.

"Faster, *please*," she begged, desperate for release.

But she was just going to have to wait. Because she was giving something to me right then, something I knew meant a lot from her, something I knew she could refuse to give me again at any time- her vulnerability. So I was fucking milking it for all it was worth, even if my own need for release was begging me to start slamming into her hard and deep.

"Shh," I whispered when she begged again, her walls so tight that it was hard to move at all and I knew she was going to come. "Right there baby, let go..."

Her body was shaking slightly with the intensity of feelings coursing through her and just as the first spasming started around my cock, a single tear slid out the side of one of her perfect hazel eyes. I leaned forward, kissing it away as she cried out, holding me so tight it was hard to take a breath as the pulsations kept coming in a seemingly endless wave for a long minute.

Then and only then, on the tail-end of her orgasm, I pressed deep and came with her name on my lips, taking perhaps way too much pleasure in the idea of my cum inside her, in knowing it was a privilege she never afforded another man before.

Afterward, her body started trembling with aftershocks, overwhelmed. I rolled to my side, pulling her with me, tucking her head under my chin, my fingers trailing down her back, through her hair, as they rolled through her, lessening slowly over time.

She took a slow, deep breath when her body finally settled down, pulling slightly against my hold so she could look at me, her eyes a little heavy-lidded still, but knowing.

I knew it too.

Things had just changed.

Things had just gotten a fuck of a lot more serious.

Then her lips parted and when she spoke, her voice was a little small, a little shy. "You're still inside me."

"Mhmm," I said, tucking her hair behind her ear.

"I like that," she admitted, and I knew how much that meant. It didn't scare her like she expected it to- to take away the last literal boundary between us. She didn't regret it. She *liked* it.

"I like it too," I agreed, giving her a small smile. "And you can have that literally anytime you want from here on out. Bed, shower, car, in the glass fucking room on the roof- whatever gets your gears turning," I smirked, running my fingers down her arm.

"We should be getting back," she said, sounding unhappy at the prospect which made me feel fucking good about myself in turn.

"Yeah," I agreed though, because it was true. We might have been building something between us, but we still had lives and a job to do. So as much as I wanted to take to bed with her for a goddamn month, I recognized that that was not a possibility. "Alright," I said, slowly pulling out of her. "You get cleaned up. I will save you some pancakes."

She sat up, smiling. "You're going to eat without me?" she objected, snagging her shirt when I tossed it to her.

I pulled up my pants and zipped them. "If you hustle, I won't have to," I told her, pulling on my shirt as she jumped up and scurried to the bathroom, legs pressed tightly together and I couldn't help but smile at that as I sat to put my shoes back on.

By the time I was laced back up, she was walking out, dressed. But no amount of primping was going to take that post-fuck glow off her face.

And I wouldn't want it any other fucking way.

FOURTEEN

Mina

Two days.

We had gotten two full, amazing days.

After we left the bed where I had done something I hadn't known I was capable of. I had given him something. And, judging by the way he looked at me while he accepted it, he knew just how huge that was. That meant something. Maybe for most women, it was no big deal to take off the condom when you knew both parties were safe and pregnancy wasn't an issue. But for me, it was a huge deal.

He simply got that.

Like he seemed to just get a lot about me.

The day afterward was a fury of activities. We ate. Lo came back, beaming ear-to-ear, picking up Malcolm and bringing him to see his father. From there, the kids were going stir crazy and Summer and Maze were clearly reaching their limit.

So me, Renny, and all the probates took turns trying to occupy them. Me and Cyrus occupied them for short bursts with video games.

Laz managed to get a *very* interested Ferryn involved in cooking lunch because unlike her mother and father, Lazarus let her work with the stove.

And Reeve, well, the damnedest thing happened.

Having had shown absolutely no interest in the kids before, or any of us really, we hadn't expected him to really pitch in on the 'give the mommies a break' plan. But he had disappeared for a minute then he had walked over to Fallon who was clearly lost with his age-mate Malcolm gone and feeling Reign's absence pretty hard, sat down beside him, pulled out a children's book, and started *reading to him.*

I elbowed Renny hard at the sight, making him make a grumbling sound before I jerked my chin over toward the pair and his gaze followed. He turned back to me, brows low, and I shook my head. I had no idea what it was about either. Or where he had gotten the book.

Granted, it wasn't *exactly* age appropriate.

It was Gary Paulsen's *"Hatchet"* that I myself had read when I was closer to the protagonist's age, at ten. It was the story of a boy who survives a plane crash in the wild and is alone and needs to learn to survive. Some of the subject matter was a bit out there for a six-year old. But, then again, I imagined Reeve figured that a kid growing up in an MC compound surrounded by arms dealers and their

197

lawless counterparts, he could handle a little literary violence.

And, judging by the way Fallon moved closer and seemed completely apt, it had been the right choice.

"I hope he knows what he's getting into," I mused aloud, but mostly to myself. "Fallon is going to be on his case to finish that book every day now."

Cyrus looked over at his brother for a second, face much more guarded than I had seen it so far, then back at me and declared, "Reeve is good with kids. He wouldn't start the story if he didn't plan on finishing it."

Again, my gaze went to Renny and, again, neither of us had a clue.

Reeve, the anomaly.

Reeve, the loose end that needed some serious tying up.

But not right then.

There would be time for that later.

That night, Laz was called in to fight. Renny told me that he wanted to take me but that it would have to wait until the next one because we couldn't leave the compound. And, as excited as I was about the prospect of going out somewhere with him, I was equally happy to be locked in with him. So Laz was walked out and Cyrus and Reeve were locked into their room.

And we went to bed.

He gave me hot and fast and sweaty, but only after he had "dessert".

The next morning, I got up before him and showered then was, yet again, had for another meal. Really, his appetite for oral sex was genuinely impressive. I was definitely not complaining.

I walked outside with my coffee to find Laz at the gates, waiting to be allowed reentry. He was a little beaten up- his left eye swollen half shut, his lip cut, and cuts broken open on his knuckles. But overall, seemed like he was likely the victor.

"Hey Mina, how'd breakfast go without me?"

I laughed at that. "Penny was in charge of it this morning."

"Aw, come on, honey, you could have handled it. I have faith in you," he told me as I nodded at the guys at the gate to let him in.

"No one wants pancakes two mornings in a row. Besides, Penny is stressing out about Duke. I don't think anyone thought this trip would take as long as it is apparently taking."

We had heard from them. Reign called Renny; Cash called Lo; Repo called Maze; and Duke called Penny. But all the conversations were short and sweet. So we knew that everyone was still alive, but they didn't give anyone much more than that and we all knew that they were likely outnumbered and in danger until they were home.

And being that Penny was the newest girlfriend of The Henchmen MC, if I was not being counted, she was the least used to the aspects of danger, to her man being away from her.

"She kind of needed the distraction," I told him as we walked back to the compound. "She's worried about Duke."

"Lucky man to have a good woman worrying about him."

"Do you have a woman worrying about you?" I asked, surprised that hadn't been something I had asked him before.

"Nah, honey, no woman," he said, and if I wasn't completely mistaken, he didn't sound happy about that fact.

Which was interesting for a probate.

199

Usually they were all gassed up about the idea of clubwhores and sowing their oats.

Laz was a pleasant surprise.

After that, we ate; the kids got occupied; Renny and I hung out with the probates, mostly asking Laz about his fight which he had, indeed won.

A while after that, I found one of the bedroom doors open in the hall, one of the ones that didn't belong to one of the core members, catching my attention. I moved toward it, brows drawn together, to find Renny standing at the foot of the bed, staring at the bathroom, in the middle of a room that was in a suspended form of chaos. Clothes were tossed everywhere. Three beer bottles sat on the nightstand. A pair of boots were on their side in front of the closet. The garbage bin was overflowing with paper and, unfortunately, condom foils.

The room of a fallen brother.

"Renny?" I called, my voice tentative, knowing he had been the one to find all his brothers. And, judging by the hollow look to his eyes as he stared into space, he was running over the memory, likely of a brother dead in the bathroom he couldn't stop looking at. "Hey, Renny?" I called, a little softer as I moved closer, putting my hand on the inside of his elbow, making him jerk hard, almost elbowing me in the face as he turned quickly.

"Fuck, Mina, sorry," he said, shaking his head as I flinched back. I knew he would never purposely hit me, but if he was dealing with some kind of post-traumatic thing, he could do things without really realizing he was doing them, without knowing it was me he was hurting.

"It's okay," I said, moving closer, putting my hand on his stomach. "Are you alright?"

RENNY

He looked over my shoulder, past me, thinking it over for a genuine moment. Then he exhaled hard as his arm slid around my shoulders and his head ducked to look at me. "Not right now, no," he admitted, surprising us both, I think.

I moved even closer, resting my head under his chin and putting my arms around him, letting him squeeze me tight without any objection even though it was borderline painful. "Tell me about him," I prompted.

"Jazz," he supplied, resting the side of his face to the top of my head. "He joined around the time Repo did. He was a fucking slob and he was constantly purposely trying to make the clubwhores jealous of each other by being nice to one one day then another the next day. Just a shit-starter really. But he was loyal. He never bitched about walking the grounds or being left behind when the others went on a drop and he had to stay and watch the clubhouse. Found him in that bathroom," he went on, voice going low so that I had to strain to hear. His hands had started rubbing up and down my back absentmindedly, like I was an anchor for him and he needed to keep touching me to remind himself he was here, in the present, and not back in that God-awful night.

"He must have been getting ready to shower. The place was steamed and the water was running still when I came in. He was facing it too, shot in the back of the head three times. There were pieces of brain matter fucking everywhere," he added and I could feel him swallow hard at that.

I wanted to tell him it was okay. I wanted to offer hollow comforts. But Renny wasn't the type of man to accept them. He knew it wasn't alright, that *he* wasn't alright about it and that he likely wouldn't be for a good,

long time. People didn't just get over things like that. It was
a mark on the soul. It was a source of nightmares for years
to come, no matter how hardened a criminal you were.

So I gave him what I felt. "I'm sorry, Renny," I offered,
tilting my head up slightly, planting a kiss under his jaw.
His arms squeezed me even tighter for a second. "Why are
you in here?" I added a minute of silence later.

From what I understood, since the cleaning had been
conducted, a large part of that done by Renny himself, the
poor soul, the doors had been closed and the rooms had
become somewhat of a memorial to the fallen brothers.

He took a long minute to answer and when he did, his
tone was resigned. "Got three potential new members.
Eventually, they are going to need rooms."

"But they're usually probates for..."

"A year, give or take," he answered for me. "But there's
a lot to fucking do. Figured I would start packing up, get
the clothes and shit to Goodwill at least."

Really, it made more sense to get the rooms taken care
of. If, for no other reason, to have more places for the kids
to hang out. But, on top of that, keeping the rooms like
shrines kept things in suspension. If they wanted closure,
they needed to get things taken care of.

But it was unfair for Renny to take that all on by
himself.

"Want some help?" I asked, pulling back slightly to
look up at him, wanting to gauge his non-verbal reaction.

He looked down, his light eyes seeming suddenly soft.
"Yeah, sweetheart. I'd like that."

So then we boxed up clothes for Goodwill. And, on a
roll, emptied the garbage and the drawers, tossing anything
that wasn't of some personal significance, and putting the
things that were into a separate box that we eventually kept

filling up as we went to the next room where the bed was missing both the boxspring and mattress because the brother who occupied it had been killed in his sleep on them. Then, finally, we finished a third room before calling it quits, deciding three rooms for three new members was plenty. Eventually, they would move in and put their own marks on the rooms, taking away some of the bad memories with their personal stamps.

We stopped there for the night.

We had dinner.

We went to bed.

We woke up.

And everything changed.

Because Renny was in a mood.

Meaning- one his his *moods.*

I walked out of the bathroom, post-shower, and he was in the room, sitting off the side of the bed, all shut down.

The thing was, nothing and happened. There seemed to be no trigger. We had woken up, he had gotten his "breakfast", we had hard sex, we both came, then I went to clean up.

That was it.

And all during the physical activities, he was fully engaged and open.

"Everything alright?" I asked, stopping short as I reached into the closet to pull out my duffle bag and place it on my side of the bed, digging out the galaxy-print leggings, a tank, and the red wine-colored shrug along with some underthings.

"Fine," he said in that creepy dead tone of his. He was watching me as I piled my clothes, his face guarded, eyes cold.

RENNY

I had a strong urge to take my clothes and go into the bathroom. But, at the same time, I knew he was watching me. And he wasn't watching me in the way I often found him doing over the past few months and, especially, since we hooked up. That was the kind of watching where he was trying to catch my smile or trying to imagine me naked. This was a completely different kind of watching. This was invasive and clinical and it seemed to leave my body cold and my skin slimy.

But it felt like a test.

It felt like he wanted me to take my clothes and walk away, like in doing so, I was somehow proving some silent point of his.

So I reached for the tuck in my towel and I pulled it, grabbing the towel and tossing it on the edge of the bed as I reached for my panties. He watched every single move I made, hardly blinking, and I tried my best to not be bothered by it.

I was bothered.

But I didn't want him to know it.

I was hoping that maybe it was just some little bullshit thing that got him in a pissy mood and that if I didn't focus on it too much, it might go away on its own.

I should have known better.

Problems didn't just go away.

Anytime I saw Renny for the rest of the day, he was always further away from me than usual, not smiling, and barely interacting with anyone.

"Come on," he demanded sometime around midday right after I finished straightening up the mess the guys had all left around, trying to remind myself not to be pissed about it seeing as it was a clubhouse and was never known for being immaculate before.

"Come where?" I asked, turning to find him waving keys at me. "We can't leave. You're in charge here," I reminded him.

"Lo said she would hold down the fort."

"Why?" I asked, knowing very little was more important to a Henchmen than loyalty. And he was supposed to be protecting the women and kids.

"Because I have a surprise for you."

I should have been thrilled.

When men spontaneously had a surprise for you, you were supposed to be excited and happy and just about bursting.

But instead, my stomach twisted almost painfully and my heart seemed to freeze in my chest.

"What kind of surprise?" I asked cautiously.

"Get your purse and let's head out," he said instead of answering, making me all the more sure that something was up.

But I went to grab my wallet, slipped into the flats Ash had packed, and followed him into the garage where we loaded into the SUV and headed out onto the main drag.

He pulled to a park just barely two minutes down the road in front of a storefront with a sign that was unfamiliar to me, but the name on it was familiar.

She's Bean Around.

It was the coffeehouse Cyrus worked at.

"Renny, you really shouldn't be..." I started, but he jumped out and walked toward the sidewalk, "in public until we are sure the threat was gone fully," I added to myself as I reached for the door handle and let myself out. "What is this? A date?" I asked as he moved silently toward the door and held it open for me.

205

But he didn't answer, just let me inside and followed behind.

The inside toed the line between intimate and packed with about ten small tables of two lining there walls and a couch seating section in the center around a coffee table. There was a counter along the fourth wall with a giant blackboard with multi-colored chalk outlining the menu.

Two women were behind the counter- a stunning redhead and an equally stunning black woman, both in black pants and a black tee with the store's name across the front.

The music was loud and almost overwhelming, but according to the sign near the register: "Our music keeps us from slapping rude customers. No, we will not turn it down or change the station. K, thanks."

I turned back to Renny only to find him several feet away, standing near a table where two people were crammed in the space where only one was supposed to be sitting, watching me.

And those people?

Yeah, they would be my parents.

Parents I hadn't seen in eight years, mind you. Parents I had purposely walked away from. Parents who were to blame for every bit of coolness I wore like a shield.

And there they were sitting with Renny bouncing on his heels behind them, excited to see his little experiment play out.

The mother *fucker*.

My hands curled into tight fists, my fingernails biting into my palms painfully. I took a breath and forced my feet to move forward, giving them the best imitation of a smile I could muster.

"Mom, Dad, what are you doing in the United States?"

Last I heard, they had been settled in England. I would say happily, but I wasn't entirely convinced either of them had a capacity for happiness. What my father had was his obsession with work. What my mother had was her obsession with my father. Obsession was not a happy thing to base your life around.

"We were on business in New York and we got a call from your young man," my mother started, lifting her chin a little, clearly objecting not only to my choice of a 'young man' but also my outfit, my hometown, and likely the coffee shop we were sitting in.

I didn't look a lot like my mother. She was full Japanese where I was only half. My skin was darker, my hair lighter, my eyes that of my father, and my body more curvy than hers. But my face had the same roundness she had.

And I didn't inherit any of her strong opinions on cuisine, clothing, music, or theater. It was a fact that always annoyed her. Why, she would bemoan, would I want to play with silly little fake animals instead of sit and watch Les Mis in French?

My father was always a bit more laid-back, more workaday, less pretentious. He never cared enough to notice that I even had a Gameboy, let alone lectured me about how much I played it.

"Renny," I said, forcing a smile but it was all ice, "why didn't you tell me you called my parents?"

"It was a surprise, Mina," he offered, watching me closely. And I just knew he was reading way too much into my stiffness, into the fact that I hadn't sat down.

So I sat down. "How have you been?"

"Perhaps you would know that if you called, Minny," my mother chastened.

"I have called." I called every single mother's and father's day just so they couldn't say I never called.

"Twice a year," she scoffed, shaking her head. "After all we have done for you. The best schools, the right contacts..."

The best schools across eight different *countries* over the course of my childhood. And the only contacts I had were the pampered, snooty offspring of the women she befriended in the 'right' circles in each of those countries.

"I'm sorry, Mother," I offered, swallowing past the bitter taste of that apology because I didn't mean it in the least. "I have been traveling a lot for work," I said, looking to my father who would not only understand, but approve, of that. "I will make more of an effort." Say, on Christmas or New Years when I knew they wouldn't be around to pick up the phone anyway.

"How has work been?" my father broke in, interested.

He looked older than I remembered. Eight years would do that to a person, but it was almost startling to see. His hair that had always been a rich medium brown was graying. His eyes that were so much like my own had crows feet around them.

"Work has been good. Constant. I have been all over the place the past year."

"But your headquarters is here, correct?" he asked. "Hailstorm Industries."

I almost corrected him before, at the last second, I remembered that was exactly what I had told him many years before when Lo took me in. The 'industries' I thought made it sound more legitimate. I knew he would never look them up. He wouldn't care enough.

"So how long have you and your *young man* been dating?" my mother broke in, always trying to steer conversation away from work, the only thing my father and I were comfortable discussing.

"Oh, ah..." I started.

"A few months," Renny supplied, moving over toward me, borrowing a chair from the table behind us, and sitting down, his knees touching me.

And, for the first time ever, I wanted to pull away from his touch. Not because I was fighting an attraction like I had been at the beginning, but because I genuinely did not want him touching me right then.

Or ever fucking again.

"Is it serious?" she asked, one brow raising.

It was seriously over at least.

"It has been steady," I improvised.

"You are getting too old to not be serious, Minny," she chastened.

I hated being called Minny. She hated the name Mina because it was my paternal grandmother's name and my mother blamed her for making my father emotionally distant. The joke was on her, though, seeing as my Granny Mina was the only bit of warmth I had ever known my entire childhood.

"She is focusing on her career now, dear," my father cut in. "She has plenty of time to have children if she *chooses.*"

That was less for my benefit and more his way of landing a blow to her. He had never wanted children, had never wanted me. Sure, he had done the right thing and provided for me and occasionally interacted with me, but it was painfully clear that I was a mistake. Or, more accurately, a manipulation.

"Of course she will be having a child," my mother scoffed, doing a completely ridiculous hair toss as she waved down the waitress as she passed to get the bill. "You want children don't you... Reggy?"

"Renny," I corrected, knee-jerk, defensive.

It was right then that Renny's hand landed on my knee, squeezing, reassuring. I knew that if I looked, I would find the coldness gone. I would find my old Renny back. Because he got the answers he wanted. He got to push my button and watch me squirm.

But I didn't want my Renny back.

It was too late.

And he fucked up way too much.

The hand on my knee didn't feel comforting; it felt like a shackle that I desperately needed to pry off before I got stuck forever.

"Let me," I offered, reaching for the bill.

"Don't be silly, Minny," my mother scoffed, passing the bill to my father.

"Yes," Renny broke in then.

"Yes?" my mother prompted.

"Yes, I want to have children. Blank slates," he added and I was a mix of pleased that he remembered I had made that comment and disgusted that he would bring it up in front of my parents, people who had a squishy little blank slate once upon a time and turned it into me.

"That is quite the... clinical way of looking at it," my mother said, reaching to put her purse in front of her on the table. A lifetime of prompts told me that she was signaling the meeting was over.

They drove over an hour to spend less than five minutes with me. Eight years and I got five minutes.

It shouldn't have hurt, not after so many years, not after me knowing to expect nothing else. But it hurt.

210

RENNY

And it hurt double right then because their coldness wasn't the only thing I had to deal with.

I had to deal with Renny too.

Just the thought of it made bile rise up my throat.

"Well, you'll excuse us, darling," my mother said, standing, straightening her dress, "but your father has a meeting back in New York in three and a half hours. Had we known you were nearby ahead of time, perhaps we could have given you more time."

It took about every drop of willpower to not blurt out- why start now?

So I stood and I accepted the cold kiss to the cheek from my mother and the cup to the shoulder from my father, wished them a good trip back, and watched them leave.

"Sit, sweetheart," Renny's voice said, his hand touching my thigh, making me realize I had been watching the closed door for a long minute after they walked out it.

I looked down at him, at his perfect, beautiful face and his amazing, impossibly light blue eyes, his charmingly copper-red hair, and the pain to my stomach almost doubled me over.

"Don't call me sweetheart," I demanded, pulling away from him and tearing through the store and onto the street, making my way on foot back toward the compound where I knew I could find a car and a way back to Hailstorm. Renny caught up to me just a couple storefronts after.

"Mina, let me..."

"You probably shouldn't be on the street right now," I cut him off. "Some people might be upset if someone put a bullet in your heart. Not me, of course," I added, viciously, too hurt, too offended, too shocked to be anything other than cruel, "but some people."

"Mina, I thought..."

211

RENNY

"You thought what?" I snapped as we came up toward the gates of the compound. I turned to face him, finding his face remorseful. But it was too late for that. There were some screw ups that couldn't be wiped away by sad eyes. "You thought that I would somehow allow you to press my buttons and watch me squirm while you jotted down notes about me?" I almost shrieked. "For someone who loathes his parents so much, you sure fit into their shoes perfectly!"

That was a bit of a low blow and I could see the impact it made when he winced.

"You won't talk to me," he said oddly, a long second later.

"I talk to you all the time! When we aren't having sex, we're *talking*."

"You talk about Hailstorm and your friends there. You talk about the places you've seen, the profiles you've done, the foods you hate and the movies you love. You don't tell me anything."

"Has it ever occurred to you, Renny, that we are more than our pasts? Our fucked up childhoods? That that is only a small part of the whole picture? All the other parts- my friends, my travels, my preferences, my job- those things make up a bigger part of who I am than the fact that my parents don't fucking love me!"

That last part was said on a scream that had the guys at the gates stop pretending to not be listening and fully gave us their attention as I slammed my hands into his chest, pushing him back against the gate.

"I think you're fooling yourself if you don't think that them not loving you doesn't have a huge, life-altering impact on your life."

212

"Oh for fuck's sake, Renny. It hasn't stunted me. I love people. I love Lo and Janie and Malcolm and Ashley and..."

"You love people platonically," he cut me off. "You don't love anyone intimately."

I felt myself jerk back from that, from the truth of it.

Because, fact of the matter was, I did love people who, if my love was not reciprocated or if their love was stripped from me, it wouldn't devastate me. It was an easy love.

"Have you ever been in love, Mina?" he asked, knowing damn well he knew the answer to that already. "Or have you been too afraid that no matter what you did, they could never love you back?"

"I have never been with someone long enough to love them," I defended, knowing it was true. It was always easy, casual. Not quite one-night stands, but not quite relationships either. Dalliances. Flings. That was what I allowed men to be to me. If I was able to trivialize their presence in my life, it made it easier to refuse to allow my feelings toward them to be anything other than that- trivial.

"Why? Because you wouldn't let them? Because they got tired of waiting around for you to let them in? To give them pieces of yourself?"

"Because I didn't want them to be a bigger part of my life, Renny. Not every woman needs to have a man all the time. I have gotten along without one just fine for a long time."

"Sure, baby, but why the fuck would you ever settle for 'just fine' when you could have more?"

"Have more... what? This? Arguing?" I shot back. "This is so much fun and so damn fulfilling!" I added dryly.

"It's fucking *real* at least," Renny countered. "It's not carefully chosen words that fit the carefully constructed

213

puzzle you want your life to be, everything neat and tidy and in its place."

"It's ugly," I said, shaking my head. "You see that you did that, right?" I asked, swallowing back a sob that tried to escape me. "You took something that had been nice, it had been good and kind and mutually beneficial, and you made it something else entirely."

"I didn't want fucking *nice* from you, Mina. I didn't want you because of your perfections. I wanted you because I just fucking wanted you, flaws and all. But you wouldn't give them to me. You wouldn't trust me with the things that matter to you."

"You don't under..."

"I don't understand?" he snapped, pushing off the fence and towering over me. "I gave you the whole sordid story of my upbringing. You know shit that I have never told another fucking soul before. You got all my flaws, all my ugly. I trusted you with that. And you wouldn't give me the chance to show you that you could trust me with yours."

"So you... what? You forced me to? You dug up my parents and you dragged them out here and you dangled them in front of me and you made me go in there completely unprepared. I haven't seen them in *eight* years, Renny! Don't you think I maybe had my reasons? Don't you think I, I don't know, maybe would have liked to have brushed my goddamn teeth and straightened my fucking hair before I saw them again and not gone in there in leggings some teenager would wear that my mother was silently judging me for from the second I walked in that door?"

"Mina, calm down," he said, voice low and soothing and it was just about then that I realized all the probates had walked outside at the very loud scene I was suddenly making.

"Don't tell me to calm down. Don't tell me that I am overreacting. How would you like it if I found your parents and dragged them here? If maybe I fished out a copy of *Raising Renny* and got to know everything you never wanted anyone to know and then used those facts to get a rise out of you? How would you like that? You know exactly what you would have done, exactly what I am..."

"Don't," he cut me off, shaking his head. And, had my rage not been blinding me, maybe I would have seen the pain in his eyes. "Don't do this, Mina."

"I didn't do this," I said, blinking hard because I felt the tears stinging in my eyes, completely humiliated that they existed at all. "I didn't do this. You did this. You made me do this."

"We can..."

"We can, what? We can work this out? No, actually, we can't. You wanted me to trust you and then you went ahead and did the one thing you could have done to ensure that I could never do that. Did you think this through at all? Or was this one of your 'I'm in a mood and therefore I can get away with anything I want' things? Because, I am not one of your *brothers* here. I don't have to grin and bear it. I don't have to put up with it. And I won't."

"Don't be a coward, Mina," he said, shaking his head, tone defeated. He knew I was right. He knew he was absolutely in the wrong with what he did. He was even sorry about it.

But there were times in life when sorry, while the only thing a person could say, still wasn't enough.

This was one of those times.

"I'm not being a coward, Renny," I said, feeling one of the tears slide hot and unstoppable down my cheek. "I'm saving myself."

"From what? From me?"

"From someone who would willingly do something he knows will hurt me. If you were just any guy, Renny, maybe I could have looked this over, chalked it up to you being an idiot. But you're not an idiot. And because you are who you are, you knew exactly what you were doing and exactly how much you could hurt me. And you went ahead and did it anyway. You hurt me *on purpose*. To prove a point. So, yes, Renny, yes. I am saving myself from you."

His face fell at that and he looked away for a long second before looking back, his face accepting. "That's really a shame then, Mina."

I didn't want to ask. The bigger part of me knew I needed to cling to self-preservation above all else right then.

But the words came from somewhere deep, a place I didn't want to analyze because I knew exactly what I would find there.

"Why's that?"

He moved a step closer, making me have to turn my head up to keep eye-contact. His hand raised slowly, tucking my hair behind my ear and gently swiping the trail the tear had left down my cheek.

"Because I fucking love you, Mina."

With that, his hand dropped and he made his way toward the gates that the guys had already opened, likely anticipating one of us at least would be storming that way eventually.

I watched him.

216

I hated to admit that, but I watched his back as he made his way up toward the front door, punched in the codes, and disappeared inside.

Then and only then did I turn away from the compound.

That was the precise moment that the dam broke too- the tears streaming down frantically, my breathing going shallow, my sobs a strangled little noise from trying to keep them in.

"Come on, babe," came a voice from behind me, very possibly the last voice I expected to hear. I could have anticipated Laz with his seemingly big heart. And I could have expected Cyrus with his easy-going sweetness. There was no way I could have guessed that Reeve would be the one to come to me. His hand went to my lower back, putting firm pressure there and pulling, making me fall into step with him as he walked me away from the compound.

"Where... are," I started, my voice breaking before I took a deep breath. "Where are we going?" I asked a little less pathetically.

"My car is down the side street. Figured the last thing you'd want is everyone gawking at you when you're trying to have a moment."

"A... moment?" I asked, reaching up to wipe my hands down my cheeks.

"A strong person like you doesn't have break downs. They have moments. You're having one."

Somehow, that helped.

He had, with just a few words, compartmentalized the entire situation for me, made it easier for me to box it up and seal it, then put it on a shelf to be taken down and dealt with later.

And I knew, I just knew that it was because he, at some time or another, had had a moment of his own, had needed to box up something and seal it and store it.

I had the distinct feeling, too, that he had never taken it back down, that it was still sitting there waiting to be opened.

"Here," he said, letting his hand drop and he bleeped the locks on a black pickup truck that was just a couple years old and dented and dinged. He wasn't one of those guys who made you take off your shoes before you got in. He was one of those 'a car is just a car' guys. I had always much preferred those. "Hop in," he added after he opened the door for me.

And with no other real option and, in that moment, feeling rather close with him, I hopped in and he shut the door and made his way around the hood to hop in himself.

"You need a drive? A drink? Or home?"

I laughed humorlessly at that. I needed them all. "Well, Hailstorm is a thirty minute drive away and it's home and I can have a drink... or five, there."

"Hailstorm it is," he said, throwing the car into reverse, backing out of his spot between two very close cars with an almost careless precision that made me queasy, then started up the road toward the hill that was, for all intents and purposes, home.

"You alright?" he asked a long five minutes of silence later as I stared out the window.

And then I did the damnedest thing.

I gave him the truth.

"Not really," I said, looking over at him.

He nodded at that, like he understood exactly how I was feeling. "Well, you will be," he said casually, but with so much certainty that I found myself believing him- this man

218

who was all but a stranger to me, a complete and utter anomaly, someone I didn't even begin to understand, I believed him completely.

I would be okay.

Even if I had just pushed away the only person, I was sure, who had ever actually loved me.

FIFTEEN

Renny

I was such a fuck.

I knew that.

Hell, a part of me had probably fucking known that while I was making the damn phone call to her parents.

I don't even know what I thought my endgame was there. I had known going in that there were issues there, especially with her mother. But I had figured maybe her avoiding them had made her intensify them in her head.

I should have known better.

Her mother, for all intents and purposes, was a fucking ice queen, a stone cold bitch. I didn't like throwing the 'bitch' word around too often, but if there was ever a woman who deserved the term, it was Akari Piek.

I had anticipated her being cold and withholding toward Mina. That sounded par for the course. I hadn't exactly expected the judgment and condescension that dripped from every syllable when she spoke.

Dedrick Piek, though, I had him wrong.

I expected a workaholic. I was both right and wrong when I first met her and called her an army brat. Her father wasn't in any army, but he did a lot of contract work with different armies all around the world. His specialty being intelligence extraction.

I hadn't expected him to genuinely not give a shit about his daughter. That was a wholly unexpected, unpleasant surprise. I had figured that with a cold and withholding mother, any decent man would step up and try to fill the void. I was completely off on that. Dedrick Piek didn't want children and he didn't care if his offspring knew that.

I could sympathize with the coldness she experienced, having ice cubes for parents myself, but I had always been wanted at least. I was never seen as an inconvenience or made to feel like a chore. If anything, my fucked up parents got their kicks raising me.

And, being that my parents read into everything I did, they rarely criticized little things like how I dressed or did my hair, choosing instead to theorize on what made me do such things.

I'll never forget the fucking look she had on her face when she saw them. All her guards, they all fell away. She was vulnerable. But not in the good way like when I was inside her. It was a raw, awful kind of vulnerability that made it clear exactly how awful she felt and how much she hated me for forcing her to confront those feelings.

RENNY

I saw the decision before she even did. Her mind was made up the second my hand hit her knee, trying to comfort her. She didn't want me touching her. And, quite frankly, if someone's touch suddenly disgusted you, there was no chance at saving things.

I had tried.

But she was beyond that.

I didn't even wait around to see what response she had to me telling her I loved her. It wasn't some coercion tactic on my part. I just wanted her to know.

Because it was the fucking truth.

I loved her.

I wasn't sure when it happened. Really, it could have been anytime between her showing up during mine and Duke's fight that afternoon and the night before in bed with her. It could have been the first time she let me kiss her or put my hands on her or take her without anything between us.

I had no idea.

But there was no denying it.

I hadn't recognized it right at first or was just chalking it up to being attraction or some superficial shit like that. But the warm feeling in my chest, the way just hearing her laugh made me smile from across a fucking room, or how hearing her threaten to 'put a cap in my ass' on Grand Theft Auto made me happier than any goddamn sexual experience ever had. It was the way sex wasn't just sex anymore. Even when we were fucking- dirty, rough, hot, even *then* it wasn't just fucking. It was deeper than that.

I loved her.

And as the cliche went, I lost her.

222

RENNY

I had looked back out the slot in the door to see Reeve, of all fucking people, come to her rescue and lead her away as she broke down.

I walked behind the bar, going right to the bottle of whiskey and drinking out of it.

"That ain't gonna help," Laz warned as he walked past. But he left it at that. There was no lecture. The last thing I needed was a lecture of the evils of alcohol from some holier than thou recovered bastard.

It wasn't going to help; but it was going to numb the stabbing feeling in my chest a bit. I knew that at least.

"Hey Renny," Lo's voice called, curious, as she walked up to the bar, head cocked to the side.

"'Sup, Lo?"

"Do you have any idea where Repo keeps the pickling spices?"

It went over my head for a second before her brow slowly raised and I remembered a threat she made before things finally started for me and Mina. She had made a veiled threat about pickling my cock like Rasputin.

"I fucking tried, Lo," I said, tipping up the bottle for another long swig.

"Did you?" she asked, brows drawing together. "Because it looks a hell of a lot like you woke up in a mood this morning and conned me into letting you take Mina out to give her a 'surprise' and obviously led her into some kind of fucked up scenario. That doesn't sound like trying to me. It sounds like you just want to be able to do whatever the fuck you want to do and everyone else is just supposed to deal with that. Well, news-fucking-flash, that isn't how relationships work."

"She wouldn't give me anything, Lo," I said, shaking my head, feeling the booze start to kick in, leading me

223

more toward the dark side than the happy drunk I was hoping for.

"What are you talking about? She gave you everything. I have known that girl since she was nineteen years old. If you think the Mina you first met was cool, Renny, the one who came to me was about as warm as fucking liquid oxygen. It took her years to be able to do something as simple as laugh around most of us. The girl that has been in this clubhouse the last few days is the Mina I always knew she would be if she let her guard down- warm, sweet, fucking *happy.* That is *everything.* What more could you have wanted from her?"

"Her past," I admitted, suddenly not understanding why that had been so important to me in the first place.

"Right," she said, eyes angry. "Because heaven fucking forbid Renny doesn't get the answers he wants right when he wants them. It's only been a couple days. You couldn't have given her more time than that?"

She was right.

She was fucking right and I had nothing to defend myself with.

There was no excuse.

"Maybe this is insensitive," Lo said, her tone holding no apology, "but maybe consider some fucking therapy."

With that little death blow, she stormed away toward the basement where I could hear one of the kids in the middle of an epic shit-fit.

"Alright, what we got here?" Cyrus asked, walking behind the bar, tilting his head up at the shelves of liquor on the back bar. "I'm usually more of a whiskey guy myself, but you've had your mouth all over that one. Brothers or not, we're not swapping spit. So... vodka it is," he said, taking the bottle off the shelf and grabbing a glass.

"What are you doing?"

"Day drinking is fine. Drinking over a woman is fine too. But those things can't be done at the same time and alone. So, here's to those who wish us well; the rest can go to fucking hell," he declared, clinking his glass to my bottle, and throwing it back. "Mother fucking shit," he declared when he slammed his glass back on the bar. "Forgot how much vodka burns."

"You realize we're bikers, right?" I asked, shaking my head. "We don't have to do the responsible drinking thing. I can drink alone during the day over a woman."

"Yeah, well, I'm fucking bored," he shrugged. "Besides, that looked brutal. She wasn't even yellin' at me and I think my balls shrank."

I snorted at that, shaking my head, and raising the bottle again. "Yeah," I agreed.

"Mina doesn't strike me as the crazy chick type so I'm assuming you actually fucked up."

"You have no idea."

"She also don't seem like the forgiving sort either."

"Nope," I agreed.

So then we drank. We drank until goddamn every part of me was numb except my fucking brain which just kept rolling over the events of the day over and over until I blessedly passed out on the foot of my bed.

I was pretty sure I only made it there because Cyrus half-carried me.

He was shaping up to be a good brother, all said and done.

"Up," a curt voice demanded a while later, kicking my boot hard enough to make my body jolt.

"Fuck off," I growled, my head slamming, every bit of me feeling dried out.

"Sorry to break it to you, but you're a goddamn grown man with responsibilities," Laz's voice said, sounding as casual as ever and when I craned my head to look over at him, he was relaxed, hands down at his sides, face almost expressionless. "You want to get shitfaced, that's your business. Lord knows I can't judge you for it, but you need to get your ass up and function."

"Thanks for the lecture, probie," I growled. "You can kindly fuck off now."

"See now," he said, clicking his tongue. "I would. Except Reign and the guys are half an hour out and I believe your ass was supposed to be in charge. Get up. Get some ibuprofen. Drink some water. And at least pretend you were keeping an eye on things all day like you were supposed to."

"Shit," I hissed, pushing up to a seated position and cradling my head in my hands for a long minute, still mostly-drunk.

"Half a bottle of Jack," Laz observed, kicking it with his boot. "You're going to be suffering for a while."

With that, he grabbed the bottle and headed out and I dragged myself into the bathroom, drinking handfuls of water and splashing it on my face. I reached into the cabinet and took four ibuprofen then went back into the other room to change, fairly sure I reeked of booze.

When I walked into the common room ten minutes later, feeling not quite so dead, but not anywhere near sober, I found Cyrus still holding his bottle of vodka and Reeve with four beers in front of them.

"You stopped drinking before I did," I said to Cyrus, brows drawn together.

"Figured it'd look a lot better if we were all trashed when they got back. Like we did some brotherly bonding or some shit," Cyrus said, saluting me with the bottle and taking a swig that he clearly didn't want.

"Renny, you look like shit," Maze said as she walked up, shaking her head at me.

"Thanks, Violet. Always the charmer."

Penny walked out after her, excitement like a live wire inside her, her body too small to be able to contain it all. She was practically bouncing.

"Who got the call?" I asked, not seeing Lo anywhere and my phone wasn't in my pocket.

"Well after your cell wouldn't stop ringing for ten minutes straight," Summer said, walking over to where it was sitting on the bar, "I answered it."

I didn't try to defend my actions and I knew I was bound to be dealing with some coldness among the women when they figured out what happened so I might as well get used to it.

"Everyone alright?"

"Yeah," she said, nodding, reaching up to put her long red hair into a ponytail. "Reign said it was bumps and bruises."

I didn't want to tell her that Reign's version of bumps and bruises likely meant Superglue stitches and broken ribs. She would see soon enough anyway.

"That'd be them," Cyrus observed as the sound of car doors met us.

It was all of two minutes before the front door burst open and brought our brothers back in.

"You said bumps and bruises!" Summer snapped as soon as Reign crossed the threshold, the entire front of his white tee dripped with dried blood, most of which was likely his if his black eye that hinted at a busted nose and the huge gash down his cheek was anything to go by.

227

"Babe," he said, giving her a very tired smile and holding his arms out.

And she fucking flew at him, big belly and all.

"That's sweet and all, but where the fuck is my woman?" Cash asked, walking in next, looking less blood-stained than his brother but walking slow and favoring his right side like he had bruised or busted some ribs.

I had no fucking idea where Lo was.

"She's on her way back," Maze supplied, giving me a knowing look. "She had to deal with something. Where is, oh," she breathed out when Repo walked in- all kinds of fucked up.

See, in the crazy anger department, Wolf took home first place. But Repo was a very close second when he was pissed. And if his bruised and bloodied face was anything to go by, he had gone in whatever he had gone into way too hot and bloodthirsty.

"You can shoot the top off a bottle of beer at like a thousand yards and you go in using your fists," Maze said, rolling her eyes at him for a second before smiling and stepping into his arms.

Penny moved in beside me, genuinely seeming like she might jump out of her skin with anticipation as we waited for the final member to walk back in.

Then he did.

But he wasn't alone.

No, he was pulling a man along with him. A man with his hands cuffed behind his back.

He was tall and strong with long dark hair that he had in a bun at the crown of his head and a full dark beard. His eyes were dark too- almost black. Everything about him elicited the immediate feeling of danger.

The man was dangerous.

228

It was also almost painfully clear he was not Italian.

If I had to put my money on anything, it would be Romanian.

"Reign..." Summer said, stiffening, pulling away from her husband. I could practically hear her brain screaming: *there are kids here.*

"This fuck is Edison. We found him chained up in Little Ricky's basement," Reign supplied, waving a careless hand toward the men.

"Smells like a gin joint in here," Repo observed suddenly. I stiffened, thinking it was chastisement, before he broke into a grin. "Forgot what that was like. It's like old times."

"Penny," Duke said suddenly and I realized the bouncy, happy Penny had deflated beside me.

Because if I thought Repo was a mess, Duke took the cake. One of his eyes were almost swollen shut; his lip was split; there was a long gash down the side of his neck, and his hands were so ripped open that the healing process was going to be long and painful because anytime he stretched his fingers, it was going to rip scabs open.

Her head turned, looking up at me a little hopelessly.

"Fell in love with a biker, blondie. Get used to blood," I told her, pushing her forward and she slowly closed the space between her as Edison moved out of the way, watching Penny with an interest that wasn't sexual in the least as she walked up to Duke, refusing to step into his arms.

"I don't want to hurt you," she insisted about half a second before Duke grabbed her and lifted her off her feet by her ass as his lips claimed hers.

"Since when do you guys take prisoners?" Lo asked, having come in from the garage unnoticed, her eyes looking over Edison.

"Long story, sweetheart," Cash said, giving her a small smile. "I can tell you all about it in bed," he told her, grabbing her and pulling her down the hall.

"Lame ass party with only three of you drinking," Reign declared, tucking his woman under his arm and walking toward us.

"Is is a victory one now?" Cyrus asked, looking almost green from the booze he had been downing for my benefit.

Reign looked over to me, nodding. "We can walk around again without having to worry," he said. "We gotta go wash up and see our kids. After that, we'll fill you in. Whoever is sober enough to be trusted around fire, make some food. It's going to be a late night," he added before moving off toward the hall.

"Yeah, I better clean up too," Duke said, putting Penny back on her feet as Repo and Maze disappeared. "You can keep an eye on him for a bit, right?" he asked as he reached into his pocket for a key and unlocked one of Edison's wrists, moving them forward and cuffing them in the front. "Give him something to drink too," he said as Edison walked over toward us.

"Vodka, whiskey, gin, beer or tequila?" Cyrus asked as the silent, intimidating presence moved to stand beside where he was sitting.

"Vodka," he ground out, his voice so low and gravely it was almost hard to understand.

"Here you go, man," he said, handing him the bottle he had been holding. "Think I'm cured of vodka for the next year or five."

RENNY

Edison closed both his hands around the bottle and brought it up, tipping his head back and chugging the contents.

"That's not juice, man," Cyrus half-laughed as he kept downing the clear liquid.

He didn't bring the bottle down until the crazy mother fucker drank almost all of what was left- which was two-thirds the bottle.

"Haven't had a drink in three months," he supplied in that same guttural growl of his.

"It'll do you no good if it all comes back up though," Cyrus said, shaking his head.

"Been drinking since I was thirteen. Save for that first time, I've never been sick. But thanks for the warning. Where the fuck am I right now?" he asked, looking around the room with its lack of windows or any real decoration.

"The Henchmen MC compound," I supplied, motioning toward my cut as I did so.

"Fucking Jersey?" he asked, grimacing.

"Where you from?" I asked.

"Everywhere," he hedged.

"Drop a pin," I suggested.

"Philly, when I am not on the road."

"What the fuck did you do to get yourself locked up in Little Ricky's basement for three months?"

"Got a real problem with pimps, especially the type who use fists on their women. He didn't like that I had a problem with pimps and therefore had a problem with me."

"That got you three months?" I asked, brows drawing together.

"My dislike of pimps might have led to one of them eating through a straw."

"Nice," Reeve said, almost too low to be heard.

231

"And you're still breathing?" I pressed.

"*Little* Ricky was a paranoid fuck. Figured some rogue asshole with an ax to grind must have belonged to some bigger organization bent on bringing his pathetic army of rapists and baby fuckers down."

"You seem to know a lot about his organization," I observed.

"I know a lot about a lot of organizations."

"Why's that?"

"Alright," Reign said as he walked back in, showered. "Reeve," he said, making the man in question straighten in his seat slightly. "You're reading my kid *Hatchet*?"

Reeve got a bit more guarded at that, but lifted his chin slightly. "I am."

"Thanks, man. Summer said he was struggling since I left. I appreciate you taking some time out for him. Secondly," he said, looking over toward me. "Where the fuck is Mina?"

"Oh, man," Cyrus said, jumping up and wavering on his feet for a second before Edison's cuffed hands grabbed his forearm to steady him. "Thanks, bud. You weren't here for this, but let's just say the Mina topic ain't a good one and we might be better off in the kitchen for a bit."

With that, Cyrus, Edison, and Reeve all shuffled off as Reign raised a brow at me. "What'd you do, Renny?"

"I got the girl," I hedged, my headache seeming to intensify at just the mention of her.

"Then you lost her. Fucking great. Did you at least compare notes before you scared her off or were you too busy doing other shit?"

"We're on the same page about Laz and Cyrus and are both clueless about Reeve."

"When did she leave?"

"Just late this morning."

"Lo know you hurt her girl?" he asked, smirking slightly.

"She's looking for pickling spices," I supplied. At his drawn-together brows, I laughed humorlessly. "To pickle my cock."

To that, he threw his head back and laughed. "Shoulda known when you were getting involved with Hailstorm."

"So why do we have Little Ricky's prisoner here... still in cuffs?"

Reign shrugged at first. "We got down to the basement, saw him, but didn't have time to ask him any goddamn thing so we just took him and ran. With the amount of shit that went down in that building, the cops were definitely on their way. We didn't want to risk it. On top of that, he saw us and could finger us. And we didn't know who he was so we couldn't just fucking kill him."

"Not worried he's going to flip shit?"

"You've seen the fuck," Reign said, chuckling. "I swear to fuck if I didn't know better, I'd think he was perpetually high. How he lost his shit and almost killed one of Little Ricky's guys is beyond me. I don't think I've met anyone that laid back."

"He claims to know a lot about a lot of organizations. When I said the name of our club, he already knew he was in Jersey. Even though his home space is apparently Philly."

"Good to know."

"What's the plan with him now? We got women and kids here," I reminded him. "And I don't think it'd be fair to lock him up with the rest of the puppies in case he's got rabies."

"Puppies?" he asked, smirking again.

"I dunno, man. I said it once and it stuck," I admitted, reaching up to rub at the bridge of my nose.

"So you thought that jumping into a bottle was maybe better than driving up to Hailstorm, huh?"

"I fucked up bad, man," I admitted. "Swear to fuck she might have put in an order to have me shot on sight."

"Well, I suggest your start racking that brain of yours to try to figure out how to get her to forgive you, because I'm thinking I want her opinion on Edison before we make any decisions on what to do with him. For now, I don't fucking know, we can lock him up in that glass room or some shit. There's no escaping from there."

"Hey, ah, Mr. Presidentè or whatever," Cyrus called from the doorway, getting our attention. "The new guy and Laz are, well, let's say they're having culinary differences."

"Jesus Christ," Reign said, shaking his head, running a hand across the back of his neck. "What the fuck is happening to my club?" he asked, walking toward the kitchen with me in toe just in time to see Edison shove his cuffed hands into Laz's shoulder.

"Keep your hands off me, *frate*," Laz shot back, shoving his own hand into Edison's shoulder.

"Frate?" Cyrus asked and I shook my head. I had no fucking idea.

Really, even cuffed, there was only one way that conversation was going to go. And we stood there and watched as the men hit the ground and fought for dominance.

"That's more like old times," Reign said, nodding.

"What's the..." Cash started, stopping short at the sight of Edison clasping his hands together and using them both to slam into Laz's jaw. "Huh, wouldn't have believed either of them were fighters if I didn't see it myself. What'd they get into it over?"

I looked at Cyrus who looked at all of us with a shit-eating grin and declared, "Basil."

To that, we all couldn't help it after so many tense months, we laughed.

"Oh for Christ's sake," Maze said walking in. "Lay them out on the table and measure them," she declared, moving to step over the grappling duo on her way to the fridge, making them both freeze.

Didn't matter how serious a fight was, when a woman as pregnant as Maze was stepping over you, you settled the fuck down.

"Are we having dinner or fucking what?" Reign asked then. "Leave the goddamn basil out if it is going to lead to a mother fucking brawl. Jesus Christ. I need my woman," he declared, waving a dismissive hand toward us and walking out.

"What, you *beat* prisoners now too?" Lo asked, shaking her head as Reeve reached down to help Edison back onto his feet.

"Reeve," Repo said, all business, reminding me of the days when he was in charge of all the probates even though he hadn't been much older than most of us. "Why don't you show Edison to one of the bathrooms so he can clean up. Here," he added, pulling a key out of his pocket. "He can uncuff to shower then cuff him back up after. Cyrus, why don't you see about helping Laz or just sitting at the table and nursing that hangover and minding your own fucking business while I fill-in everyone?"

With that, and not waiting for a response because the way he said it left no room for argument, he turned and walked out into the common area, dropping down on the chair with a sigh, patting his leg until Maze sat down there.

"Alright," Lo said, sitting down and giving me a glare when I moved to sit near her, making me decide to stand instead. "So, is it over?"

"That's what took so long," Repo said, absentmindedly stroking a hand through Maze's purple hair. "We got to the place and realized it was a fuckuva lot bigger than we planned on and we were too out-numbered. We stopped to regroup and called Janie for some background on the guys, what Ricky's numbers were, that kind of thing."

"Had Repo pick off the night guards before we decided to go in," Cash added. "By the time we fought our way through the inside guys, Little Ricky was nowhere to be found. Pulled a fucking Lex Keith with a mother fucking panic room. Had to go *back* through all the guys who were still breathing until we found one who knew the code and then, ah, find a way to get that information out of him."

Didn't take an idiot to know that information was beaten out of him. And, judging by the look of his hands, it had likely been Duke who had done the extracting.

"And?" I prompted when no one continued.

"And Little Ricky was inside the room with one of his poor fucking women, beat to shit, clothes ripped, a real mess," Repo added, shaking his head. "Cash got her out of there and Reign made him pay for what he did to our brothers."

I knew Reign enough to know that behind the take-charge or alternately laid-back persona of our president, he was as dark as the rest, had more blood on his hands than most save for maybe Wolf.

Whatever fate Little Ricky met with was brutal and bloody and totally fucking justified if you asked any of us.

"That's about when we came across Edison," Cash added. "We were doing one last look around to make sure we didn't miss anyone or anything and behind some steel door, there he was, chained to a metal chair."

"What the hell possessed you to bring him back here? If he was a prisoner there, he wasn't likely to try to take you guys down for rescuing him," Lo said, ever the strategist.

"Reign kind of liked the fuck," Duke offered, walking back in, his hands and face all bandaged up and I knew it was Penny who had insisted on it. Duke likely would have poured alcohol over the whole of it and called it a day. But, no, he had a woman who loved him and wanted to take care of him.

Never was much of a man for envy until right about then.

"He's in rebuild-mode," Cash supplied. "It was like this after Pops got killed too, along with half the other men. Any guy he came across who seemed the least bit capable of handling this lifestyle, he kind of just pulled them in and had them prospect."

"Well, four new men in the course of a week isn't too shabby," Lo mused. "If they all pan out. Bet you'd be ahead of figuring that out right now if *someone* would get his head out of his ass..."

"I know I fucked up, Lo," I said, shaking my head. "No use squeezing lemons into the wound."

"Well, apparently there is a need for it since you spent the afternoon trying to numb your pain instead of figuring out a way to try to make it up to her."

"Make it up to who?" Edison's deep, unmistakable voice asked, coming up behind us.

I turned to find him cuffed again, but freshly showered, likely feeling a fuckuva lot more human than he had ten minutes before, and dressed in clothes that must have belonged to one of our fallen guys, just black jeans and a black tee.

"Renny pissed off his woman this morning."

"My advice, frate," he said, clamping a hand on my shoulder. "Fucking grovel."

"You don't even know what he did," Maze insisted, giving him a strange smile as he dropped down next to Lo as casually as you please.

"My experience with women, love, is that it don't fucking matter what you did. Whatever it is, you need to fucking grovel."

"But what if..." Maze started.

"You like the woman?" he asked, leaning forward, putting his elbows on his knees and looking at me.

I don't know why I said it, least of all to him, a perfect stranger, and surrounded by people who barely even knew the situation, but I did. "I love her."

"Then you grovel. You love her, you fucked up, you make it up. This ain't fucking rocket science here. Besides," he added, going for a little levity if the way his lips turned up into a smirk was anything to go by, "can't have you drinking this away when you can't hold your fucking liquor."

It was right about then that I remembered how much he had drank.

And the man seemed sober as a judge.

It was fucking impressive was what it was.

I looked over at Maze. "Any idea how late the mall is open to?"

She had been taking a sip of Vitamin Water when I asked and started to choke on it. "The... mall...?" she gasped out between chokes as Repo slammed his hand into her back.

"Yeah, I have to pick up some socks."

"Socks?" Cash asked, lips twitching. "Yeah, man, that's... ah... romantic."

"Trust me. It's a thing," I said, standing. "You gonna make your guys let me into Hailstorm are are there shoot to kill orders on me?"

She looked up, brown eyes warm, because if there was anything Lo was, above a certified badass, it was a hopeless romantic. And she was a sucker for a good romantic gesture. "I suppose I can have that order lifted for a little bit."

"It's going to have to wait," Maze said, making me freeze. She waved her phone at me. "The mall is closed until ten tomorrow."

Of course it was.

"Eh, maybe it's good," Edison put in. "Let her work through the anger first."

"She wasn't angry," Reeve said, drawing everyone's attention. He had been so silent I had forgotten he was even there. He looked at me then, face guarded, and gave me all I needed to know. "She was heartbroken."

SIXTEEN

Mina

"What'd the leggings ever do to you?" Ash asked, walking up behind me as I stuffed them into the garbage in the bathroom.

"My mother saw me in them. For that, they need to burn," I supplied, ripping off the shrug while I was at it and letting it follow the leggings into the garbage heap.

"You know," Ash said, watching my reflection in the mirror, "I've known you, what, five years now?"

"Sounds about right," I agreed.

"I've never seen you cry."

"Don't analyze me, Ash," I begged, shaking my head. "Believe me, I've had about enough of that today."

"It's just an observation," she said, shrugging. "Your nose gets red," she added, smiling when my eyes widened at the comment.

"Gee thanks for pointing that out," I said, laughing a little as I made my way back to the barracks to grab some new clothes. I dragged up my old, familiar utility pants and a somewhat roomy Army t-shirt I stole from one of the guys when they shrank it in the wash, and moved to sit down on my bed, reaching under my pillow and freezing.

"What's the matter?" Ash asked, sitting down on the edge of her bunk and looking at me.

"I left it there."

"You left what where?"

"My Gameboy," I supplied. "I left it on Renny's nightstand."

In fact, it had been there since that first night when he first pulled it out of my hands. I hadn't touched it since then. There was no need. I was calm there, comfortable. I had slept like a baby.

Ash looked at me for a second, knowing as well as anyone else in the barracks that I was never without it, that I all-too often could be found up playing it at night when sleep wouldn't come.

And I had just had a hell of a day.

I had needed to deal with my parents. That, in and of itself, pretty much guaranteed sleepless nights for the next month.

But on top of that, I had had that God-awful fight with Renny.

In general, I didn't have fights. Granted, I disagreed with others plenty. It would even come to words on occasion. But those words were always calm and carefully chosen. I didn't just... shriek and screech and say whatever

241

came to me. That wasn't how I operated. It was ugly and
messy.

And I liked my life as neat as possible.

So amid having that fight like a CD on a loop going
around and around in my head, making me cringe at the
things I had said, the volume at which I had said them, the
carelessness with which I had done it all, and the sick-
stomach feeling that all gave me, I also had to come to
grips with what the argument had ended with.

It had ended with Renny telling me he loved me.

A part of me wanted to shrug that off, roll my eyes, say
it was silly, it was too soon. It was impossible.

But it was possible. It wasn't like Renny was some guy I
met at a bar and went back to his house for a long weekend
and had some fun.

I had known him for months. I had gotten to watch him
from afar and interact with him on pretty much a daily
basis. I got to know his quirks, his flaws, his positive
attributes. I had a begrudging respect for his skill set, one
that, despite what I had told him upon meeting about how I
was way out of his league skills-wise, if I was honest,
surpassed mine. He was funny and charming and forward-
thinking. As a whole, he was good with his brothers as well
as the kids and women. He was, bad moods and all, a
favorite of Maze's and Penny's. He was a worthy opponent
in a video game and by leaps and bounds, the best sex I had
ever had.

I *knew* him.

And, in turn, he *knew me.*

It was entirely plausible that he loved me.

And, even as I tried desperately to find some kind of
reason that it wasn't possible, the bigger part of me knew
that it wasn't only possible, it was the damn truth.

He loved me.

He loved me and no one had ever really loved me before.

That was a hard horse-pill to swallow.

It was lodged in my throat and choking me.

It was dissolving and leaving a God-awful bitter taste in my mouth.

Ashley watched me for a long minute, likely seeing a range of emotions cross my face. I wasn't going to cry again. I was pretty sure I had gotten that out of my system before climbing into Reeve's truck.

He had been a surprisingly good companion while I was trying to put myself together. While I still didn't *get* him, I was starting to understand parts of him. In that car, his presence was calm and comforting. He didn't ask me questions. He didn't expect explanations. He just let me have my 'moment'. He just instinctively understood that not everyone needed or wanted to talk things out.

I didn't need to talk things out with people. If ever there was someone who understood their reactions and the motives behind their reactions, it was me. No amount of jaw-jabbing would change that. It was useless noise.

I appreciated Reeve's silence.

And when he pulled up to the gates and I thanked him and moved to grab my door handle, his hand had slammed down on top of my other hand and made my head snap back at him.

"You've had your moment," he told me. "You needed that to clear your head. Now you need to give this some thought, Mina. I don't know a fuckuva lot, but I know that some shit, shit like I saw between you and Renny, it's not common. You gotta decide if one fight, one fuck up, is worth throwing away something rare like that."

With that, he released my hand and I jumped out, uncertain.

I hadn't pinned him as sentimental, as wise. To be honest, I found that almost more unsettling than thinking he was just an enigma.

"My father said something really interesting to me when I was younger," Ashley said suddenly, breaking me out of my own swirling thoughts. When my gaze found hers, she shrugged a small shoulder. "He told me that the people who make the biggest impact in your life, the ones who shake you to the core, who make you really *think* and *feel* are usually the ones we desperately try to push away.

"Somewhere along the way, and he blamed Disney for this," she added with a smirk, "and romance novels, we have been convinced that love is pretty and flowery and heart-warming. But it's none of those things. Anyone who has ever been in love, truly, magnificently in love, knows that it is *torture*. It is ugly and messy and brings out the absolute worst along with the best in you. It hurts because it forces you to confront every aspect of yourself. It forces you out of your comfort zone. And people, well, we love our comfort zones. In fact, we tend to love our comfort zones more than we love our partners. So anyone who comes in and tries to drag us out of them, well, we make sure we push them away so we can jump right back into that comfortable feeling."

"How old were you when he told you this?" I asked, wanting to change the subject instead of agreeing to the truth of the statement.

"Twelve. When he first suspected I was gay and I had told him that I wasn't going to be friends with Jenny anymore."

"Because you had feelings for her," I guessed.

244

"Exactly."

"I think I'd like your father," I said, meaning it. It was so rare to find a parent who not only accepted their kids as they were, but tried to convince said kid that it was okay to be how they were amidst a society that was telling them anything but.

"He is a wise man," she said with a nod. "As such, maybe you should think on that, yeah? Because I think you're mad right now because you have been yanked right out of your little comfort zone and you are scared and unsure of yourself. But you need to stop and consider that in twenty-someodd years, nothing and no one has been able to do that, to drag you out of that comfort zone. So what does it say about Renny and your feelings toward him that he was able to do that?"

With that, she stood and walked out.

I was apparently surrounded by very wise people without knowing it. And they were all *really* good at that 'say something awesome and walk off like an action hero walking casually away from an explosion they just set' thing.

The worst part was she (and her father) weren't wrong. I knew enough of people to know that love was rarely pretty. Love was a murder-suicide. Love was slit wrists. Love was a depression that never went away.

Because love, well, love was scary. It was so terrifying that your knee-jerk reaction was to hide from it or go toe-to-toe with it and ultimately blow it up from the inside out.

Affection was easy. Comfort was too. Then because somewhere along the way, we learned it was better to not feel too deeply about anything, we began to take those two things and call it love. And, to be fair, many people pulled it off. Many people built lives and new generations on the back of affection and comfort.

But affection and comfort weren't love, they were safety.

Love was brutal and bloody and, above all, *risky.*

When faced with it, too often we realized we weren't willing to take that risk.

We were cowards.

I was a coward.

I threw myself back onto my bed, pressing my palms into my eyes.

As a whole, I wasn't one for regrets. Though that, for the most part, was because I never acted without thinking. I never said something without weighing my words. My entire life was a expertly played game of chess.

Then Renny came, grabbed the board, and shook all the pieces out of their places.

I found out something about myself when he did that too- I found that I didn't so much like my life neatly arranged as I didn't honestly know of any other way. Until he showed it to me.

Had he given me some time, I would have given him what he wanted- my past, my scars, my damage. I probably would have given him anything he wanted. I had already given him more than I had given any man before.

My heart, I realized as I felt the hollow spot in my chest.

He had ripped it out and shoved it in his own.

As I lay there, I started to wonder if it would always be there, if I would never get it back.

I had a sneaking suspicion as I slowly drifted off sometime late that night, that I was just going to have to get used to no longer feeling that beating in my chest.

RENNY

--

"Mina," Ashley called, making me jump. I had been entirely too focused on writing down my notes on Cyrus, Lazarus, and Reeve for Reign. Just because I had needed to leave the compound didn't mean I was going to leave the job unfinished.

I was better than that.

"Yeah?" I asked, looking over at her, slow-blinking a few times because, I tried to convince myself, I had been staring at my own writing for too long. The reality was my eyes were swollen from all the crying from the day before. But I didn't want to admit that, not even to myself.

"Lo wants to see you in the spare room," she said, walking away before I could even question her.

The spare room?

As a whole, we all slept in the barracks. It was what was most familiar to most of the ex-military members of Hailstorm. And it was just prudent. But Lo kept a spare room with a single bed and a nightstand and a dresser off all by itself. Occasionally, she would find someone who was suffering some severe form of PTSD and had raging nightmares that would keep everyone awake. Or sometimes we would even need to offer a safe haven for someone we had come across in an operation who couldn't be expected to sleep in a barracks full of strangers. So that was why we had the spare room.

RENNY

Seeing as it literally had nothing in it aside from those three items mentioned, I couldn't fathom a reason Lo wanted to meet with me there. There were offices all over if she wanted to get some privacy to talk to me or yell at me.

I felt my stomach twist, remembering how she had gotten me to go back to The Henchmen compound in the first place.

She had threatened me.

No, worse.

She had threatened my *job.*

I couldn't help but wonder if my relationship and subsequent dissolution of it and departure from the job she sent me on was why she wanted to see me. To fire me. To kick me out. To tear away the one true constant in my life.

Hailstorm, for all intents and purposes, was my comfort zone.

It was all I had in the world.

She couldn't take that from me.

"Lo?" I asked, walking into the empty room, dark, as most of the rooms at Hailstorm were since we had no windows, save for one lamp. "I knew she couldn't have meant the spare room," I said to myself, shaking my head.

Then the door slammed shut behind me, making my stomach drop to my feet, my hand instinctively going to my pocket where I kept a small self-defense keychain with slots for my fingers and very sharp points meant for serious eye-gouging.

I whipped around, throat tight.

And I didn't find Lo.

Oh, no.

I found Renny.

RENNY

Seeing him, my belly did an intense little fluttering thing that I tried to ignore or find any explanation for aside from happiness.

But I could find none.

"What are you doing here?" I asked, forcing myself to cross my arms, maybe the only way I could prevent myself from walking over to him and wrapping my arms around him.

In that moment, I was starting to wonder if Ashley was right, if I was pushing him away for the wrong reasons. True, he had screwed up. But everyone screwed up. Never having been the type to overreact to, well, anything before, it had been hard at first for me to see that that was exactly what I had done.

"I think my past behavior has proven that I'm not exactly the kind of man who gives up easily."

I felt my lips curve up slightly at that. "You mean your borderline obsessive flirting?"

His smile went a little boyish at that. "I like to think it was me knowing exactly what I wanted and aggressively pursuing it."

"Call it what you want, it was obsessive," I said, trying to not be quite so taken with that smile as he moved closer, stopping just a couple feet in front of me.

"Knew it would be something special," he said, shrugging. "I wasn't wrong."

"Renny..." I said, shaking my head as he got a little closer.

"I fucked up," he offered without even the slightest bit of hesitation, something not like him. He didn't joke; he didn't hedge; he didn't try to make light of it. "I have no excuse. It was a shitty move and I was thinking of myself and not you and that's fucked up. But I can't take it back,

249

Mina. Doesn't matter what I say or do, that's something that is always going to be between us if you can't forgive it and let it go."

"Us?" I croaked out, my voice a strange, raspy version of itself.

"Yeah, see, way I figure it, there's going to be an us. Maybe you'll see I am genuinely sorry and want to make good right now and you'll take me back. Maybe you're going to be pissed for a while and I will have to wait it out. Maybe you're gonna be stubborn and take off and not come back to town and see me for fucking years. But there's not one situation where I don't see this being it for the both of us. True," he allowed, "we could try to move on, fuck other people, try to get to know other people. But you and I both know it wouldn't be the same. It wouldn't even be fucking *close*. Maybe you're willing to settle for that. I'm not. That's why I'm here."

"To... what?" I asked, choosing my words carefully. "To try to convince me to give you another chance?"

He smiled slightly at that, sitting down at the edge of the bed, making me have to turn to face him. He pulled something wrapped out of his pocket and put it down beside him, drawing my attention to the small, thin, rectangle shape, completely at a loss for what it could be.

"I'm not going to try to convince you of anything, Mina. First, because I respect your decision more than that. And second, you can't convince someone of shit. Either they want something or they don't. You either want me, sweetheart, or you don't. It's that simple."

"It's not that simple. You..."

"Fucked up. I admitted to that. And I apologized for it too. Now, if you're worried that I might dangle your parents in front of you again, let me assure you, that won't

250

be happening. One, because I didn't like that look it put on your face. Never felt lower than I did when you looked at me like you didn't know who I was anymore, angel cakes. I would willingly relive the memory of the night I found all my brothers dead before I would go over yesterday again. I never want you to look that hurt or betrayed again. And two, well, they're fucking assholes and I would be totally fine never seeing them again for the rest of my life."

I couldn't help it; I laughed at that.

"I could go the rest of my life without seeing them again too," I agreed.

There were some people who believed blood above all else. But people like me and Renny, people who found places like Hailstorm and The Henchmen, they learned that it wasn't about DNA; it was about who loved and supported you no matter what.

That was what family was.

And it had nothing to do with blood.

"So we're agreed," he concluded, giving me a smile.

"Well, we're agreed on the my parents being an asshole thing," I allowed.

"Sit, Mina," he requested, patting the spot on the other side of the small package that I wanted to pick up and shake like a Christmas present. I moved and sat down, pivoting toward him slightly. "Look, I can't promise you that is the only time I am going to fuck up. We both know there's no guarantee of that. But I can tell you that it's the last time I fuck up that epically. That look you gave me and that argument and the subsequent drinking and hangover and realization of how bad I screwed things up for no good reason? Yeah, I am pretty confident saying I won't push like that again."

RENNY

"You're supposed to be some badass biker and you got a hangover?" I asked, smiling a little at the idea. "You guys are getting soft."

"Don't think you'd be saying that if you met Edison."

"Who the hell is Edison?"

"Long story," he said, ducking his head a little. "So what do you say?"

"About what?" I asked, stalling, not sure how I was supposed to be handling the situation. It was clear to me right then that, while I was good at telling others how to act and respond and make decisions, I was horrible at doing that for myself.

I tried to detach myself from it, consider what I would tell someone else in my situation to do. At the end of the day, there was nothing more someone could say than sorry. It didn't mean you had to accept the apology, depending on the offense, but you had to acknowledge that no amount of repeating that phrase would change the meaning behind it.

I certainly didn't need a man on his knees, crying, begging me for another chance. And, if that was what Renny came at me with, the decision to kick him to the curb would have been solidified. Because it was fake. Renny wasn't that kind of man. But he was the kind of man who usually never apologized, never tried to make amends for his fuck ups. He always thought his actions were justified, no matter how irrational that seemed to anyone else. It was how he was programmed. So the fact that he came to me and gave me a genuine, heartfelt apology, that meant something. It meant everything for someone like him, someone who previously never considered someone's feelings as important as knowing the truth, suddenly realized how in the wrong he was.

252

And I even liked that he told me he couldn't promise he wouldn't fuck up again. I hated empty declarations. I hated when someone promised something there was no way they could say with one-hundred percent certainty they would never do again.

His apology was possibly the most genuine one I had ever heard.

"About not using this situation to prove a point instead of doing what you really want."

"And what do I really want?" I asked, wetting my lips and watching as his eyes moved there for a second.

"Me, sweetheart. You want me."

My eyes went up, landing on his light blue ones.

He was right.

I did want him.

I wanted him more than I knew it was possible to want another person, in a way that I wasn't sure was even healthy.

"Renny..."

"Admit it."

There was no denying it. I wasn't even going to try.

"I want you," I said, nodding. "But I'm not sure..."

"You can never be sure," he cut me off. "I'm not asking for you to be sure. I'm not even asking for you to promise me anything except a second chance."

I looked down at my hands for a second, taking a deep breath, then looking up at him. "Okay."

"Okay?" he asked, smile rising slowly. "How about a little enthusiasm here? It's not an execution. In fact, you should be squirming in your seat since you are signing up for the best mother fucking oral sex just about every day for the rest of your life if you're signing up for me."

I smiled then- big, happy, expectant.

Because he might have been full of bravado, but I had experienced enough of his skills to know it was not *false* bravado.

"What's in the package?" I asked instead, not being the type to get all mushy even if my insides were suddenly all warm and smushy.

"Figured if my world class charm, notorious pussy eating skills, and love for you weren't enough, I should have a backup," he said, picking up the gift and handing it to me.

It was as light as it looked and bent in my hands like fabric. My brows drew together as I looked at him for a second, before my hands went to the nondescript but pretty silver paper, slipped into a hole, and ripped it open.

What did I find?

Socks.

But, wait.

They weren't just socks.

They were *Pokemon* socks with little Picachus and Balbasours and Charmanders and Squirtles all over them.

If I hadn't been sure before then, I was absolutely one-thousand percent certain right then as my heart did a squeezing thing in my chest and my lips curved up enough to make my cheeks hurt.

I loved him.

"That's a good look," he said, eyes warm. "I like me a low maintenance woman," he added, reaching out to run his hand up my jaw. "Give her a pair of socks and she lights up like a mother fucking Christmas tree."

"It's the thought," I insisted. Flowers and chocolate and diamonds said nothing but 'I am obligated to get you something'. A gift that had personal significance, this case not just knowing I played the video game to cope with my unhappy childhood, but also the fact that you could put a lot of emphasis on the conversation in The Henchmen basement that included talk of my Pokemon socks being the real start to our story, meant so much more. It meant they cared, they paid attention, and they knew you well enough to do better than generic.

"So, we're doing this?"

"We're doing this," I agreed, nodding.

"Well, it's about fucking time, don't you think?" he asked, pulling the socks from my hand, grabbing me, and pulling me close. "So you gonna tell me or what? I told you a couple times already."

"How do you know I feel it?" I countered, lifting my chin a little.

"Well, see," he started, lips twitching from holding back a grin. "It all starts with a little dopamine. You saw me, you got all excited. Your brain kind of liked that feeling. Then we move onto stage two. This is where your system started getting flooded with adrenaline, epinephrine, norepinephrine, getting you all doped up on that high you got when you..."

"Renny, I know what goes on in the..."

"Hush, I am giving you a science lesson," he said as his fingers started tracing up my thigh. "Then you know, you started getting addicted to me. I know, I know... I am a hard habit to shake. Then, of course, we can't forget that your amygdala shuts down, you know, because you're obsessed with me and don't want to see any of my flaws. Tricky little fucker that, makes you really unprepared for when I screw up. But you don't care about that because then, oh then, it's all about the cuddle hormone."

255

RENNY

"Also known as oxytocin," I smiled. Then my head slammed back into his shoulder as his hand slid between my thighs and pressed in with perfect pressure.

"Gold star. Anyway, I tend to shoot you up with that anytime I give you an orgasm. So, let's just say," he went on as his fingers started tracing my clit, "I plan to keep you coming as much as possible until we get to the final stage where your ventral pallidum is so used to all that shit that you never ever want to give me up. And then we live happily ever after. The end."

I was sure there was some sort of flaw to his argument somewhere, even with all the correct science thrown in, but I was suddenly too distracted by his fingers to care about any of that.

But I wanted, before I came and he or I could blame all the hormones on the fact that I felt it, I turned my head on his shoulder. "Renny?"

"Yeah, sweetheart?" he asked, ducking his chin down and looking at me, eyes intense.

"I love you."

--

EPILOGUE

Renny - 2 weeks

She was all but moved into The Henchmen compound. Really, the woman didn't have very much. I guess that came from both living on the road a lot and then having your home be a barracks where you only had a foot locker to store your shit in.

But my closet filled up with all her tees and tanks and utility pants and boots. My dresser drawers had her bras and panties and socks, including the ones I bought her that she wore first every time they made it out of the dryer.

To the new puppies, well, it all came off like we had a lovers spat and made up.

It wasn't exactly wrong.

But there was no more faking it, no more covert operation to profile the guys. They learned about my skills and Mina's skills and all seemed to take it with a grain of salt, understanding that we couldn't afford to allow anyone into the organization who hadn't been properly vetted.

All in all, they were a pretty laid back group.

"So, you travel a lot," Cyrus concluded as we all sat around the common room relaxing.

Relaxing.

It was something I almost forgot was possible.

But, the fact of the matter was, after Janie went all rogue and then the guys headed to Long Island, they did a good job of ending the Abruzzo empire. They missed a few lower-level guys who would likely try to rise from the ashes, but they were low level and a long way off from being any kind of threat. Besides, we were all pretty confident that they got the message to stay the fuck out of Navesink Bank.

"Yeah, for the most part. There aren't a hell of a lot of jobs around here that need my set of skills," Mina agreed from where she was perched half on my lap, my arm around her lower back.

"What about Renny?" he pressed.

"Don't fucking own her, man," I said, shrugging. "She's got a job that takes her away, I'm here when she gets back."

Lo came walking in just about then, face warm and soft.

"How's the kid?" Cash asked, patting his leg and she moved over to him without hesitation.

"Fat. Squishy. Green-eyed. Loud," she added, leaning back into Cash's shoulder.

Summer had gone into labor four nights before, doing so without any fanfare, without actually waking anyone up at the compound aside from Maze who she asked to keep an eye on Ferryn and Fallon because it was her 'third kid and she didn't need everyone worrying about her'. By the time everyone got up in the morning, she and Reign already welcomed a second son, Finn, into the world.

With the threat neutralized, they had every intention of welcoming their new addition back to their house, not the compound. In fact, Cash and Lo were supposed to drive Ferryn and Fallon there the next morning and help them settle in.

Right then, there was an unexpected, loud, four pounds to the front door, making everyone stiffen. Lo and Mina hopped to their feet so we could too, Cash getting up and making his way toward the door, hand going toward the waistband of his jeans where he kept his gun, even though the only way someone could get past the guards was if they were approved.

We still weren't expecting anyone.

Cash went up and looked out the window, freezing for a second before ripping the door open.

And there was Wolf.

Really, it was a miracle that Janie had managed to keep him in the hospital as long as she had. Especially when all the tests came to the same conclusion- he was healthy. Aside from major fat and muscle loss and the weakness accompanying it, he was in tip top shape.

Everyone had gotten the chance to visit him in the hospital, save for the new guys who were still kept primarily at the compound, Edison included.

After about four nights cuffed in the glass room followed by days where he was nothing but comfortable and, at times, helpful around the clubhouse, Reign ordered his cuffs off and said he could crash with the other probates if he was so inclined.

Apparently, he was.

"I figured I would bring him here," Janie announced, shaking her head at him. "At least I have you guys to back me up and keep him from doing too much too soon. He's too fucking stubborn for anyone's good."

"Love you too, woman," he growled at her, giving her a small smile as he made his way across the room, looking like each step hurt just a little more than it should have. "Lo, Maze," he said, giving them each a nod as he sat down. "Penny," he added when he spotted her in the doorway to the kitchen where she and Laz were getting some food ready for everyone.

His eyes moved over to Mina, his brows drawing together.

"Mina," she offered, giving him a smile and offering him her hand which he took and completely swallowed up with his huge mitt. "I'm..."

"Mine," I offered, making Wolf's gaze snap to me, dark brow raising.

"That was quick."

"Yeah, well, what can I say? I'm fucking irresistible, man."

"Good luck with that," he offered Mina who smiled at him.

"I'm gonna need it," she agreed.

"So you're Wolf," Edison said, walking in, head cocked to the side.

"I'm Wolf," he agreed.

"Edison," he offered, giving Wolf a nod.

"*The* Edison?" Wolf asked, making Mina and I share a look.

From what we could gather after we got his full name and ran him, he wasn't anyone special. He had a few arrests when he was younger, usually associated with his criminal father and uncle, then drunk and disorderly as an adult. Aside from that, nothing.

"Yep," Edison agreed, leaning back against the wall, crossing his arms.

"Nice."

"We missed something," Mina said quietly as the conversation shifted.

Mina- 1 year

"Seriously?" I asked, sitting at the very large round table in Maze's dining room, the entire surface of it covered in magazines and computer print outs.

"I thought we were done with this," Alex declared, shaking her head. "But, *no*, of course not. You had to go and get shacked up with a Henchmen and join the girls club."

"You guys are the ones making it complicated," Summer insisted, jiggling Finn on her hip.

"It's only complicated because this whole thing is ridiculous," Janie insisted.

"Just because you wanted a small wedding doesn't mean everyone does," Lo chastised.

So... I was getting married.

It had been a natural progression of things, but I had been shocked when Renny asked me.

And of course, he did it in true Renny-style.

There was no silly trip to a nice restaurant where he had the ring put in a cupcake or anything like that.

Oh no.

He got me a new game for my DS, telling me it was an advanced copy of some game not slated to come out for another six months that he had Janie and Alex get for me.

And, along the lines of *Pokemon Go*, it was a real time, real life game where I had to chase not Pokemon, but little serial killers and try to cage them based on some clues that led me from place to place.

The last of which led me to She's Bean Around and right to a table that was very familiar to me.

It didn't click.

Really, I was genuinely in the dark, too wrapped up in my new game to see that maybe the location was a bit *too* pointed. I sat down, tired from running around all morning, and opened the little envelope on the screen that was supposed to give me clues to the next tidbit of my profile.

But it wasn't a clue.

It was a demand to look up from my screen already.

Like he had somehow known I would be too into the game to notice anything else.

My head jerked up to find Renny kneeling next to the table, boyish smile in place, hand up, with a diamond ring between his fingers.

It was exactly the kind he somehow knew I would like too, despite the fact that I never wore rings so he couldn't have just observed a preference. It was a single cushion-cut diamond on a thin platinum band- nothing crowded or over the top.

"Didn't figure you for the rose-petal trail kind of woman," he said, breaking a long silence as I sat there too stunned to say anything.

"So you had a video game made for me?" I finally asked when I found my voice.

"Only got one chance to do this, figured I might as well do it right."

"That must have taken months."

"Let's say I had Janie hook me up with some people pretty much as soon as you moved into the compound. I didn't want some cheesy C-level game."

Right after I moved into the compound? He knew he was going to marry me a *year* ago? Hell, a year ago, I wasn't sure if I could last a week of him *never being able to hang up a wet towel*. Let alone spending the rest of my life with him.

"Come on," he said, breaking through my swirling thoughts again, "what do you say you spend the rest of your life dealing with me fucking up, huh?"

Thrown off, maybe expecting a bit of cheesiness after all, but pleased that wasn't the route he took, I laughed. "Well, I've dealt with you pretty well this far," I offered, extending my hand toward him.

He slid the ring on and I felt the tears sting at my eyes when he leaned down and kissed it before moving up and sealing his lips over mine.

It was an important moment for me.

Not only because he loved me. He had loved me for a while. But because he was telling me that he never planned to stop. And, being someone who never had that kind of promise before, it meant the world.

But... I was rethinking my agreement to the whole marriage thing.

Not because I changed my mind about Renny.

Oh, no.

Let's just say... I had been completely unprepared for the girls club.

See, they were sneaky. They came up on me slowly, one by one or two by two, never letting me see what, exactly, it was like when they got all together.

For me, Janie, Lo, Alex, Maze, Summer, and Penny were all old news. But with Janie, Lo, Alex, Maze, Summer, and Penny... came the rest of the girls club. That introduced me formally to Amelia, Shooter's wife, and Elsie, Paine's wife.

I was sitting at a table covered in bridal magazines full of wedding gowns and centerpieces and venues and floral arrangements and different fonts for invitations and bakeries to taste test cakes at.

But they weren't the problem. Oh, no. I had all of that figured out in less than twenty minutes.

The problem?

That would be the fact that Alex and Janie would not wear dresses. And Elsie and Lo really preferred to not be in heels. But, then again, Penny would like the highest heels possible given that she was practically child-sized. Then we had to add in body shapes. Because Amelia would prefer something that drew attention away from her thighs and Lo wanted something to understate her breasts and Elsie and Maze, well, they were fans of their legs.

Really, the list of considerations for bridesmaid dresses was starting to make me genuinely think that, hey, hopping a plane and getting married in Vegas by Elvis wasn't *that* cheesy, right?

My gaze shifted over toward Ashley who had been sitting there perfectly quiet watching the goings-on with no small bit of amusement. She looked over and shrugged a shoulder. "I say you move this whole shindig to the beach and, if they don't quit their bitching, make every last one of them wear a G-string bikini."

That effectively shut up a lot of the conversation, Janie's gaze going to me. "You wouldn't."

"Wouldn't I?" I asked with a small smile.

"Why not just make it simple and say... everyone wears something black that they feel hot as shit in?" Alex supplied, always being the more impatient and level-headed of the girls club.

I looked down at my notes, scratching out the theme colors, for which I had chosen white (obviously) and a sage green and scribbled in black instead. "Alright. That's the plan then. Wear black. And for God's sake, I don't want to hear another word about hemlines or necklines."

I would swear, even giving them all the license to dress how they preferred, there was still some upset among the group.

I had a feeling that maybe by giving in so quickly (though it felt like the argument had gone on for days), that I had somehow ruined a tradition among the women.

But I was hoping, for all future members of the girls club's sake, I was making the tradition an easier one.

RENNY

Renny- 1.5 years

"I'm not fixing the fuckin' thing again," Shooter supplied as I tugged at my tie for the fifth time that afternoon.

I hadn't worn a tie since I was a teenager. I had somehow gotten away with just a suit at all the other weddings I had needed to attend over the years. No one was ever paying that close of attention to me.

That couldn't exactly be said of my wedding day though.

As a whole, I was never a nervous person.

But standing in the room down the hall from the spot where I was going to marry Mina, yeah, I was freaking out a little.

Not because I wasn't sure I loved her and would continue to love her. I had never been more sure of anything in my life.

It was something deeper than that, more long-buried than that. It was some old demons rearing their ugly heads.

"Renny," Reeve's voice called, making my head snap up to find him standing in the open doorway.

"Yeah?"

"Mina wants to see you," he said, jerking his head toward the hallway.

Mina and Reeve had seemed to form a certain bond after the afternoon she dumped me a year and a half before.

266

And after she finally learned his history, because one night he trusted her enough to tell her, well before any of the rest of us found out, it had gotten to be an even deeper connection.

As such, it was almost fitting he was the one walking me toward her room, that he was actually going to be the one giving her away since there was no way in ever-loving hell we were going to have her actual father do so or even be invited to the wedding.

"She alright?" I asked as we got closer to her door.

Reeve stopped just outside it, giving me a long look. "Nope," he declared, but did it with a smirk before clamping a hand on my shoulder and moving away.

Curious, I reached for the handle and went inside. At the sound, Mina swiveled around from where she had been sitting facing the triple vanity mirror.

"Marriage is stupid," she declared, her voice edgy.

"Alright," I said, nodding, trying to not smile.

Cold feet.

She was having fucking cold feet.

It was so unlike her that I wanted to laugh.

"Seriously. I mean... look at your parents. Look at *mine*. What are we thinking? If there are ever two people who could royally screw this kind of thing up, it's us. We had literally no good examples of happy and successful marriages growing up."

That wasn't untrue.

I exhaled slowly and walked over to her, kneeling down in front of her little wooden seat and putting my hands on her knees. "True, but that doesn't mean we don't have good examples to look to. For fuck's sake- we have Reign and Summer and Cash and Lo and Wolf and Janie and Repo and Maze and Duke and Penny and, if we want to dig a

RENNY

little deeper, there is Breaker and Alex and Shooter and
Amelia and Paine and Elsie. We're fucking surrounded
with successful and happy marriages, Mina."

"Sure, but if there are ever two people to break a perfect
track record..."

"Mina," I said, waiting for a long second before her
perfect fucking hazel eyes landed on mine. Then I felt my
smile tease up a little. "You know what the problem is?"

Her brows drew together slightly at that as she shook
her head. "No."

"See the girls club whisked you away last night and
never brought you back..." I paused there, fingers sliding
up her thighs. "Neither of us got to have breakfast," I added
with a wicked smile and I started moving apart the ends of
her short silk robe, watching as her eyes went a little
heated. "I've been a little edgy this morning too. Figure
maybe it's because I'm hungry," I added, pulling the sash
and the entire thing parted to the sides. "Fucking famished
actually."

"You know," she said, her breathing getting heavier as I
leaned down and started to kiss up her thigh. "I think you're
right. That must be it. We should... oh my God," she
groaned as my mouth sucked in her clit through her pretty
little silky white panties that I knew were supposed to be a
surprise for me later.

I reached up, snagging the sides of the waist as I backed
up slightly, pulling the material down her thighs and legs
then off her feet. Her hands reached out, deftly untying the
mother effing tie and making it so I could finally breathe
again, before her hands started in on the buttons to my
shirt.

268

"You know," she said as she pushed my shirt and jacket off my shoulders, "I think we're supposed to wait until after we're married to consummate it."

I laughed, unfastening my pants and pulling her down onto my lap, reaching between us to line my cock up with her hot, wet pussy. "Fuck that. I want you at that alter with my come still inside you," I declared, pulling her hips down so my cock slid in her tight pussy. "It can be our little secret," I added as she started to ride me, slow and sweet at first, but ending hard and rough and frantic, fucking up her hair and makeup and making it so there was no way the girls weren't going to know *exactly* what I did to calm her down when they came back in to finish getting her ready.

"See you down there, right?" I asked as she tied her sash back into place, her face post-fuck rosy, her entire body more lax than it had been twenty minutes before.

"Wouldn't want to be anywhere else," she said with such confidence that I knew that, among other places, I had warmed up her cold feet.

As I walked back down the hall to my room, I was a fuckuva lot calmer too. And when Shoot retied my tie for the sixth time, I knew without a doubt that we weren't going to be the exception to the rule.

We weren't doomed to repeat our parents' mistakes.

We weren't somehow unlovable because we had never been loved.

And there was no one, fucking no one in the world who could love Mina better than I could.

And, I was pretty fucking sure, no one would ever even want to love me the way she did.

We were going to be fine.

Mina- 4 years

"Blank slate," Renny declared, climbing into the bed with me, pulling back the blanket from her little pink face.

"I still can't decide if that is a good thing or not," I admitted, knowing it wasn't what you were supposed to say while holding your baby right after it got cleaned up, but preferring to be honest.

I had gotten the implant out of my arm almost two years before I got pregnant. It was due to come out and I just... never got it replaced. We were in a committed relationship and we figured whatever happened, happened. We weren't going to plan it, but if it happened, we would welcome it.

The month I missed my period, though, had been one of the most stressful in my life. It suddenly didn't matter how far Renny and I had gone, how much we had opened up and exposed our wounds so we could let them heal. It didn't matter that we were stable and Renny very rarely, if ever, got into one of his moods. Somehow, faced with impending parenthood, every single little flaw of mine felt amplified, felt insurmountable. And I couldn't help but worry that I would take our little blank slate and instill my own shortcomings on her.

RENNY

"Mina, look at what we came from," Renny said, leaning down and kissing her little scrunched-up forehead. "And we turned out alright. We are going to be fine."

I didn't want to be fine. I wanted to be able to give her every advantage, every bit of encouragement, every bit of love that neither Renny or I got.

"Here's hoping," I agreed, smiling down at her face as she started wriggling and squirming and opening her mouth to scream.

I hadn't realized then that I had, inadvertently, named our daughter.

Because we knew from that moment that what we had most, along with a love neither of us believed we would find and the best of intentions, was hope.

Hope that we could do better than our parents.

Hope that we had learned from all our mistakes.

Hope that we could break the cycle.

Hope.

"Oh, I forgot," Renny said, climbing off the bed as I situated Hope for feeding. He went over to the windowsill where he had a small overnight bag and pulled out a very small, very familiar, rectangular package.

I knew what it was.

For any big event- birthday, anniversary, Christmas, along with a normal gift, I always had my little rectangle. I also got one anytime he was apologizing for something.

I had the kind of sock collection even a hoarder would look at and tell me I needed to thin it out a little.

But each and every pair represented a moment, a milestone, a time when he was thinking of me and the traditions we had started all those years ago.

So I didn't care that they were 'just' socks.

Every pair was the best present I ever got.

He moved back to the bed, sitting down on the edge and holding the package, ripping the edge for me so I could pull the rest of the paper off with one hand, the other holding Hope to my chest.

I pulled out the plastic holder and found a pair of very pink socks with print all over them: #1 Mom.

I looked up at him and that was about the moment that I finally believed it. I believed I could do it. *We* could do it.

I reached for him, pulling him down until he was laying beside me on the bed, his arm wrapped over my belly and his hand resting on our daughter.

"See?" he asked, looking over at me. "Aren't you glad I wore you down?" he said, giving me a boyish smile I had gotten so used to, so attached to.

And I was.

I was so incredibly happy that he hadn't given up, no matter how many times I shot him down, no matter how many times I fought my own attraction, no matter how I tried to push him away.

Because if he was any other guy, he wouldn't have hung in there and won me over.

And neither of us would have known what it was like to be truly, unconditionally loved and then make the decision to share that love with a new generation.

"Yeah," I agreed, giving him a smile. "Now all we have to worry about is moving out of the compound. Things are getting a little crazy over there with all the new blood..."

XX

DON'T FORGET

If you enjoyed this book, go ahead and hop onto Goodreads or Amazon and tell me your favorite parts. You can also spread the word by recommending the book to friends or sending digital copies that can be received via kindle or kindle app on any device.

ALSO BY JESSICA GADZIALA

The Henchmen MC
Reign
Cash
Wolf
Repo
Duke

The Savages
Monster
Killer
Savior

--

DEBT
For A Good Time, Call...
Shane
The Sex Surrogate
Dr. Chase Hudson
Dissent
Into The Green
What The Heart Needs

274

RENNY

What The Heart Wants
What The Heart Finds
What The Heart Knows
The Stars Landing Deviant
Dark Mysteries
367 Days
Stuffed: A Thanksgiving Romance
Dark Secrets
Unwrapped

275

ABOUT THE AUTHOR

Jessica Gadziala is a full-time writer, parrot enthusiast, and coffee drinker from New Jersey. She enjoys short rides to the book store, sad songs, and cold weather.

She is very active on Goodreads, Facebook, as well as her personal groups on those sites. Join in. She's friendly.

STALK HER!

Connect with Jessica:

Facebook: https://www.facebook.com/JessicaGadziala/
Facebook Group:
https://www.facebook.com/groups/314540025563403/

Goodreads:
https://www.goodreads.com/author/show/13800950.Jessica_Gadziala
Goodreads Group:
https://www.goodreads.com/group/show/177944-jessica-gadziala-books-and-bullsh

Twitter: @JessicaGadziala

JessicaGadziala.com

RENNY

<3/ Jessica

CPSIA information can be obtained
at www.ICGtesting.com
Printed in the USA
FSOW01n2036010617
34924FS